Seeds of Disorde

Barvalus de Hoop finds herself dra~~ ~~
and deceipt involving a the race bet~~ ~~
identify and patent the choicest bits of human genetic material
being churned out by the Human Genome Project.

About the Author

Sean Badal is a former journalist and technology specialist who has written for a wide range of publications, including *Wired*. His first book, Dead Sanctities, was published in 1999.

This book is also available in e-book format at:
www.authorsonline.co.uk

An AuthorsOnLine Book

Published by Authors OnLine Ltd 2001

Copyright © Authors OnLine Ltd

Text Copyright © Sean Badal

The front cover design Alia Syed ©

The moral right of the author has been asserted

All rights reserved. No part of this publication may be reproduced, stored in a retrieval system, or transmitted in any form or by any means, electronic, mechanical, photocopy, recording or otherwise, without prior written permission of the copyright owner. Nor can it be circulated in any form of binding or cover other than that in which it is published and without similar condition including this condition being imposed on a subsequent purchaser.

ISBN 0 7552 0052 7

Authors OnLine Ltd
15-17 Maidenhead Street
Hertford SG14 1DW
England

Visit us online at www.authorsonline.co.uk

Acknowledgements

Many thanks to:

Ian Mckillop (as usual!),
Professor Elizabeth Fisher (for the belated insights),
Nicole Columbine (for the sufferance),

and to

Jonathan Taylor, Renee Grawitzky, Joel Jacobson, Mara Scop and Edward Powys.

To Mirri Kanaye, for the fun, laughter and friendship

Seeds of Disorder

By

Sean Badal

PROLOGUE

Europoort, in Rotterdam, is the largest port in the world. Completed in 1968, it was ideally placed to handle the new range of sea-vessels, the supertankers that had started to plough the oceans of the globe. Today it is a conduit for most of the tonnage that enters and leaves Western Europe. It is thus extremely susceptible to acts of terrorism, and has adapted appropriate countermeasures should such events ever occur. This has been largely unnecessary, though, because the are hasn't even been the subject of a fictional drama, let alone a real one.

One would imagine a Euro-thriller of this kind would be quite exciting - lots of buildings blowing up, ships sinking in the harbour, politicians on television portentously discussing the spectre of a starving Europe...

By virtue of their size, the buildings at Europoort have a surrealistic quality about them that is hard to comprehend. It is as if they were built for a race of giants. In millennia from now they might be unearthed by our dwarfish relatives, who will ponder in awe at the size of their ancestors.

The silos, the warehouses, even the trucks that weave doggedly in-between the buildings, dwarf the humans, making them seem like industrious ants. At night it is even worse. The gigantic lights illuminate the sky, and from a distance the whole area looks like a landing strip for alien aircraft. Inside the sprawling complex, the tall buildings cause the lights to create dark, cavernous shadows between the harshly lit-up areas. Even if you know your way around, it is easy to get lost. According to the harbour police reports, amongst the people that have died there since 1977 two are listed as having died of starvation, that is, they couldn't find their way out. These days, it is much more difficult to get lost; workers carry mobile phone, bleepers, even watches with GPS systems built into them.

At 3am, a man, X, stumbles around Silo 357. He desperately feels the smooth walls, as if hoping to find the end, or a least an opening hatch. The silo is, of course, circular so even if he was able to go around, he would only return to his starting point. The openings are high up, way beyond his reach. They are built for the funnels of the large transport vehicles that ply the area, not for humans. X can see the bright lights above, but it is like being lost at sea with only the stars for company. It is a desolate and empty brightness, like Las Vegas.

Behind him, three men attempt to catch up. There is a small blue van of nondescript vintage and make crawling behind them. It keeps its distance. They walk slowly, fully aware that his screams will be unheard. The man who is running away from them pauses. The terror on his face has transcended into resignation, or perhaps surrender. The sweat pours from his face, glistening on his dark skin. His lank, thick black hair is damp and plastered in strands down his forehead. There is a lifelessness in his limbs too. It is not just physical. His body has been emptied of soul.

He notices that there is a needle still stuck in his arm. He looks at it for a moment, profoundly unable to comprehend his predicament. Then he wrenches it out with a grimace. In a futile gesture, he hurls it at his pursuers. Then he slumps down against the wall, arms at his side.

They catch up with him. There are no triumphant gestures on their part.

They have work to do. One of them feels his pulse, looking at his watch. He nods to the other two. They open the back door of the van and haul out what looks like a cooler bag used for picnics. One of them reaches inside again and drags out some sort of long shiny, metallic implement. He presses a button. It hisses softly, small red dots blinking in the dark. A pencil-thin beam of sheer white light emanates from the instrument.

The driver of the van gets out, walks over, and holds X down firmly, just in case he attempts any last-minute acts of desperation.

There is a growing stain emanating from between X's legs. The man with the implement moves closer. One final nod and he neatly slices off the left and then the right hand, just above the wrist, of the man on the ground. X has fainted even before the first hand was cut off. The men are careful to avoid the two streams of blood that gush out violently from where X's hands used to be.

They place the hands carefully into sealable plastic bags, fill the bags with a transparent gel, and then place them into the containers. Without looking back, they drive off. The man lying on the ground will bleed to death.

Barvalis de Hoop, on vacation, Miami, Florida.

Chapter 1

'You MUST...' The Tae Kwon Do instructor takes my arm and thrusts it exaggeratedly over her shoulder. The bone snaps out of the socket. An electric shock of pain jolts through my armpit and down the muscles over the rib-cage. It is a sharp brutal stab of pain, which also serves the purpose of jolting me out of my reverie.

I feel the flush of embarrassment spread from my neck up to my face. Even my olive-coloured skin cannot hide what must be a dark blush spreading over my face, like the foreboding shadow of gathering storm clouds.

Then anger.

Not at the gratuitous act of violence I've just been subjected to, but at the fact that the fine stitching in my Colleen Dinnigan bra has undoubtedly been broken. Classy Australian underwear is hard to find in Amsterdam. And I'm no seamstress.

Everybody is staring. Round heads peering at the still body on the ground, burying sweaty sniggers into the folds of their white, floppy jackets. I hate all-girl groupings. Put a group of women together for an extended period of time and they regress back to schoolyards and boarding houses. Ask anyone who's ever attended a baby-shower.

The instructor pulls me forward brutally, her pitiless eyes boring into me.

The next thing I know is that I'm on my arse. Seeing stars. There are flecks of white light floating dreamily around me.

'Do it like this...' she steps back triumphantly, hands on her pathetically skinny hips, acknowledging the polite murmurs of approval.

They're still staring at me. Ritual humiliation is an integral part of all martial arts, except probably Tai Chi, but this, I suspect, is payback time. Martina Schaarf, militant lesbian and martial arts instructor, has disapproved of me even before she set eyes on me. Like all Europol sub-contractors, she has been thoroughly vetted, but why the agency chose to hand its personal defence courses to a woman who specialises in what looks like lesbian-only classes is beyond me. The poor men who attend must suffer more than I do. A little humiliation for the lone heterosexual.

Something she has taught us comes to mind. How to defend yourself against a mad rapist who has thrown you to the ground. Go for the legs. Bring him down. Hard. Break bones, take his breath away. And his power.

She lands next to me with a thud. I enjoy a split-second frisson of pleasure at the look of pain and anger in her eyes.

I get up before she has a chance to roll over and smother me with her rippling thighs. Walk rapidly but elegantly to the change-room without making eye contact with the other viragos. Make sure to swing my hips.

*

At the office Josef Boehme is standing at my desk with an exasperated expression on his face, as if waiting for me to materialise out of thin air. Which is what I do.

He pointedly looks at his watch.

'*Schnell, schnell.*' He growls softly at me, like an old dog supremely sure of its dominance. I offer him the chocolate bar that I have purchased for him on the way back. He pretends to be even more exasperated, rolling his eyes at me.

'Herr Boehme,' I address him politely, 'why do I have to subject myself to humiliation, mental torture and physical pain in the interest of my work?'

'So that we can turn you into an efficient killing machine,' he answers, without a trace of irony.

Then again, you can never be too sure with Boehme. He has a way of upsetting all your Germanic notions and prejudices.

'The only unarmed combat I can relate to is a witty riposte,' I say.

He frowns at me. 'Are you being funny again?'

Through the windows, the muted squalling of seagulls rises above the whirr of the fax-machine, the photocopier and the clatter of the typist's metal extensions on her fingernails hitting the plastic keys of the keyboard.

The buildings along Prins Hendrikkade are prime real estate. When it comes to office space, and other perks, the members of the European Community spare no expense. Below and above us are equally expensive offices, teeming with preening foreigners in dark business suits working for "consultancies". There are always gorgeous Lebanese men in Import/Export standing at the elevators, chatting earnestly into their mobile phones, eyes never failing to follow the women that come into their line of vision.

Nearby is my little secret, the Maritime Museum. I spend my lunchbreaks here, amidst the ancient, yellowing maps, the sextants, the various unidentifiable brass instruments. It is a good place to lose oneself. Even the musty air is invigorating.

We are not allowed to open the windows - suicide - but the salty air seeps in nevertheless. You can taste it on your lips first thing in the morning. Before too many cups of scalding coffee blunt the taste buds and kill the brain cells. The view is nice. When they bother to clean the windows, and the weather is good, you can see the big ships moving into the harbour. It is a sight that never fails to warm my heart. They may be carrying logs from the Amazon, refrigerators from Taiwan, or iron ore from Ghana, but in the sunlight they are stately and dignified, like cruise ships arriving from exotic destinations.

We call him 'Helmut' behind his large back, in deference to the fact that he comes from Ludwigshafen-am-Rhein. The same place as the former German chancellor.

He's also sensitive about his weight, so we take care to address him directly as Herr Boehme, and not Helmut.

They call me 'Dutch' behind *my* back. But I pretend not to know.

'Scotland Yard.' He says portentously to me, handing me a note.

It's actually the Metropolitan Police Service in London. Scotland Yard is simply the headquarters at No. 10 Broadway, London, but not many people know that. Newspapers and books have been peddling the myth for so long that the service has simply given up doing public- relations exercises.

'Oh good, they want me to investigate traffic offences for the British members of the European Parliament.' I smile sweetly at him, lest he thinks I'm being cheeky.

Sometimes Boehme's proprietorial airs over me are really irritating. I have been with the organisation for five months and he still hovers over me like an overprotective father. He has supervised my training with such fine detail that I feel as if I'm part of a grand experiment, being prodded, examined, dissected.

I enjoyed it when I first started, but now it is beginning to chafe. Besides, I was in a very vulnerable state then. Now it's different. I am my own again. To be honest, for three of those five months my foot was encased in plaster of Paris, which would have made lessons in unarmed combat difficult anyway. It did mean, however, that I spent an inordinately large amount of training time in the company of various automatic firearms. The end result is that I can discuss the finer points of the new Glock G30 as opposed to Heckler & Koch's new Universal Self-Loading Pistol. However, I still tremble when I pull the trigger.

'You shouldn't read other people's messages.' I grab the slip of paper from his hand.

'Snappy, snappy,' the secretary, Ilsa Memert, chips in, 'you ought to find yourself a boyfriend. Then maybe you won't come into the office like a bear with a sore head.'

Ilsa is the same age as me, thirty, but singularly lacking in ambition, which explains why she's been a secretary since she was seventeen. She's also very strange looking, in that exotic sort of way that's likely to tempt magazine editors to declare her "the face of ..." whatever. In her case, it's probably "the face of Death". She dresses in black every day. She wears black neoprene trousers that reveal the slit of her cunt to the whole world. When she steps into the building elevator the other women, in their neat, tailored executive suits, move away, as if afraid to be tainted by the blatant sexuality they've spent so many years trying to suppress in the interests of their careers.

Weekends she spends in various Amsterdam rave clubs picking up young boys. Unlike me, she gets laid pretty regularly. And lets everyone in the office know it.

Maybe I'm just jealous of her degage behaviour.

I call her a slut under my breath. And a heretic. She wears a crucifix around her neck with a topless Mary, instead of Jesus, nailed to the cross. During weekends she has her hair teased into two ridiculous horns on the top of her head. I saw her once at 2 am in a café, surrounded by waifish sixteen-year-old boys determined to get into her trousers. I was walking my neighbour's dog, worrying about my pension fund.

Josef Boehme had spent twenty years working for the *Bundeskriminalamt*, the German police network. They say that he worked his way up from being a patrolman on a bicycle in some fishing village on the outskirts of Hamburg. But that is really a malicious lie.

He actually rode the autobahns on a powerful BMW motorbike in the late Sixties. He showed me photos of his former svelte self, sitting atop his bike with his buddies in a photograph disturbingly reminiscent of elite Waffen SS troops taking a smoke-break from their rampages across Europe. That's another nasty thing they say about him. That his inherent Teutonism is detrimental to the welfare of his colleagues. That he lays flowers in the cellars of 8 Prinz Albrechtstrasse, the former headquarters of the Gestapo where his grandfather worked as a *Hauptsturmfuehrer.*

All lies.

He is simply a workaholic and a slob utterly devoid of any social graces. He is like a hungry pig rooting in farmyard muck, except that he roots out thieves, blackmailers, smugglers, killers and, on occasion, spies. Although he doesn't like to talk about it, in 1984 he singlehandedly rounded up a nest of East German agents in the border town of Gothastadt, at great personal danger. The East Germans had set up some kind of communications centre there, from which they were relaying information back to East Berlin. It was all quite brazen. Boehme was on one of his rare holidays, a cycling tour through the picturesque German countryside, when he spotted antennae sticking out of the barn of an old farmhouse. From enquiries in the village he learnt that the farmhouse belonged to a wealthy couple from the city, and that they only occasionally used it.

That ought to have put his mind at rest. After all, it's perfectly normal for wealthy people to have satellite dishes. But that explanation didn't assuage Boehme's doubts. The next night, he simply stormed into the building and arrested everybody. One look was enough to tell him that they weren't a rich couple enjoying a few days out in the country. They were too astonished to believe that he was on his own.

For his actions, he was reprimanded. The authorities said that he didn't follow the rules. The case turned out to be something of a cause celebre for him, with the media taking his side and entering into a predictable round of self-flagellation about the German character. About how it was stifling initiative, enterprise, the gung-ho spirit.

He was thus promoted and awarded Germany's second highest police honour.

Having reached the zenith of his career with the *Bundeskriminalamt*, Europe beckoned. In his case, it was Interpol. There was also the slight personal matter of him having an affair with the wife of a local politician. It's something you don't do in Bonn, and, had he stayed, it would have meant the end of his rise within the German police force, irrespective of how wonderful his record was. The politician whose wife Boehme had been screwing would have seen to that. Law and order was in his portfolio.

How do I know all this? Ilsa of course. She specialises in being Miss Nosy Parker. She even showed me the newspaper clippings that she had surreptitiously removed from Boehme's desk when he was away in Berlin.

Boehme remains unmarried. And, although I have looked, I have been unable to find traces of any woman in his life.

In France, where the International Criminal Police Organisation (Interpol) is headquartered, they turn a blind eye to marital infidelity, and other similar ethical transgressions. This is a country, after all, where the prime minister, Francois Mitterrand, ordered his country's secret police to bug the flat of Carole Bouquet so that he could find out what his favourite actress was up to.

Boehme's old boss, Antony Dierdorff, as anyone who's bothered to read the hundreds of missives that the EU spews out in the interests of democracy will know, now heads Europe's latest crime-fighting machine, Europol.

I snatch the message from Boehme's stubby fingers. The fresh smell of Boss for Men tells me that he has had the second of his twice-weekly baths. He bathes on Thursday and Monday mornings. The aftershave was a present from me. An impulsive purchase from the duty-free shop in Zeebrugge. He must be nearing the end of the bottle. It will be Christmas in two months. I resolve to get him another bottle. Something redolent of pine trees and the ocean.

I have grown to love him.

He has saved my life.

The message is from Terence Helm in London.

'He says it's not very urgent, so you don't have to call him right away,' jabbers Ilsa.

'How charmingly Anglo-Saxon,' I observe.

Time is not a problem. I haven't done any work since I arrived. I let Boehme know this fact as discreetly as possible. It is as though I have been suspended in a jar of some particularly viscous liquid, unable to move, me staring at everybody, everybody staring at me.

Boehme's jowly face is up close to me. His head is almost shaven, and his eyebrows are thick but well-groomed. He has Bismarck's bulbous eyes. If you look closely, you can see the little snips that he has made with scissors to shape his eyebrows. Other than this little weakness, he doesn't really take care of himself. He is not as fastidious as most Germans. This must be his only weakness. His breath smells of toasted cheese and onion sandwiches. He has the distinctly un-Western habit of invading your personal body space. It is a gesture that is a summation of his personality and his life.

Reduced to its simplest core, he lets nothing get in his way.

I tell him that he's nicked himself shaving again. That throws him off balance for a second.

'Better phone Helm. Now,' he growls at me. 'It's probably about crooked money again.'

Boehme is being sarcastic. Ever since the single European currency was introduced, the National Criminal Intelligence Service (NCIS) in the UK have found themselves in a situation where organised crime gangs are starting to plan to convert chunks of their cash assets (mostly Deutschmarks and Dutch Guilders, if you exclude the dollar) into pounds. This is due to the fact that six months after the introduction of euro-notes and coins, all citizens of the euro will have to present their original currency at their country's central bank in person. Naturally not many criminals are prepared to stand in line to do this. So, in addition to buying up large quantities of gold and diamonds, they are buying pounds, banking on the obstinacy of the English. This has horrified the London-based Financial Action Task Force (FATF) who has started to put pressure on the NCIS to do something.

'Of course it would be easier if the English simply joined up,' he adds bitingly.

*

Detective Inspector Terence Helm seems to think that I'm his European connection, all on the strength of one lazy, hazy phone call he made to the organisation about three months ago. It was a Friday afternoon, and he had phoned in to enquire about some corruption issue or the other. We'd ended up chatting about films. He'd told me that his favourite line in a movie was Michael Caine as Harry Palmer in Funeral in Berlin.

German waiter: *'Bitte, Mein Herr?'*
Palmer: 'No, Lowenbrau, please.'

Since then I've become his unofficial liaison. He's phoned me for all sorts of commonplace queries, stuff about the smuggling of cargo - mostly cigarettes - into the UK from Europe. It's astonishing how much of it goes on in this day and age, and on the very threshold of a united Europe.

I know very little about him - name and occupation, to be precise, but I like his other bits. His voice, his habit of asking me about the weather. His endearing self-deprecation.

Somewhere between a polite casualness and flirting there is another zone.

We inhabit that zone.

I have worked out that he is about thirty, between five and a half and six feet, thin, fit. Don't ask how.

*

Ilsa hands me a cup of coffee in her usual fashion, that is, in a manner that makes it clear that she would rather perform this particular chore for Boehme only. In my office I dial the London number. He answers.

He apologies profusely for about five minutes for having disturbed me. Then he sighs as though he's about to deliver bad news.

'Bodies,' he breathes heavily.

'Last week we fished out six bodies from the Thames. Five of them had been chained together and dumped overboard. Forensics has shown that they drowned. Water in the lungs.'

He pauses, as if afraid to disturb my refined feelings.

'I'm made of stronger stuff,' I reassure him.

'They also had their hands chopped off, or should I say sliced off. All of them. So they would have died from loss of blood anyway. The sixth person was simply shot. In the head. His body was found a few feet away from the others. Snagged in an old anchor chain. Hands intact, by the way. There were no papers, or any other items of identification on their bodies. It looks like they were searched before they were killed. They weren't stripped of clothing though. From what we have established, some of the men were wearing items of clothing made in Sri Lanka. Sandals and shirts to be exact. Which in itself doesn't mean much these days, but the physical characteristics of the men denote that they are of Indian origin. Decomposition hadn't set in. There's a strong possibility that they're Sri Lankan.'

'Illegal immigrants?'

'Or Tamil Tigers. Or possibly both. I did a bit of checking up on the national computer. About three days before the murders in London took place, the Dutch police fished out a body from the Rotterdam harbour. Same story. No documents. No hands. The Dutch police have chalked it up as a drowning. An illegal immigration smuggling operation gone wrong. It happens all the time. There are two possibilities; they were smuggled in via the land route - eastern Europe, Germany, Holland, UK, or they came on a ship that docked in Rotterdam. It's possible that they came in on a ship that arrived in London, but the person in Amsterdam was killed first. If there is a pattern, that would be its natural progression.

What we would like to know is whether there's a connection, and also what ships came in from the east over the period. The police stuff I have asked for help from the Dutch police, but I was wondering if I could bother you to check up on the shipping. They tell me that you're the maritime liaison. And something of an expert.'

Helm adds the last bit a touch disingenuously but I forgive him.

'I'm a liaison officer, and a maritime lawyer in my previous life,' I say gruffly. 'I know nothing about dead bodies floating in rivers.'

'Liaison officer' sounds like the most boring title in the world. Sounds like I work in a supermarket. My previous life flashes before me. It is unsettling, only supposed to happen in moments of extreme terror.

I push it away.

'Boehme has told me otherwise,' he continues. I can see him smile at the other end.

'Boehme likes to get his pound of flesh from his employees. It's the Protestant work ethic. Don't trust anything he says.'

'You have to help me,' he implores jocularly, 'we're part of one big happy family.'

'And which family is that?' I ask.

'Why, Europe, of course.'

I don't tell him that it's a screwed-up, dysfunctional family.

'"*All happy families resemble one another, but each unhappy family is unhappy in its own way.*"'

'Where's that from, a fortune cookie?'

'Anna Karenina. Tolstoy.'

'Don't read books, I'm afraid, but I did see the movie.'

'I have a quote for every occasion,' I say.

He laughs loudly into the phone. 'What we would like to do is see if there is a connection, if any. What we have in London could simply be gang-related, but I doubt it. There is very little Tamil gang activity in the UK.'

'What about the terrorist angle?' I ask.

'Strong possibility. And the one we suspect most likely to be the right one. In which case we will not need your services. The Liberation Tigers of Tamil Eelam have a strong history of exploiting the social services in the UK and indeed the rest of Europe. It ranges from obtaining grants under false pretexts, to defrauding the DSS. They're also into money laundering, drugs and illegal immigration. You can throw in intimidation as well. So we have our work cut out for us. We're trying to establish if the murdered men were associated with either the Tamil Tigers or opponents of theirs. You can't tell if it's a fallout of comrades or a wiping out of enemies. Either way, it's a horrible death. Anyway, I'm sending you the video clip. Or rather, I'll tell you where to find it. You can view it on our Intranet. I presume your organisation has access to our databases? What is your e-mail address? I'll mail you the video directory of the Forensic Science Service.'

I give him my details, ignoring his little petulant aside.

Chapter 2

When I go sailing I get seasick. The rocking of the boat, the waves weaving in slow motion around me like an army of witches casting a spell, drives me insane. The physical manifestation is an uncontrollable urge to vomit. Which is what I do in copious amounts, and for a sustained and painful period. The superstitious might say it's a sign of possession.

I do not like sea-sand either. Feeling its squishiness between my toes makes my flesh creep. And I swim very badly, only when I absolutely have to, never for pleasure.

And yet I cannot do without the sea. It is my daily fix. I need to walk along stony shorelines on cold days, warm days, in-between days. I need to go sailing too, because once the vomiting is out of the way I feel purged. The rhythm of the boat as it cleaves the water is ineffably soothing. A panacea for the soul.

My last boyfriend - about a year ago - wanted to go to the Bahamas for Christmas. The sun, the sea, the bathing, the skin-diving, he'd cajoled desperately.

He went on his own.

I need glimpses of it, the smell in my nostrils, the feeling on my skin of the salt-tinged wetness that makes my hair bristle.

On the motorway to Rotterdam, between the factories, the oil refineries and the cheap housing blocks, the North Sea shimmers in the distance, casting a silvery glow over the dark landscape. The rising sun is an alien blot on the horizon.

I stop at a dingy trucker's café to buy a cup of dishwater muck masquerading as coffee. The truck drivers in the parking lot mistake me for a hooker. There are other girls wondering around, screeching at each other, chatting, getting stoned. These sorts of places attract the worst girls in the business, girls desperate for cash to buy drugs.

A few of the drivers flick their lights at me from the cabins of their trucks. I swear profusely at one who is brave enough to stick his head out of the window but he just laughs and makes an obscene gesture with his fingers. He sticks his head back quickly into the cabin of his truck though. An interesting sociological experiment is taking place here. There is a woman, an artist, who goes around photographing truckers in the act of picking up prostitutes. She has put up some of the pictures in an exhibition in Amsterdam. At least one trucker has gotten into trouble with his family, but the exhibition has aroused a great deal of controversy, both for her and against. The result is that some of the truckers go around behaving as though there's a serial killer out to get them. It is fascinating to see the shoe on the other foot, so to say.

Boehme does allows me certain improvisational freedoms. Like taking long lunchbreaks, leaving early on Fridays, driving down to Rotterdam when it would be easier for me to sit on the telephone for a couple of hours. It didn't take much to convince him of my need to extract information on a one-to-one personal basis, that more effective results could be obtained as a by-product of a casual conversation than a cold interview over the telephone, that I have 'contacts.' He is aware of his limitations, which endears him to me. In his heart, he knows that he is not - as described in the business journals, a 'peoples' person.' He doesn't know that I know that he has been reading How to be an Effective Manager. I saw it jutting out of his battered crocodile briefcase in the front seat of his car in the parking lot.

Although we're on different floors of the parking lot, it's a deliberately excursive trip I occasionally make purely to check what's inside his car.

Spying, they say, is as much about hard work as it is about serendipity. Besides, I am immutably curious, like a cat.

His inability to forge a constructive solution for this self-perceived defect both humbles and infuriates him in equal measure. Perhaps humble is the wrong word - it is more of a frustrating recognition of an inalienable flaw in one's character.

In August we all had drinks in a bar to celebrate Boehme's 49th birthday. Boehme bought drinks, as he thought it was his duty, with all the gravitas of a man about to be hanged. Attempting bonhomie, he cracked jokes, made a stab at levity, laughed a lot, all the while chafing under the constraints of his innate weakness. It was only at 3 am, when everyone was utterly drunk, that the barriers were removed. I watched him mournfully surveying his subordinates, his drink-addled brain still somehow conscious of its failures. That he lacked Grace.

*

Rotterdam. City of broken dreams. My old city. My home for most of my life.

There are parts of Rotterdam that still look as though they haven't recovered from the bombing the Germans inflicted in the Forties. These are the parts that I love. The old Oostpoort has been subjected to gentrification. Tourists trawl through the streets for the 'authentic' Dutch experience. Brochures exhort them see one of the oldest sea ports in Europe. To suck in the musty odour of the ancient water-routes. All they smell is their own expensive sweat.

Coonrodt lives on his boat, North Star, in an old canal, the Bloemgracht [Flower canal] near the Oudehaven, Rotterdam's old harbour. It is not really a canal, more of a little inlet that somehow finds its way to the Meuse. There are so many of them in Rotterdam, hidden away like old, abandoned roads. Geriatric canals, silted up with three hundred years of junk. The ironically named Bloemgracht - it is also full of old rubbish and stinks of rotting fish - is Coonrodt's hideaway, away from the prying eyes of marine inspectors and social service workers.

It is half boat and half barge, a clunky old hybrid that is at home - barely though - at sea or in the narrow canals. Coonrodt says that his boat is unsinkable, that the worst that can happen is that it will capsize, and even then the watertight locks will prevent him from going down.

Sometimes I wonder how he manages to get his barge out into the ocean, but he succeeds. Often, I wonder how he manages to navigate through the bureaucratic jungle of port fees (exorbitant), rules and regulations, pompous officials, but he manages this too.

I have to park my car near a row of derelict buildings and walk the badly cobbled alleys. I'm glad that I'm wearing flat shoes. There is nothing living about, except a couple of rats looking for breakfast. This place is so deserted that not even the drunks bother to frequent it. Sometimes I worry for Coonrodt's safety.

Coonrodt is standing on the deck, savouring his second cup of coffee.

He is still lean and handsome, his crewcut hairstyle and tight black polo-necked sweater making him look younger than his sixty-eight years. Unlike my father, who used to be good-looking, but now looks like the sleek plumpish businessman that he is, but thinks that he isn't. Coonrodt had more wrinkles on his face though. He's also very well-tanned. Coonrodt reminds me of an eagle. A kindly, old eagle soaring high above the rest of us.

He usually wakes up at 4 am. It is now a little later than that. Strange cries emanate from his direction. Violent, strangulated screams.

His deck is overcrowded with small metal cages. Inside the cages there are beautiful Persian cats. Very frustrated, highly strung Persian cats all caterwauling to the heavens.

'Taiwanese restaurant in Paris.' He kisses me on both cheeks.

'Only joking,' he adds.

Coonrodt makes a living transporting whatever he can get his hands on. Or whatever people will let him. I'm sure that if the owners of the cats had seen his barge they wouldn't have given him a consignment of expensive and delicate creatures to transport. Not that he behaved in any way less than exemplary. But these days appearances count for everything. And neither Coonrodt's battered barge - 1947 vintage - nor his physical appearance would win him any lucrative contracts. The barges that ply the waters of the coastline of western Europe are sleek, steel coffins these days, carrying vacuum-packed cargo. Coonrodt is a modern-day version of the biblical boatman.

He transports anything and anyone, as long as it is legal. Sort of.

In times of financial hardship he has transported cigarettes to the desolate Cornish coast. Mostly though, it is anything from tricycles to truffles. Surprisingly he transports a lot of perishable food items. It is one of his mainstays. Shops and restaurants are starting to use him because he doesn't have strict schedules, and he's available at short notice. Mostly, he deals in mussels, which he ships in gargantuan quantities from the Dutch coasts to Brussels, a nation that consumes more mussels than any other group in the world. Food is big business these days. Piles of boxes of Parmesan shortbread, jars of El-Alhen figs, packs of T'yn Grug cheeses, Farinata from remote Italian villages. Not since the glory days of the Roman Empire has there been so much trafficking in exotic foodstuffs. Sometimes I wonder if there an augeral message in this. When nations develop all-consuming passions for the finery of dishes, a nitpicking obsession with ingredients, does it portend an end to civilisation?

His territory is small. The northern part of the French coast, Belgium, Holland, the remoter ports of England, and sometimes the Scandinavian countries. He has been doing this for more than twenty years. He is a drop-out, opting out of the fast lane of global shipping to be a sea-going tramp. He does something that most of us spend lifetimes trying to achieve. Getting paid for doing the work he dearly loves.

*

The first time Coonrodt came into my life he seemed like an old man. I was seven years old when my father started inviting him home for dinner. They had been colleagues for a few years before that. With his grizzly beard, ever-present pipe and smelly jerseys, he became a permanent fixture in my limited landscape. Now, twenty-three years later, the only difference between the man I knew as a child and the one that stands before me is that the lines have etched deeper into his face, his hair a shock of white and grey. His beard is white and wild.

'How's your father, mother?' He knows very well that I haven't visited them yet, that I always visit him first.

'Fine.' I stand at the cages making soothing cat noises. It is true anyway. I had spoken to my mother over the telephone. Told her I was going to be in the neighbourhood.

The cats can tell that I am not a cat lover. They turn up the volume. I prefer dogs.

'You need a wife,' I say to him, looking pointedly at the shoddy washing on his makeshift washing line.

'If you were a woman, would you come to this?' He sweeps his hand over his domain.

'I *am* a woman, in case you hadn't noticed. And no, I wouldn't come to this. You should get yourself a nice little flat with an ocean view.'

There was a time when Coonrodt used to joke about me taking care of him in his old age. But as he gets older he does it with less frequency. As if he's afraid to tempt fate.

Once, when I was eighteen, Coonrodt and I went on holiday together.

It wasn't meant to be a holiday. He went Malacca to sort out a house that he had there. Somebody was exploiting the fact that he was Dutch and didn't live there, and was trying to expropriate the property. He ended up selling the house. I went along for the ride.

It was to the sea of his youth, far, far away from Europe. It was a totally different world for me. Culture shock would be a gross understatement. The brilliance of the sun, the exotic lives of my mother's people. It was as if someone had stripped away a Vermeer to reveal a Monet underneath, all sunshine and brilliant light.

We met all his old comrades that he had sailed with in his distant past. Days and nights we went out with them, fishing, coasting, swimming.

I felt like Magellan, cruising the Flores and Celebes Seas. We even sailed as far south as Babar Island in the Arafura Sea.

He took me to Christ Church, built in 1753 to commemorate one hundred years of Dutch rule. It was where my parents met one rainy Sunday morning, and where they married exactly one year later. We were even attacked by pirates, firing wildly with semi-automatic weapons. Even now my heart still thumps wildly when I think about it. The acrid smell of gunsmoke smarting the eyes, the primeval screams tearing through the air. It was a kind of ferocity that strikes into the core of one's heart.

I give him the package that I have brought along. He holds it to his nose and sniffs ecstatically. Coonrodt and I share the same taste in coffee. A taste for Sumatra Mandheling. In his small cabin below, he has an ancient coffee grinder, its insides darkened with more than a hundred years of grinding beans. I'm not sure if it's the grinder, or his equally ancient coffee *plongeur* that makes his brew taste so special. The intoxicating aroma fills the tiny space. We saviour it in silence.

'I need information.'

'What kind?'

'Ships with special cargo. Immigrants.'

'There are hundreds of those in any month. You know that. Are you looking for trouble again?' Coonrodt coughs and puts down his coffee cup.

I explain my problem to him.

'Ha. Then it's slightly different. You're looking for a ship with a problem. Those are easier to find out about.'

Coonrodt knows everything along his stretch of coast, sometimes even beyond. Rumblings of mutiny, captains that have dumped illegal immigrants into the ocean because they can't be bothered to face all the paperwork, ships that regularly smuggle drugs into Rotterdam harbour. Plus all the trivial gossip.

I explain the details of my particular problem. The body in Rotterdam harbour. The missing hands. Also that the immigration angle might be only half a clue.

'Not a drowning that one. The man was taken out on a boat and thrown overboard. As he couldn't swim he drowned. Happens all the time. Didn't know about the hands. I mind my own business, so I don't know who did it, or why.'

'And nobody heard him scream?'

Coonrodt runs the palm of his hand across his mouth.

'He was taped?'

'Yes. And his hands were tied when he was on land. That is, his wrists were.'

'How do you know all this'

'Everybody was talking about it in the Richter.'

The Richter is Coonrodt's favourite - actually the only - bar that he frequents. It is a thirty minute walk from his boat. It is a seaman's bar, a Tower of Babel. There are sailors there from all parts of the globe, and places I didn't know existed. The only thing they have in common is that they all look as though they'd slit your throat in the dark without a second thought. The prostitutes also seem to reflect all nations of the world. The place is however, surprisingly violence-free, and serves some of the best seafood in the city.

'Nobody went to the police?'

Coonrodt shrugs his shoulders at me in mute abjectness. He looks away.

Immediately I feel contrite. The code of silence is not his fault. It is part of the culture of the docklands. It is changing, part of the ebb and flow of moods and alliances in this part of the world. Rapid movement means that there is less and less loyalty to ships, gangs, organisations. Already it is a microcosm of a society that is lagging behind with the times.

'Can you find out more?'

'For you, anything.'

I give him a hug.

When I was about fourteen, Coonrodt stopped coming to the house. It was about the same time he opted out of society. Naturally I assumed it was because of the sharp divergence in career paths between him and my father, although I really couldn't see why that would have a bearing on what to me seemed like a solid and eternal friendship. Career-wise Coonrodt had always been one step behind my father.

Always vice-captain to the captain, so to speak. Suddenly my father's career took a quantum leap. Instead of becoming captain of a bigger and better ship, he was appointed director of operations, in charge of the whole fleet, and the associated problems that go with the job. Ironically, this nominally desk-bound job meant that he stayed away from home more often than when he was a mere captain.

Coonrodt quietly slipped into the background. I still used to visit him once a week, on his barge. Gradually though, I became aware that his absence was not the sad outcome of a steady dissolution of a friendship. At home he wasn't talked about anymore. It was as if he didn't exist. If I mentioned that I had visited him, a deadening gloom clamped over the atmosphere. From then on I knew better than to ask questions.

An idea fomented in my mind. That Coonrodt and my mother had had an affair. It was the only plausible explanation I could think of. I had seen her face on the occasions his name was mentioned. A barely perceptible tightening of the jawline, the sudden rigidity in her posture. I couldn't say for sure, but I was fairly certain. Then I would think of her insufferable rectitude and dismiss the notion from my mind. Occasionally temptation floods over me like an endorphin rush, and I want to blurt out to Coonrodt, to ask him all the questions I have wanted to ask him over the years.

But I control it.

*

The old lady is stooping over her roses in the garden. Her skin looks so beautiful, so smooth in the dusk. Her hips as narrow as a sixteen year old. Only her breasts distort her shape. They are very large, and sag uncomfortably. At least, it looks that way to me.

I, unfortunately, inherited my father's bone structure, which means that at certain angles, and depending on the light, I can look like a farm-horse.

If it weren't for the relentless dowdiness of her clothes, the severe hairstyle, the old Dutch air of moral righteousness that hangs around her like a cloud, she could pass for a woman of forty instead of sixty-five.

'I arrived just a short while ago.' I lie glibly.

The smell of supper wafts out into the garden. I have starved myself the whole day for this. She takes my hands and leads me down the garden path.

'You look as though you're not eating.'

'I don't.' I'm just as susceptible as the next person to a little feeding and fussing over.

Her husband is sitting in the lounge watching soccer on the television.

He looks very comfortable surrounded by the trophies of his past, his certificates and photographs on the wall, his souvenirs from around the world. I know that the cupboards contain boxes of his service medals. When he dies I suspect everything will be buried with him, like a Viking sailor.

He picks up the newspaper when I walk in. He doesn't even unfold it. It is a nervous reaction, enacted to put a barrier between him and me. Most people simply fold their arms. On the other hand, a newspaper is less harsh, less intrusive.

He is polite and friendly though, as befits father who hasn't seen his only daughter for seven months. And a father who still harbours a residual measure of disapproval for his daughter's recent conduct.

Like so many figures of authority, he doesn't look so distinguished without his uniform on. Just another medium-sized Dutchman on the eve of retirement. With his captain's uniform and his high-crested cap, he is another person. A captain of captains.

Watching his inexorable rise through the shipping ranks was like watching a movie and wilfully disengaging from the plight of the leading character. One does this for a particular reason, mostly perhaps because one loses sympathy for the hero.

And he had been my hero - even if only for a short but important period in my life.

Now he is a stranger.

*

I wouldn't say that the case of Jools vs. Transline Shipping enthralled an entire nation. It did however generate a fair bit of debate within certain circles in the country.

The details are as follows:

Captain Dawid Jools chartered a ship from owners Transline Shipping (owned by Dakonite Corporation), as he had been doing regularly for the past fifteen years. The ship was then hired by an English company, Williams Electronics, for the transport of goods to China. The bill of lading showed the goods listed as 'electronic equipment'. Before the ship departed from Liverpool, customs officials boarded the vessel and found a wide range of illegal weapons. Batons, electric prods, gas containers, even water cannons. They arrested the captain.

According to the Cargo of Goods Act, codified in The Hague-Visby Rules of 1968, the captain, as the one party of the contract of carriage - the other being Williams Electronics - was liable for checking the bill of lading which is meant to identify the goods he is transporting. Normally, the shipping company is the liable party, but as the captain had chartered the ship on his own volition, he was the sole bearer of responsibility.

Under duress, the captain broke down and made all sorts of allegations. That he had taken the goods under implicit instructions from Transline, and that he had often been asked to do this. That if he refused, they would revoke the extremely favourable terms (so favourable, we found, as to be downright charitable) at which he was allowed to charter their ships. He also alleged that Dakonite Corporation was the chief mover, as both Williams and Transline were wholly-owned subsidiaries of the corporation. They functioned entirely independently, but the lines always ended up with Dakonite.

The firm of lawyers I worked for was hired by Greenpeace to represent the captain. I was Jools's lawyer. After a lengthy battle, we were, as predicted, annihilated in court. We did however win the hearts and minds of the people.

When you get neatly parcelled excrement put through your door, when old boyfriends and neighbours are questioned about your personal habits, when the tax man comes calling because of an anonymous tip he's received that says you're running a brothel from your place of dwelling, it's hard not to imagine that someone might be after you. Did I mention the fact that I had a broken foot because someone pushed me down the stairs of the court building and didn't bother hanging around to find out how I was?

My father had flicked his head in annoyance when I told him all this, as though I was a malingering child unwilling to attend school. Perhaps my head in a bag on his doorstep would have convinced him. He said I was "paranoid".

The strange thing - perhaps it's not so strong - was that not a hint of anything personal was ever brought up in court, not a hint of subtle coercion. The corporation's lawyers were models of decorum and nicety. I refuse to believe they couldn't find anything nasty about me, that I have lived a life of such propriety. Consequently, I can only assume it was all a show of strength, of what they could do if they wanted to.

Captain Jools found it all too much. He hanged himself shortly after, leaving a wife and three children with very little in the way of financial security. Like Coonrodt, he had been an acquaintance of my father's before their career paths diverged.

My father, the fleet captain (one hundred and fifty vessels) of another of Dakonite's shipping groups, Euroline, was in a tricky situation. I was sympathetic to his position, but not prepared for what followed.

I don't think Dakonite would have been foolish enough to put pressure on him to get at me, but he clearly disapproved of my actions. I received no support from him. None whatsoever. He didn't tell me outright what he thought, but his air of suppurating frustration spoke volumes. The way his mouth twisted into curlicues of distaste when I had attempted to discuss the matter with him made me want to punch him.

I stopped going home, spoke to my mother on the phone when he wasn't there, put the phone down when he was. Planned my visiting trips by scanning the shipping reports to see when he was out of town.

Nothing was the same again. It was as if sloughs of ice had descended upon our shoulders freezing us into pillars of silence.

'What are you doing in Rotterdam?' he says with barely feigned disinterest.

'Relax dad, I'm about to embarrass you and your precious career again.' I want to say to him, but the words don't come out.

'Business. My new job.'

I haven't officially told him who I work for, so he doesn't officially ask. My mother knows, so she must have told him something. The absurdity does cross my mind. The sheer stupidity of two adults behaving with such pig-headedness, such stubbornness. It is shameful, that we perpetuate a drama that started long ago, when, as a teenager we rowed in similar fashion. My mother was the centre of gravity then. She had the power to chastise me. Now, I don't care much for her entreaties. Her fretting and silent fuming. But then, I have a greater measure of self-awareness now.

Yet we are both trapped in this endless cycle.

He asks me a few desultory questions, then goes back to his newspaper.

In the kitchen my mother talks to me about her relationship with God as she ladles out her roasted pumpkin pie, hot bread, mustardy mashed potatoes. My mother holds no brief for people who blanch at overdosing on carbohydrates.

As if reading my mind, she tells me that she has already packed a food basket for me. I thank her, in that excessive way that usually has its roots in guilt.

In the garden I make a quick phone call to Boehme. He tries to dissuade me from seeking an interview with the chief of police in Rotterdam.

'You're not Van der Valk. It is not your job. We can file an official report when you get back. We don't want to cause any trouble with the police.'

'This looks like gross negligence to me. This man had his hands severed. The information I'm requesting is one hundred percent legitimate. You know that. Besides, I've already made an appointment.'

'Okay, okay.' he relents, 'but none of your aggressive bullshit. This is not Hollywood. You're there to find out about a dead man, not to hang the police for incompetence.'

'That's fine by me. Just one thing. How do I bring up the subject of a man whose hands were chopped off and his mouth taped over when the police describe it as an 'accidental drowning'?'

Boehme slams the phone down. He's always a sore loser.

'The problem with you, Boehme,' I say to myself, 'is that you are only a slightly good person. And that is a bit like being only slightly pregnant.'

Pity he's not around to hear it.

*

The police captain, Ton van Kessel, is a big, charming man in his fifties. He's over six feet tall, with a ruddy, happy face. He looks like an overgrown schoolboy, with his bad haircut and naughty grin.

He pulls my chair out with a flourish, offers me coffee and biscuits and seems more distraught than I am that the air conditioner in the office is not working. Naturally, I'm swept off my feet.

There is another man in the office. The section head of the harbour police, Guus Antes. There's nothing friendly about him. He's straining on an invisible leash, exuding an air of palpable hostility, one hand drumming rapidly on the desk, as if he's getting ready to tear at my throat. I can tell that he's not a seafaring person, that he has no affinity for the ocean. His skin is a ghostly pallor. He's much younger than the captain, a yuppie on his way up. His shoes are a giveaway. They're a pair of black Italian loafers. Clean and shiny. And delicately flimsy. Not the sort of shoes to wear at the docks. That tells me he doesn't like his posting. He'd rather be in some smart detective outfit, or in commercial crimes.

When he shakes my hand, his palms are soft and flabby. For a moment it looks like it might be one of those good cop/bad cop routines that they show on television, but there isn't the slightest bit of affection from captain Van Kessel. He's just a big puppy.

'What can we do for you?' It is the hard-as-nails harbour captain. Van Kessel is still gazing at me adoringly.

'A man was found in the harbour...'

'A drowning. As we've said in the report.' Mr Hard-as-nails leans forward, as if about to challenge me to a head-butting competition. My icy glance shuts him up.

'I haven't finished yet. According to my information, he was minus both his hands and his mouth was taped over. There is nothing in the report about this.'

'Forensics didn't find anything out of the ordinary. It was listed as a drowning.'

'That may indeed be the case. But rope marks on a body would be pretty easy to spot. What about the missing hands? Do you think they were neatly bitten off by a shark perhaps?' I have no idea if this is true or not. It's a chance I take.

Hard-as-nails is foaming at the mouth. His temples are throbbing dangerously. He is a candidate for a stroke. I don't know what I have done to provoke him, but then again it could be very generalised rage. Against the people I work for, against the government, the EC. There is a wedding band on his finger. His wife must really suffer his bursts of anger.

'The cut was consistent with a ship's propeller. You are aware that corpses in the sea often get mutilated in this manner. You must realise madam, that we cannot thoroughly examine every single body that comes into the morgue. We are chronically understaffed.'

Van Kessel looks shocked by the behaviour of the two of us, his face getting redder by the minute. He grips the side of his chair and half-stands up.

'It has nothing to do with the fact that the victim was probably an immigrant. We treat all of the dead the same. As a matter of fact, we are not one hundred percent certain that he was an immigrant. We treat all bodies the same.'

'I understand. Perfectly. I'm only questioning the police procedure in assessing the cause of death.'

'The body has been cremated. There is nothing more to do.'

It is the creep again, exultantly flourishing this bit of news at me, twisted pleasure written all over his face.

'Besides, it could have been terrorist related. Tamil Tigers for all we know.'

A flush of real anger overwhelms me for the first time.

'What you're saying is, it's okay if they kill each other, as long as no Dutch citizens are involved. That they can wilfully murder each other on our soil. You're a first-class prick. And you always will be. You ought to try and get out more often. I will get Brussels to write to the commissioner. Your job is on the line.'

It is another bluff on my part but it is worth a try.

He gapes at me with his mouth open. I like good exits. It gives me a fleeting sense of power.

The captain ushers me out, his eyes silently imploring contriteness. I shrug my shoulders reassuringly. I have no intention of carrying out my threats.

'If there's anything I can do to help you further...'

'How about breakfast?' I say.

The initial look of shock on his face is quickly replaced by a beaming smile.

'Give me five minutes.'

In the small coffee shop across the road, he apologises again for his colleague's brutal behaviour.

'He's young and ambitious. You know how it is.'

'No, I don't,' I answer. 'Who says you have to behave like that? What rule is there that you have to behave like a bastard to get ahead in life?

It is a perversion of our sense of values that we have to stomp on people to assert our superiority. That is why we have wars. Anyway, you don't look as though you got ahead in life by trampling on other people.'

His eyes light up at my compliment.

'Ah, what is it you want from me,' he asks almost coquettishly.

'A little information. Is it true that the body has been cremated?'

'I'm afraid it is.'

He looks at me intently. Then I see my mistake reflected in his eyes. In thinking that this portly, avuncular man was somehow less of a policeman than my expectations required.

'There is something else.' He is a different man now. Intense, stronger, steely. His body is tense, the muscles in his shoulders hunched up like a rugby player's.

I lean forward expectantly.

'There might be a blood sample floating around somewhere. It's usually taken from the victim as part of the autopsy. The report could be anywhere. It's also possible that it hasn't even come back from the lab. There's a huge backlog. The usual story, shortage of staff. The technicians often queue jump with the more urgent cases. I have no idea where it is.'

'Can you find out?'

He picks up his coffee cup without looking at me. He's thinking, weighing the pros and cons of handing me information that, legally speaking, I'm not entitled to. Not without the necessary paperwork anyway. It would earn him a rap on the knuckles. Or something worse.

'I'll keep quiet.' The hint of desperation in my voice makes him break into a bleak smile.

'Okay, I'll see what I can do.'

He takes my business card gingerly, as though it has strange talismanic powers.

'I'd better get going.'

'Do you really need to?' The sheer guilelessness of his voice disarms me.

'Have another cup of coffee.' he adds hastily, lest I misconstrue his message.

We chat about this and that. He tells me about his wife and children, his life in the police force. Shows me pictures. A man of common decency, a committed civil servant, implacably devoted to his family and his job. There are not many of those around.

I leave him to spend the rest of the day with Coonrodt. He's taking me fishing. Ironically, for a pastime that values solitariness, I have never been able to do it on my own. The silence of his company is a rare pleasure. Coonrodt knows some interesting spots. Deep artificial gullies in the canal where large, ancient fish lurk. The view is not edifying though, deserted warehouses with broken windows, abandoned railway tracks running into nowhere. The pervasive smell of rotting wood. The seagulls wheel noisily above us, breaking the silence. An occasional Boeing streaks slowly across the high skies, vapour trails lingering like wispy tails. If God was a European existentialist, this would be his idea of heaven.

Chapter 3

'I said you could go to Rotterdam, but I didn't say that you could spend two days down there.' Boehme's studied truculence flies completely above my head.

Quietly I outline the results of my investigations. I stick to the facts, leaving out the personality clashes. His bulldog face relaxes only marginally, but it's the best he can summon from within himself. I also leave out Van Kessel's offer of the results of the blood test. Boehme is unpredictable when it comes to maintaining law and order. He has no qualms about bending the regulations when it comes to himself, but he doesn't like anyone else to do it. It has to do with control. It is a principle he applies to excessive alcohol consumption. He will drink himself to into a stupor but woe betide anybody else in the office who does. It is worse if you are female.

'You'd better phone your London boyfriend.'

'Jealous, Boehme?'

The door slams after him.

Two seconds later he pokes his head out again.

'Give the data to him and tell him to hand it to immigration. Where it belongs.'

I phone Helm.

'Oh, so glad you called. I've been checking out Hermes, the new pattern recognition software we have installed at head office. It seems that we may be onto something. I found another body that matches the general description of the others. In France. Cherbourg, to be precise.'

'Do me a favour.'

'Yes?'

'Run a similar pattern check for Chinese corpses, and then for Africans. Call me back.'

*

I go shopping for new clothes. Unlike other people, I am an inspired shopper only when I'm happy.

On the way back, I slip into the building and take the elevator to the underground parking so that Boehme doesn't see me. He doesn't like his staff running personal errands while at work. He even frowns if you come back from lunch with your arms full of parcels.

The phone rings as I reach my desk. It is Helm. He is contrite and subdued. He has found similar patterns, he says. Many similar patterns.

I go easy on him.

'It's not your fault. Deaths at ports involving illegal immigrants and foreigners are very high.'

'I thought you said that you didn't know much about criminal activity.'

'I don't.'

The reason I know this little fact is that when I was working on the Transline case I had to wade through a lot of eye-opening documents about life outside our cosy, cosseted middle-class little environments.

Sifting through all the official documents relating to shipping conditions at the various Dutch ports, another less romantic picture slowly formed. They were dull papers, couched in technical speak, listing mishaps, injuries and deaths at the ports. The overwhelming majority of these "mishaps" happened to foreigners, either crewing ships legally or illegally.

'It doesn't necessarily mean that your theory is wrong though.' I add quickly to assuage his misery.

'But if you say that this is a regular occurrence...'

'Yes, the deaths are, but the level of violence isn't. Accidents, sheer neglect, yes. Missing hands, no.'

'Oh.' He makes it sound like he'd like to slap himself across the face.

'Are you sure you've never had any experience in detective work.'

'Nope.'

'Natural born talent then?'

'Something like that.'

'Ha. Thanks for your help anyway.'

'My pleasure.'

We say our goodbyes.

His e-mail has arrived. I log on to the FSS database and call up the video clip on my computer. It takes a couple of minutes to load.

A red warning message flashes on the screen. It reminds viewers, ie police personnel, that what they are about to see may make them ill, or words to that effect. I wonder idly if it is yet another bizarre EU directive.

The clip is dark, grainy, and badly filmed. This does not detract from its stark horror. The bodies float lazily in the ocean, upright, like a pod of sleeping whales. They are tethered by rope to the ocean floor. When the camera moves in closer, it is possible to discern their physical features. They are blurred like charcoal drawings that have had their edges smoothed away, the effect of salt water on flesh. I move my chair away from the screen. It doesn't help the feeling in my stomach, so I go to the bathroom for a glass of water. By the time I reach the sink, I am ready to retch.

Jung, in his analysis of synchronistic phenomena, stated that the unconscious wills events, and that the basis of synchronicity was what the ancients called "sympathy of all things". The negative side of this is, of course, the common, everyday occurrence of bad things happening in clusters, which is why I get a cold feeling in the pit of my stomach when Boehme summons me into his office.

His face is impassive, eyes hooded and dark. When duty calls, it's as though he shuts down all the non-essentials of his body. His brain takes over. He becomes a monolith of energy. It is an impressive sight.

'This came through on the computer.' He flings a report at me.

It is a printout of the daily collation of police activity in Europe, and sometimes the rest of the world, if the crime has international implications or involves citizens of the European Union.

There's a excursive red ring next to one of the entries. A three-line entry. Death of a Tamil subject. Body found in Hamburg. Assailants not as yet apprehended.

There's a name attached to it. Visuvanathan Rudrakumaran.

'He's the son of the Sri Lankan military attache to Germany. Or rather, he was.'

I don't say anything. I don't think Boehme wants me to. His pause is purely for effect.

'His hands are missing.'

This time I mutter something under my breath.

Boehme continues, 'Initial forensic reports show that the severance was a result of a high-heat implement. There are signs of extreme cauterisation on the skin. The forensics people are not used to seeing bodies carved up by laser, so they're seeking a second opinion. But we can assume it was laser beams. There's nothing else out there that could have caused that kind of damage.'

Boehme has a copy of the day's *Berliner Morgenpost* on his desk. He throws the paper messily across to me as well.

'The papers are already calling it a racist attack. And so are the Sri Lankans. It could be true, or it could also be some kind of revenge attack. The incident happened in the *Reeperbahn*. There are unconfirmed reports that he had gambling debts, and mixed with a rough crowd.'

'But you don't think so?' Boehme smiles wanly at me. The smile, together with his corrugated forehead, gives him a conspiring air, as though the two of us shared a dirty secret and were bent on keeping quiet.

'No.' I answer.

'What I didn't tell you,' Boehme continues, 'is that he was also garrotted, presumably to finish him off quickly. Not the usual method thugs use, or racists for that matter. No trace of the wire either. Pockets were also empty. Could have been a robbery, but then the thieves took everything, personal effects, the lot. Robbers don't do that. *And* they left his gold chain. I thought it might be related to your Englishman's incidents.'

'He's not "my Englishman", I snort, but Boehme's not listening, or pretending not to. His head is already in his papers, and he waves his arms at me, as though he couldn't be bothered with such trifles.

The temptation to reach over and slap him is great.

As I turn the door handle, he shouts at me without deigning to pick his head up, 'The captain in Hamburg is Walther Karcher. Find out what he knows.'

'Are you putting me onto a case?'

'This is no case. I want data to process.'

Before I call the captain in Hamburg, I phone Helm.

'Yes, I saw it late last night, on my way out. Interesting. Are you're going to Hamburg?

'No idea.'

'Want to come to London?' he asks.

'Why?'

'Well, I could share all the information I have with you.'

'This is the age of mass communication,' I remind him. 'We have the internet, faxes, video-phones, video-conferencing, and let's not forget courier services.'

'I heard about your trip to Rotterdam, so I thought that perhaps you'd want to further abuse government funds.'

A knock on my door prevents us from sliding further into nonsensical chatter.

'Package for you. Express mail.' Ilsa leers at me. She thinks that everyone who receives brown envelopes in the post are getting hard-core porno material or LSD-impregnated sheets of paper.

It is the results of the drug test from captain Van Kessel along with an endearingly sweet handwritten note which reads:

Dear Ms Barvalis de Hoop

Thank you for your visit. It was very nice chatting to you. May I may take the liberty of telling you that you brightened up my day considerably!

Again, I must apologise for the behaviour of my colleague. I hope he didn't upset you too much!

Here are the results of the tests. If you need any further assistance, please do not hesitate to contact me.

Yours Sincerely

Ton van Kessel

The blood sample report is very complicated. Boehme is the only person who understands what's in it. The only line I understand is the line that says "HIV-negative".

He glances at it briefly. 'It's a normal toxicology report. If there was anything unusual, they would have highlighted it. This is not going to tell you anything.'

I phone the police captain in Hamburg. After an interminable wait listening to an overwrought orchestral version of "Hey Jude" he comes to the phone. His voice is deep and hoarse. He sounds like the city, impersonal, tired, overworked, suffused with the cliched *weltschmerz* that is supposed to be "Hamburg".

He also mistakes me for a journalist.

'I have nothing to say. You'll have to call the press office. I will give you the number.'

It takes a while for me to explain who I work for and where I am.

Then he slouches back even further into his cynicism.

'He was garrotted by wire, judging by the deep marks. Not your normal method of killing, even for the neo-Nazis. Also, there were no personal effects on his person. Nothing. I'm not saying that it's not possible for a group of street thugs to strangle a man and then systematically remove all the contents of his pockets. Muggers take wallets, jewellery, but there is always something left behind. Items of no value. Tickets, receipts. This is not a random killing. And this is the professional judgement of myself and my colleagues.'

'What are you saying?'

'I'm not saying anything. I'm merely presenting a series of facts to you.'

'There is one matter to consider.'

'What's that?'

'Mr Rudrakumaran had been convicted by the police on a previous occasion. Brawling and assault on a police officer. They also found drugs on his person, but didn't prosecute on that charge. It was a small amount of marijuana. It seems that he mixed with a pretty unsavoury bunch in Hamburg. According to his father, the boy was warned that he would be sent back home if he didn't behave. He was only nineteen. Horrible way to die.'

He shudders over the phone.

'But you've seen worse, right?'

He's not sure what to make of my comment, whether I'm being impertinent or empathetic. In the end, he's overcome by his own inertia. He does however, agree to fax all the documentation to me.

Chapter 4

The woman who greets me in the foyer of the operations building for ATS, the Dutch Anti-Terrorism Squad looks vaguely familiar. She's a petite woman, older than me, I would say in her late thirties. Her face resembles that of a cherubic choir boy, except for the scar that runs from her left ear to just beneath her jaw-line. It is not a livid, dark scar but it is plainly visible. Her hair is cropped short, and is carefully dishevelled so that the gelled tufts stick out in all directions. It gives her that wild and windy look. It also reminds me of that profound statement that someone once made about Ghandi, that it costs a lot of money to keep him in poverty. Her suit has been impeccably tailored to fit her small frame. She has little bits of tasteful antique silver jewellery scattered about her person, the way a good interior designer plants objects d'art in a house. Her makeup is applied according to the same rules so that you don't really notice the clever work that makes her eyes seem so large and lustrous. Even her handcuffs look as though they born to dangle from her hips. She walks confidently, aided by her sensible flat shoes.

'It's you,' she says cautiously by way of greeting. The face comes back to me. She's in the same Tae kwon Do class as me. The fault is not entirely mine. This is the first time that I have seen her without her white suit and black beret. Before she had reached me, she had paused to stick her gum into an ashtray. Now, she unwraps a new pack pops a stick into her mouth.

'Anti-smoking gum. Sorry I can't offer you a piece.'

I smile at her weak joke.

She stares at me intensely for a moment, causing a flash of panic in me.

'So, Europol? I was wondering when I would come across one of you people.'

'What do you mean?' I ask cautiously. There is no bitterness in her voice, but there is a certain amount of disdainful bemusement in her eyes.

'Well, I hear that we now have to work together. Very soon we'll be like the Americans. The FBI fighting with the CIA, the CIA fighting with the NIA.'

There is a certain amount of truth in what she says. Under article 10, Title III of the Europol Convention, the activities of the organisation have been broadly increased. Instead of simply being a repository for data on criminal activities, the organisation now has the power to meddle in illegal immigration, trafficking in nuclear materials, corruption, xenophobia and terrorism - which, up until now, has been the exclusive preserve of member states.

Her desk is in an open-plan office. The entire floor consists of cubicles. Everything looks and smells new. Even the twenty-five year olds that scurry by look like they're auditioning for roles in an American police series. Predictably, the existence of the ATS is not something that is widely known, or publicised. Unlike the Americans, the Europeans tend to keep their elite special forces hidden away from the limelight. We don't make fancy television programmes so that the whole world can see how we operate.

Which, of course, also means that all our little mistakes and mishaps tend to be swept under the carpet as well.

Barbara Benschop-Fehr's little cubbyhole is festooned with tasteful apercus to her personality. She's a determinedly cultural individual. The Van Gogh exhibition postcards. Pictures that show she's been to the Guggenheim Museum in New York. A small bust of Voltaire sits on her computer. A woman after my own heart.

Next to her desktop computer, she has a sleek black notebook computer. Nearby, the detritus of a modern workaholic. Empty cartons of organic homemade soup from some farming co-op in the country, dome-capped cappuccino containers.

'Tamil Tigers. European activity,' she says emphatically.

She's talking to her computer. It seems to respond.

'What have we got here.' She reads her screen and then suddenly swivels in my direction.

'What would you like to know?'

'Everything.'

'Right. Follow me. Let's do this properly.'

She gets up and walks towards a glass-walled room in a corner of the floor. I follow her as ordered.

'Coffee?' she asks me without turning around.

'No thank you.'

'Ops room.'

The lights comes on as soon as we enter the room. She presses a few buttons on the computerised gizmo on the table and the room darkens as a white screen embedded in the wall shimmers to life. It's all perfectly synchronised. A little bit of theatrical showbiz to impress visitors, especially the politicians who like to see that their money is well spent.

'Boehme has briefed me about the murders.' she says, clicking more buttons.

'Do you know him?' I ask.

'Only by reputation. He's a legend.'

A picture of the island of Sri Lanka shimmers on the screen. It is green except for two red blobs.

She has one of those laser beam pointers in her hand.

'Basically, the Tamil Tigers want a Tamil homeland in Sri Lanka. They feel that the majority Sinhalese cannot coexist with the minority Tamils. Here and here.'

She points to the two red blobs.

'In the north and east of Sri Lanka. Since 1983, the liberation Tigers of Tamil Eelam have waged a war which has claimed over 50 000 lives. In Sri Lanka, it has suffered serious losses against government forces, losing its former stronghold of Jaffna - where they have been a sort of government in residence. Paradoxically, the position around the world is not the same.'

She presses another button and a picture of the world shimmers into view . It is very impressive.

'Somebody at the LTTE has been taking lessons in global capitalism. They have built up an impressive and complex network of businesses around the world that ensures a steady supply of income to finance its operations. To do this, they have drawn on the resources of the Tamil diaspora. They have built up an extensive business empire that mirrors a global corporate structure - commercial companies, small businesses, informal banking channels, a fleet of Liberian-registered ships, property, money-laundering, you name it. Politically they operate visibly in about forty countries around the world. No funding source is too small for them and they make a few million just from collections. Tithes you could call it.

'Their procurement procedure for arms is very interesting. It started off as a small-scale smuggling operation across the Palk

Strait between India and Sri Lanka. They then moved up to speedboats. With the help of a few rich Indian shipping merchants, the LTTE has purchased its own fleet of ships - registered under Panamanian, Honduran or Liberian flags and largely crewed by Tamils. They make money out of it too. Ninety percent of what they transport is legitimate goods - timber, paddy, fertiliser. The rest is, of course, arms. It has been a classic business expansion programme. They also have their own little navy - Sea Tiger Naval Wing. '

'And what is the Dutch connection,' I ask.

'Him.'

A picture of an avuncular, smiling man appears on the screen. He's dark-complexioned and dressed in a dark suit, shirt open at the neck. His face is moon-shaped and his small eyes seem deeply embedded in a large expanse of flesh. His head is crowned by luxuriantly coiffured black hair. He looks like a failed musician or an ice-cream vendor

Mr Laxman Kadirgamer. European head of operations. Based in Amsterdam for the past five years.'

She shows me a few more grainy pictures of his portly frame entering a shabby building, leaving the building, getting into his car.

'Pretty shrewd operator. Has been under sporadic surveillance by us for about two years, but has never been remotely connected with any illegal activity. Our informers say that he has demonstrated a capacity for extreme ruthlessness in his homeland. Eyewitness accounts say he has personally butchered captured Sinhalese soldiers. No hard evidence though. Apparently keeps his hands clean in Europe, no doubt terrified of our swift and just legal system.

'Spends a lot of time with Tamil expatriates in the city, the very model of a concerned emigre. Provides funds to the needy, etc. Hands out money like Father Christmas. Buys all the books, videos, pays the salaries of the 'volunteers'. Also spends time with a number of Dutch businessmen. One of them, Gijd den Baorghas, a former Congo mercenary, runs a shipping firm that imports wood from Thailand. We suspect that the company is a front and is owned by the LTTE. So far, no proof. Den Baorghas says that he got the money to start the company from gambling in the Bahamas. Who are we to argue.'

She hits the buttons emphatically to switch off the screen.

'And where would I find Kadirgamer during working hours?'

She stops and stares as if I had asked her an impolitely intimate question. Her laser pointer is trained on the ceiling of the room. She seems to fumble for an explanation.

'We have documented policy on that matter. There has to be liaison between the organisations concerned. I have to check with my boss.'

'What you are saying is that we have to fill in a lot of forms.'

She hides her sheepish smile by half turning away from me.

'Something like that.'

'What, ' I say to her politely, 'is the correct procedure for finding out whether the LTTE were behind these killings?'

'I'm afraid I really don't know. As Europol is a new organisation, we don't have a formulated policy with regard to mutual assistance and co-operation. I'm sure that you appreciate the situation, given the responsibilities of each of our organisations. I would imagine that it would be similar to our relationship with Interpol, but as Europol has a much more hand-on approach to law and order, there might be a few rather fundamental differences.'

It occurs to me that I ought to remind her of my rights as a taxpayer, but then it occurs to me that ninety-nine point nine percent of the Dutch population don't know of the existence of the ATS. And probably don't care. I try another tactic. I plead. Subtly.

'If you're thinking of doing one of those "sisters are together" acts, you can forget it.' There's no harshness in her voice, only a gentle chastisement, as if disappointed that I'd stoop so low. At the same time she brushes aside my clumsy apology. Carefully, so as not to cause me undue embarrassment.

'Would you like some coffee?' I answer yes this time, and she leaves the room. I press the buttons on the screen to have another look at the slides. This time I pay careful attention.

She returns, carrying a slightly different air about her, less formal, more inquisitive.

She shares a bit more information with me. It is nothing substantial. Most of what she says I could probably get off the

Internet or from the Economist magazine. She also tells me about ATS and how it functions. I try not to pry too much.

In the car a comment that she had made about working suddenly strikes me. She knew how long I'd been in my new job. It explains why she took so long to get the coffee. She'd been checking up on me, no doubt using her extensive network of computer connections to call up my court records, my school history, university records, and my current bank balance.

Bitch.

All the same, I like her. She has style, chutzpah, and an awareness of history.

The bridge over the Singel canal is lined with trees. At this time of year the leaves have started to fall. There aren't many of the small canal bridges that are tree-lined, and it's difficult to comprehend why someone would have attempted this engineering feat on so short a span of bridge, but they have, and it exists, for which we have to be grateful. It is a short but beautiful detour. I start to slow down at Oude Nieuwstraat 15. It is a squat, ugly three-storey building. The window panes have been painted white recently, with no thought to what it does to the aesthetics of the building. All the lights are on and I can see figures moving around on all the floors. The overall impression is of one of those cheap night schools, or acting classes.

A car behind me hoots impatiently. The Dutch are slowly starting to learn all the bad habits of American drivers, presumably from what they see in the movies. The car lurches past, the driver turning his head to glare at me. Its plates are French. So I don't feel too guilty about giving him the V sign.

There is a young Tamil man in an anorak standing outside the door of the building. He looks lost and forlorn, hands thrust deep into his pockets. After hesitating further, he opens the door and goes inside.

I drive past.

Chapter 5

To be free from the impositions of daily routines is a curiously liberating experience. It is, one would imagine, akin to going on holiday, especially if the vacation spot was your own city. Everything takes on a different hue. Things are seen through a stranger's eyes. Light, colour, sound, all seem different. I am also wearing new attire.

A short skirt, black stockings and high heels. To be honest, it is only the skirt and the shoes that are new purchases. The rest are from my one wardrobe. But they make all the difference. I keep the shoes in a brown bag and cover the skirt with a long coat, just in case anybody sees me leaving my flat. I go to the cinema first, at 10 pm. After the movie, I have coffee and think about what I'm about to do. In the toilets of the coffee-shop I apply a little more makeup.

Then I return to my car and dump the coat and my flat shoes. It is now after midnight.

At night the area takes on a slightly different character. There is a small red- light district bounded by the canal and the main street. It is a dark and occasionally ugly place. The girls that work here cater mainly to the locals from the surrounding working-class areas. There are no cheery prostitutes in houses with large glass windows. Most of the furtive fumblings take place in the alleyways. The teenage drug addicts who lie sprawled in the gutters after freebasing on heroin are another tourist deterrent.

I step out of the shadows, my heart pounding. The car is two blocks behind, in a side alley.

After a couple of minutes the walking becomes easier. A man strolls past, avoiding looking into my eyes, but at the same time gazing at my body. There is an exhilarating pleasure in both the aimlessness and in the adaptation of a new persona. A liberating joy, and an actor's freedom. At the same time it is mixed with the irrational fear that such a pleasure might become addictive.

There are two women standing under a faded awning at the entrance to a health shop. They stop talking and stare at me, suspicion and anger building up in their eyes. It is a territorial aggression. I would feel the same way if somebody invaded my workspace.

Nevertheless, I don't want a black eye or a broken wrist. So when they swagger over, I adopt a posture as non-threatening as possible. My lips end up sticking to my teeth.

'Good evening girls.' In my hand I clutch my Europol identity card. It is not as impressive as one of those shiny American badges but it works.

'What do you want here?' They say almost in unison.

Self-consciousness threatens to overwhelm me and destroy any vestige of authority I may still possess. Through smiling teeth and forced friendliness - lest anybody is watching - I tell them brusquely that I'm not there to steal their territory. That I only need the space for a few nights to observe the area. I do not make the mistake of telling them what building I intend keeping my eyes on. Surprisingly, they believe me. Their aggression melts into superciliousness.

Nicola and Katinka have been working this stretch of road for six months. They know most of the traffic and the passing trade. They have no pimps, they proudly say, when I carefully ask, in case they are working for the occupants of number fifteen. The only person that they on speaking terms with is a German marijuana dealer who lives in one of the houses. He provides them with hot chocolate on cold nights.

'The world is our oyster. We're captains of our own ship.' Katinka blows smoke into my face as if she believes in what she's just said.

Safe from the predations of the police and pimps, they start telling me, with all the outraged indignation of two old ladies, all about the drug addicts, the petty street crime, the illegal immigrants. They deliver an impassioned tirade against exotic Nigerian girls, accusing them of undercutting their trade. Under the guise of asking them about all the people in the street, I ask about the Tamils.

'They come and go at all times of the night,' says Nicola, offering me one half of a beef sandwich that she has carefully removed from her handbag. I tell her that I don't eat red meat.

'I bet you suck cock.' She laughs raucously in my face.

I don't deign to answer her.

'Only men pass through that door, no women, no children,' adds Katinka. 'They are not very friendly. They seem to hate us, which is a cheek seeing that this is our country. They are quiet and very meek. Sometimes they sing strange songs upstairs. And their food smells!'

'So, what is it exactly that you're after?' The look on Nicola's face tells me that she's tried hard, but can't control her curiosity any longer.

'Shhhh, it's a government state secret,' giggles Katinka.

I laugh along, but with all the fake ruefulness I can muster, I sadly decline to tell her.

They then start to tell me the tricks of their profession with all the passion and pride of a tradesmen revealing the arcana of his trade. It is an illuminating lesson. At around 3 am they decide to call it a night. Business has been bad. I apologise profusely for taking up their time.

On the second night, I arrive earlier, at 8 pm. This is the time the girls start working. I have brought them food, roasted pumpkin with feta cheese, stuffed in pita bread. Just to prove that vegetarian food can be satisfying. We sit on a broken bench near the canal, tying up the loose ends from the previous night's conversation.

At 8:20 an old white Toyota sedan pulls up outside the block. Laxman Kadirgamer eases his bulk out carefully from the back seat. He walks around to the pavement, leans back into the window and says something to his driver. When he turns, he meets my stare. There is in his eyes a flicker of distaste, as if I was a lump of dog shit. Katinka childishly sticks her tongue out at him.

'Told you they weren't very keen on us.' she says.

He is wearing a hairpiece, something that didn't show up in the photographs. The streetlight reflecting on it makes it look unnaturally blue. His face is even plumper, beady eyes darting from person to person. Even from where I am sitting, I can see that his blue suit is too small for him. The buttons on his white shirt are threatening to pop around his belly. The battered brown briefcase he carries is chained to his hand. His demeanor is that of a slum landlord, rather than a terrorist head.

On the fifth and sixth nights he's there again, same briefcase, same chain. Same dirty look.

*

There are many blocks in Amsterdam like my own. Sturdy solid buildings constructed during the nineteenth century for the rich merchants who ruled the oceans of the world. Naturally they wanted to live in style. The Dutch however, pride functionality above style, so, while you are made aware of the owner's wealth, there are no outlandish embellishments or florid curlicues that you would find in, say Victorian buildings. The houses are solid, built to weather the years. It suits me fine. The thick walls keep out the noise from both the street as well as from the neighbours. The two rooms that I have are inordinately large; when you lie on a low bed, the room is even bigger, the patterned ceiling a distant sky. There is a row of fading holes on the ceiling, and the owner, Mr Gervoldt, says that the Germans sprayed the walls with bullets. I didn't believe him until I leaned dangerously out of the window, looked down beneath and saw the bullets still embedded in the wall. The wood around the window had long been replaced. Nothing exciting Mr Gervoldt had said. Only a callow Wehrmacht soldier losing control of his machine gun mounted on the back of a truck while on patrol, much to the derision of his fellow soldiers. This was in 1941. Only later did it occur to me that he must have been a young boy at that time, and possibly lived in the house with his parents.

Somewhere in the back of my mind there is the notion that I may pack up and leave in a hurry. It is an inexplicable fear, and difficult to comprehend at times but it lingers. It has prevented me from making lots of purchases. Every time I pass a shop, or a stall at a flea-market and see an old ship-in-a-bottle, I have to remind myself of that irrational conviction. Consequently, I live in an apartment that has the temporal air of a migrant worker. That's not to say I don't love my flat. It is my haven, my womb. My furniture in minimal, a desk, a futon bed, microwave and fridge. Tons of books that overflow from the hopelessly small bookshelf onto the floor. It's just that empty spaces make me happy. It also obviates the need to explain why I don't have dinner parties.

The strange odour doesn't bother me at first. It is an acrid tinge in the air but it could have come from the road, or from the apartment next door. It is not as obvious as someone stealing an illicit puff in my apartment. Rather it is a wisp of a smell, a fading odour that hovers in the air. Near my bedroom door it is stronger. I can detect a distinct odour, bitter and foreign. Still, 1 only experience mild annoyance. The caretaker should have told me first if he was planning to bring maintenance staff into my flat. I would have put my underwear hanging in the bathroom away, and politely asked him to ensure that no-one smoked inside.

When I open the bedroom door, there is still, in the pit of my stomach, a residual tension, so the rope that descends over my neck is not a total shock to the system.

There are two them. They are dressed in dark jeans and T-shirts. One of them has a Nike logo on his shirt, the other one says DISNEYLAND, USA. They are short, dark men almost blue-black in colour, with thin wiry arms. Both have grey balaclavas over their heads, but I can see their eyes. Yellow, dead eyes. There is no time for reaction. They are professionals. My arms are pinioned expertly and painfully behind my back. The noose is tightened around my neck. I attempt a weak kick but it is an empty action. My legs flay about futilely. Then they simply turn to rubber. Dark spots seem to be floating in my line of vision. Nothing of what I have learnt over the past few months comes to mind. I feel myself falling to the ground with a lumpish thud. That is all I remember. That and the feeling of impotent rage as they turned their backs to me.

It is dark when I awaken. All the lights are off. I look at my watch. It has only been about fifteen minutes. The rope is still around my neck. Staggering, I switch all the lights on, in every room. Then I go to the bathroom to look in the mirror. There is an ugly welt already developing around my neck. The skin is broken and there are little drops of blood on my collar, but nothing serious. I check my cabinet and apply a drop of camomile lotion to the bruises. It hurts. Perhaps it is the wrong thing to apply, but there is nothing else. Then I try and breathe slowly and deeply.

Barbara Benschop-Fehr's card is in my bag. She has written her mobile phone number on the back of it. She answers right away, sounding as though she was expecting a call, and making me feel a little guilty.

'I've had a little accident,' I say to her. Something in my voice, perhaps the tremulousness, makes her avoid asking me any questions.

'Give me your address,' she answers sharply.

'No,' I say, 'let's meet somewhere.'

'Cafe Pushkin.' she snaps.

I know the place. We used to call it the Russian Tea House when I was at university. It is ten minutes away by taxi.

'I'll meet you there shortly.' She clicks the buttons on her phone without saying goodbye.

I wrap a scarf around my neck and close the door behind me. Then I go back in again to apply a little makeup around my eyes. Before I close the door again I spray lavender air-freshener liberally throughout the flat. I do not want to come home to that smell again.

The caretaker is watching cartoons on television. Through the door comes the sound of squeals, car crashes and loud bangs. I ring the bell. The door is opened by a spotty-faced teenager with lank blond hair. I'd seen him around before, moping on the steps of the entrance to the building, looking like he was trying to sell drugs. He even manages to slouch across the half-opened door. There is a scowl on his face, and he doesn't bother hiding his irritation, tossing his head inside when I ask about the caretaker. Teenagers today have no respect for their elders.

'The old man is cooking dinner,' he says sourly. He shouts out to the caretaker and turns to plonk himself down in front of the television.

Granddad arrives at the door, wiping his hands on his apron.

I ask him if anyone had entered my flat. He's immediately worried and solicitous. I tell him not to worry, that it's nothing.

*

She's sitting at the window , away from the students and the noise. The restaurant is warm and cosy, a perfect counter to the October drizzle and cold. It is, as usual, full of students. We used to come here often whenever we drove down to Amsterdam from Groningen. They made the best blini in town.

Breaking the news to her is not easy. It is only natural that she will be extremely annoyed with my unorthodox behaviour. Not to mention the fact that I used the information given to me by her in confidence.

I am right.

'You know, I knew you were the kind of person who'd do something so breathtakingly stupid the moment you walked into my office.' Her voice is low, firm and chastising.

'And when you checked my files, you knew for certain?'

She throws her hands up in exasperation. 'It's normal procedure. We do checks on everybody. You ought to know that.'

She sighs. 'What you didn't know is that they have another office directly across the canal. It is actually an administrative office because they are short of space in the building, but it means that they can see whatever happens on the road. So, while you were pretending to be so uninterested in Kadirgamer, someone must have spotted you from the opposite building. They now know where you stay.'

'And presumably who I work for,' I add.

'I don't think so,' she answers.

'Why's that?'

'Well, if they knew who you worked for, they would have either left you alone, or killed you, if desperate enough. Instead, they tried to scare you. As I've said, the LTTE is very careful to avoid any contact with law enforcement agencies in Europe. They wouldn't jeopardise their stay on European soil by attacking you. They probably think you're still a lawyer. I hear that you're quite famous.'

It is an attempt at a joke and I smile at her.

'Is there anything missing from your bag?' she asks.

'Didn't have it with me. I only went home to change into my gym clothes.'

I show her the darkening weal around my neck. She's immediately concerned.

'Were they wearing gloves?'

'Yes.'

'Then we need to take you to a doctor immediately.'

'It's only a bruise ...'

She interrupts brusquely, 'yes, but it could have been infected with a poisoning agent.'

'Why would they go to all the trouble?'

'Same lengths you'd go to protect your territory,' she answers.

Chapter 6

The doctor that she drive me to lives in an apartment in one of the posher Amsterdam suburbs, near Vondelpark. The properties that have not been converted into designer hotels or chic little boutiques are occupied by people with lots of money. The kind of people that have candelabras hanging from their ceilings.

'Are you sure he won't mind?' I ask.

'No, we make use of him regularly. He's always on call, so to speak.'

'And no doubt he is paid quite well.'

We're interrupting a genteel dinner party, judging from the laughter, and the exquisite smell of perfume, cigars and good food in the air.

It makes me realise how hungry I am. There is a row of expensive coats hanging in the hallway.

The doctor doesn't seem to mind. Quite the opposite, in fact. He seems to enjoy it, almost as if our barging into his home enhances his stature in the eyes of his guests. Dr Henk de Paauw is a round, gnomish man with a large bald head, and a pair of very large round glasses that dwarf his face. He looks frighteningly brilliant.

He greets us warmly and ushers us down the corridor. I sneak a quick look through one of the doors where the sounds are coming from. His ten or so guests are having pre-dinner drinks. They all look like gynaecologists, heart surgeons, ENT specialists. I feel a twinge of self-pity. Nobody invites me to chic dinner parties like this.

The doctor has turned his cellar into a fully-equipped surgery, with all the latest medical mod-cons. The walls are panelled in a light wood, with potted plants scattered around the room. Even the chairs are leather. In the corner there is a treadmill and a step machine. Only the lights are uncomfortably bright. He beckons me to lie down on the medical table. Benschop-Fehr hovers around like a worried mother. I ask her to take a seat. She gives me a dirty look. De Paauw removes a metal tube from a row of instruments and punctures my neck with a slight prick. He opens up a steel cabinet to reveal an array of shiny instruments.

Another section contains what looks like hundreds of blue bottles.

'The doctor is an expert in poisons. Actually he's an expert in tropical diseases, but somewhere along the way he has acquired this amazing knowledge of poisons,' says Benschop-Fehr, hoping to appease my growing anxiety.

'I lived in Brazil for ten years. My wife is Brazilian.' He pats me on the shoulder and takes my pulse.

As if on cue, she glides down the stairs bearing a tray of drinks. It contains mineral water and orange juice. She's a beautiful woman, with the kind of beauty that takes your breath away. Tall, dusky, with straight black hair down to the small of her back. Her cheekbones are high, and her skin so delicately stretched over her bone structure that it looks like papyrus.

'If you need anything stronger, shout.' She smiles at us, displaying perfect teeth.

De Paauw continues his examination, asking me questions and applying some kind of emollient to my neck. He doesn't seem to be the least bit surprised at my description of what happened, nodding his head sympathetically as if I had fallen off a bicycle.

Finally he swings around on his ergonomically-correct Danish swivel chair.

He addresses both myself and Benschop-Fehr. 'Nothing to worry about. Everything looks fine. If, however, you should experience sweating, erratic heart-beats, cramps, any pain whatsoever, give me a ring. Write your address down so I'll know where to find you. In any case please call me tomorrow. In the meantime, try and have a good night.'

'Come back to my flat,' says Benschop-Fehr to me outside the good doctor's house.

It's more like an order than a request. Seeing that I'm about to get into her car, it would be difficult to refuse anyway. Her flat is in the Jordaan area of Amsterdam, another rapidly gentrifying part of the city, with its cafes and smart galleries and couples dressed head to toe in black, including their babies. She lives in a building almost identical to mine. Inside, it is the exactly the way I imagined it to be. All the walls have been knocked down to create a large open space. Her floors, unlike mine which are dull with age, shine brilliantly. She has a large bed, low on the ground in one corner of the room, away from the windows. Her metallic desk is on the opposite side. Her furniture is of the same duality as her office, the fashionably old alongside the fashionably new. The computer notebook sits comfortably on the seventeenth century De Lille escritoire designed for Parisian ladies of taste.

On the long, narrow kitchen counter she has an open copy of a current French bestseller, a quirky history of philosophy.

I pick it up.

'Ever read it?' she asks.

'No,' I answer, 'I only read books with happy endings.'

She even has a cat. A lovable Siamese eminently aware of its pedigree.

It jumps on the table and condescendingly offers itself to me to be stroked. Benschop-Fehr is busy with her pots. Unlike my kitchenware, they're all arranged in descending order of size. She starts to boil the milk.

'What's a nice Jewish girl like you doing at ATS?' I ask. She has small and tasteful Star of David on a gold chain around her neck.

'I have two degrees and a masters. I speak five languages. And I was a runner-up in the Dutch national Judo championships. They thought I had potential. Eight years later and I'm still there.'

I take the cup she hands me. It is *anijsmelk*, aniseed-flavoured milk, a Dutch speciality.

She smiles over her stove, sharing a secret joke with herself. 'Besides, the only job I could find was as a research assistant at the local university. What about you?'

'There's nothing I need to tell you. You know everything,' I answer tartly.

'Okay, okay, there's no need to remind me. I did what I had to do. What I don't know is *why* you joined Europol? I mean, at face value, it would seem an illogical decision. Your fascinating background suggests that you'd be more at home somewhere else.'

I sip my milk and look away. It is not a secret, but neither have I told anyone before.

'It was Boehme,' I say finally.

'Why? Did he blackmail you? Does he have some dirty secret on you?'

'You could say that.'

'Which part, the blackmail, or the dirty secret?'

'The blackmail.'

She whistles softly. 'So he is as nasty as they say he is.'

I hold up my hands. 'It's not what you think it is. Anyway, what do they say about him?'

'He's got quite a reputation. A legend in Germany. They say that the co-ordinator hand-picked him for the job. They say that Boehme ascribes to the "Neanderthal" method of detective work because it's "nasty, brutish and short".'

It is funny, and we both laugh.

'Boehme is complex,' I say. 'He cares about his job, but he also thinks about himself as a human. And this makes him think about the way he interacts with his fellow humans.'

I start tell her about how we met. It was towards the end of the trial. Boehme simply rang the doorbell to my flat one night. When he said that magic word "Interpol" I naturally assumed it was something to do with the case, so I had let him in. Officially, he was still working for Interpol at that stage. I also assumed that he was there to ask me to stop wasting my time. I made the assumption that Interpol was working hand in glove with those capitalist bastards.

'You have reason to,' she interjects.

He'd been following the case, he said. He was like a schoolboy the first time we met, by turns awkward, diffident, arrogant. He waffled on and on about Interpol and all the good work it had been doing. Assuming it was meant to be a PR exercise to soften me up for what was to follow, I was less than polite with him. Then, out of the blue, he blurted out, 'Would you like to work for us?' I'm afraid to say I laughed in his face.

That derailed him a bit, and he was all bluster and boastfulness. I had shown him the door. It took me a while to actually comprehend what he had been trying to say, and even then I had found it difficult to believe.

A week later he was there again, this time with a thick file in his hand. He barged in, moved over to my desk, shoved my papers aside, took out a few sheets from his file, spread them on my desk and asked me to sit down. Which I did, with a mixture of anger and mounting confusion.

I sat down and started to read. After I'd finished I asked to see the rest of the file. He gave it to me. I offered him a beer and he sat down, patiently watching my back for the next hour. When I'd finished reading I'd turned to him and said yes. His face remained immobile. Then he started to tell me about Europol. To me it had sounded a lot worse than Interpol, but such is the power of revenge that I still said yes.

'What was in the documents?' asks Benschop-Fehr eagerly.

'The documents detailed Dakonite Corporation's involvement in assisting the French government in transporting nuclear weapons for detonation in the Pacific. Now, the French Government has always insisted that the transportation was done by navy vessels, and that absolutely no private ships were involved. In addition to using taxpayers money to pay Dakonite, it also showed that Dakonite had *already* been receiving hefty subsidies from the government. What the French government was doing was also a contravention of international maritime law. It was dynamite.

Boehme kept his word. A week after the trial was over, Le Monde broke the story. After that, it was all over the papers and television. The British and the Americans were not too impressed.'

'I remember,' she nods.

'The case went to the Hague. The directors resigned, the Americans revoked all shipping rights to Dakonite, which just about killed the company and they had to pay a one hundred and fifty million dollar fine. That was the beginning of the end for Dakonite.'

'Phew,' she breathes out, 'all that just to employ you.'

'I don't think so,' I answer. 'The story would have broken anyway, sometime in the future. Boehme simply played on my rage, my immediate thirst for revenge. I understand now why they say that "revenge is a dish best eaten cold". If Boehme had approached me nine months later with the same story I may not have said yes. It gave me immense satisfaction then. Now, I am not so sure.'

Benschop-Fehr pours me another cup of *anijsmelk*. It tastes subtly different from what I am used to, even better than my mother's.

It is also ineffably soothing.

'What's your secret?' I ask.

'A little dash of vanilla. It must be the artificial variety. The real stuff doesn't taste so great.'

'That's quite a story,' she continues. 'I wish my recruiting process was as exciting as that. All I had to do was go through a number of interviews with a pack of faceless bureaucrats. It makes me think of Boehme in an entirely new light.'

'The problem with Boehme,' I say, 'is that he always seems to be presenting you with a problem to which he alone seems to know the answer. It's his little party trick for life.'

'Let's get back to today,' she says, putting her cup down. 'You know, the chances of catching your two attackers are almost zero. They will be in Germany, or London by now. They certainly won't be in Holland.'

'Are you going to write a report?' The question had been at the back of my mind ever since I had phoned her. I had hoped to approach it with a bit more tact. Unfortunately I just blurt it out.

'Are you?' she asks in return.

'Not if I can help it. Boehme would kill me if he found out,' I answer.

'Well then, neither am I, but there is something you can do for me.'

'What's that?' I answer cautiously.

She gazes into her cup, as if struggling to find the right words to say me.

'Before I discuss it with you, there's something I will share with you after, but please hear me out first.'

'Okay,' I say, intrigued by her internal turmoil. It's hard to tell if it's genuine or just well-acted.

She takes a deep breath. 'What I would like from you is information on the killings. Everything that Europol has. Names, addresses, profiles, dates, reports, investigative personnel, the whole bang shoot.'

I must have stared at her with my mouth open because she shrugs her shoulders in defeat and turns away.

'Are you saying to me,' I finally say, 'that, as a major anti-terrorism operation you cannot get all this information?'

'That's exactly it. We're an anti-terrorist organisation, not a crime-fighting one. This is not the US, where we all co-exist happily with each other. The ATS still falls under the jurisdiction of the internal Dutch police. In order for us to get information from Europol, we have to fill in forms and wait. And wait. In theory,

Europol is an international organisation operating within the bounds of the EU. You have no idea of the amount of regulations we are dealing with. More difficult though, is the ability to avoid stepping on anyone's toes. The English, the Germans, all jealously guard their territories.'

'You can have whatever comes into my ambit of authority,' I say, 'but I cannot actively source information on your behalf.'

'Fair enough. Now, let me tell you what I didn't discuss with you in our meeting. We currently have a case open against a suspected gun-running operation that is hauling cheap weapons, mostly handguns and machine pistols, from Eastern Europe to the Far East via Amsterdam.

We suspect that the LTTE is involved. Normally they don't operate from Europe like this but with the current glut in small arms the Slovaks must have given them a deal too good to pass. We're raiding a vessel in the harbour tomorrow night. We don't expect to catch anyone wearing LTTE badges, but there's always someone who'll provide the right information.'

'Can I come along for the ride?'

'Yes,' she answers, 'but no gung-ho stuff this time around.'

Chapter 7

In the mist and the cold, every straggler that hurries past looks like a potential criminal. People flit in and out of the swirl, doing mundanely harmless things, exiting the pub, carrying crates, snatching smoke-breaks, and yet everything seems to be tinged with an air of menace.

Even harmless greetings sound like threats. Huge metal containers tower above us. Every now and then one of the cranes looms frighteningly overhead, a large box clutched in its claws. It moves swiftly to the hulking masses of the ships anchored along the quay. In the background there is the constant grind of the millions of gears that keep the harbour going. It is the heartbeat of the district. I shiver in my coat. We are standing between two of the containers. I'd hate to think what would happen if the container next to us was suddenly picked up. Besides me, Benschop-Fehr unwraps yet another stick of her gum and sticks it in her mouth. She then unscrews an old silver flask and offers it to me. I take a swig, thinking that it might be hot chocolate. It contains strong, harsh brandy. My choking elicits a low chuckle from her.

'The police and our team are positioning themselves. We ought to be picked up in a couple of minutes, once they surround the ship,' she says. A two-way radio is in her hand and we can hear voices sputtering softly in impenetrable police jargon.

'Let's go,' she whispers urgently, 'that's the signal.'

We stroll rapidly towards the quay, without trying to look too panicky. There are two police officers waiting for us. Silently, they assist us in boarding the police launch. The boat kicks into life and we move out towards the ocean. One of the officers points silently to a small vessel about five hundred metres from where we are.

We don't get very far. I'm not sure what came first, the blinding flash or the boom that sounded like a thousand cannons. The blast seems to shake the waves. The boat shudders and heaves violently. It is lifted out of the water and smacks down again with a sickening thump.

The officer at the wheel struggles to maintain control of the craft. Benschop-Fehr and I, standing at the aft, are thrown back, almost out of the boat, but we manage to cling to the rails. I try to ignore the excruciating pain from my head slamming against the bow.

The second officer is shouting into his radio, trying to find out what happened but there is only a confused babble on the other end. He looks at us haplessly and I scream out a meaningless stream of invective. Benchschop-Fehr is sprawled ungainly at my feet. He legs seem to be around her head. I grab her hand and attempt to pull her upright.

There is fear in her eyes.

Suddenly a large speedboat roars past, spraying us with water. It is followed by a police craft, zigzagging crazily through the waves. The policemen on board are clinging cartoonishly to the rails.

We are still in motion so the pilot of our boat gives chase, shouting at us to hang on. He grinds the gears so violently that I fear we will shudder to a stop.

All three boats are heading out towards the ocean. The speedboat in front is very fast. My judgment tells me that there is not much hope that either of the police launches will be able to catch up.

My stomach heaves violently. The temptation to let go and fall into the calm sea is great, but I hang on. Besides me Benschop-Fehr grits her teeth. There are tears in her eyes but she hangs on for her dear life.

There is another boom. We watch in horror as the first police launch disintegrates into flames. The tank blows. A blue fireball shoots up, lighting up the sky again.

It is impossible to see if there are any survivors. Before we have time to react, our craft shudders violently, as if given a resounding slap by the hand of God.

The fore of the boat bursts into flames. The two officers scramble to the back. The jacket of one of them is in flames. His colleague battles to smother them. Benschop-Fehr is so still that at first I think she might be hit. She is in shock. The front of the boat is in flames, which are rapidly spreading. It is also taking in water. I grab her hand and push her into the sea, plunging in after her. The impact of the cold water takes my breath away.

Benschop-Fehr is struggling to take her jacket off. I assist her, battling to keep my head above water. She does the same for me.

We are both spluttering, gasping for air. I kick out, trying to stay stabilised in the churning water.

The two officers are also in the water. Together we kick out in the direction of the quay. Behind us, the boat finally explodes violently. A large chunk of burning wood lands with a thud directly in front of us. Benschop-Fehr's eyes close as she mutters a prayer. I feel like doing the same, only I don't know what to say.

The stillness and quiet return as quickly as it was earlier shattered. A few fragments of wood mark what has happened. The ocean is a mercilessly quick scavenger.

Only the sound of our splashing disturbs the silence. The mist is much thicker, swallowing us. There are two bright lights in the distance, pointing the way to the shore-front. It is an eerie and frightening experience. Despite the cold, I start to feel an unnatural warmth. It's hard to tell if hypothermia is setting in, or if it's simply exertion from swimming. This is not the first time I had been lost at sea. At thirteen, I had "borrowed" a small sail boat from Coonrodt with the intention of sailing up the coast of Holland for a few hours. The mist had rolled in suddenly and before I knew what was happening I was lost. They say that a boat adrift in one of the Gulf streams can cover a distance of ten miles in an hour. That was the only thing that played in my mind, over and over again. I'm not been sure how many hours had gone by. All I remember is compulsively munching through all five of my chocolate bars. Then I had started to cry, screaming at the sea until exhausted. They had found me eight hours later. I was picked up by a fishing boat. Back home, nobody said a word to me except for Coonrodt. He had raged at me, shaking his fists, throwing things around, and finally weeping. I could never understand why my parents remained mute and he so full of anger. To this day, I still cannot explain it. My recurring worry has been the idea that he was blamed for my misadventure, but I have never been able to broach the subject with him.

There is a faint gurgling sound in the distance. It grows louder and louder. I recognise the sound. It is an old diesel engine on its last legs. I feel what everyone is feeling, the hope of being rescued turning to the fear of being mutilated by a passing ship. A loud gunshot shatters the relative quiet. Then another shot, and another. One of the officers is firing his gun frantically. The engine chugs to a halt. A bewildered voice cries out. We all shout back in unison. If it was tape-recorded and played back, the relief in the voices would be palpable. The voice cries out again. There is a splash, which must be the dinghy being lowered, then the rhythmic sound of oars hitting water. We yell again, so that they don't miss us.

I see his face first, a young, babyish face registering bewilderment.

He doesn't believe his eyes, rubbing them almost comically. Another crewman has a long pole in his hand. The police officers are closest and they are hauled aboard first, then Benschop-Fehr and finally myself.

The vessel is a tugboat on its way home from a late shift. The other members of the crew gather round and stare at us silently. One of them offers us a large, dirty blanket. It is all that they have. The five minute trip to the quay is an eternity. Above us two police helicopters circle the area, their blades thudding hypnotically in the night. Police cars, fire engines and ambulances crowd the area. The activity provides the perfect cover for me to slip away unnoticed.

*

It is 4:30 am when I reach home, wet, bedraggled and on the verge of hysteria. It is only when I drop my keys that I scream out in frustration, kicking the door violently and hurting my toe. Then a flood of tears. Inside the flat I run a scalding bath and slip beneath the bubbles. It feels like a voluptuous dream. The hot chocolate and potato cakes that follow complete my sense of deep wellbeing. Before I curl up under the covers of my bed, I phone the office and leave a message on Boehme's answering machine. Tell him that I have contracted an exotic Asian flue strain.

Then I pull the plug out.

Oblivion.

*

On Friday morning, the past seems like a long time away. It was Wednesday night when we staked out the Panamanian-registered Morning Star, Thursday morning when we were fished out of the harbour.

I practise a form of self-deception, become an observer, pretend that I wasn't there. I am in the office early with all the newspapers. One of the papers calls the incident a "conflagration" in the harbour. Most of them seem to think that it had something to do with drugs. But then again this is what the police seem to think as well. Fortunately for us, one of the captured sailors had a small quantity of cocaine in his possession. It will take at least until after the weekend for the true story to break.

Benschop-Fehr had phoned me at home the previous night. One of the men in police custody was willing to talk about the guns. She said that he was only a foot soldier but, most importantly, he worked part-time at the LTTE offices in the city. He was the one who would provide "that little gold nugget of information", as she had called it.

At 9 am Ilsa enters the office. She had also phoned the previous night, to say that Boehme "wanted my ass back in the office on Friday". I ignore her and continue reading the papers. She sings to herself, giving me one of her silent-but-sardonic looks, before eventually telling me that Boehme will be late for our weekly Friday meeting as he is at police headquarters. It is a relief, giving me a bit of breathing space.

When Boehme walks into the office, I feel a knot of tension in the pit of my stomach.

'I hope you are feeling better,' he says politely, but with what sounds to me like an undercurrent of sarcasm. It is also possible that my imagination is working overtime again.

He rubs his hands together. 'We have a lot of work to do. I have been to listen to the man in custody. He has made a lot of allegations, most of which I suspect are unprovable, but it has given us enough cause to have the police issue a search warrant for the offices Herr Kadirgamer, as well as his home.'

'What about ATS?'

'What about them?' He glares at me as if I had asked a very asinine question. 'They have their job to do and we have ours.'

I don't push my luck.

'Yes,' I answer meekly.

'You'll be working in a small collaborative team which will include a representative of ATS as well as the police. You will be in charge.

That woman from ATS, what's her name...?' He snaps his fingers.

'Benschop-Fehr,' I answer casually.

'Ja, she will be from the ATS. As I've said, you'll be in charge.'

'Why me?' I ask.

'Simple. We have international jurisdiction. They don't.'

This is what I dislike about Boehme. His air of infallibility mixed with his peculiar single-mindedness. He neither sees nor hears anyone else. Worse still, if you do manage to penetrate his thick skin, he turns on you as though you were the lowest form of life on the planet.

'An operations room has been set up at ATS. You will have the services of a computer expert, as well as a translator. Benschop-Fehr knows what's going on, so she will fill you in on the historical data. Is everything understood?'

'*Jawohl, mein herr.*' I reply.

The operations room is a small office at the ATS centre. Our translator is a Swiss woman, Martina Krebbs. Her CV says that she spent fifteen years in Sri Lanka at the Swiss embassy. She is currently working at the United Nations Commission for Refugees based in Geneva and has been seconded to us. Krebbs is a dour woman of forty-five.

Her blonde hair is pinned severely back into a small bun, giving her the look of a housekeeper from the Fifties. She arrives every morning at nine and leaves every day at 5 pm, to the second. At 10:30 am she has a fifteen minute break, and again at 3:00 pm. She leaves for lunch at 1:00 pm and returns at exactly 1:45 pm. She wears dark slacks and a white blouse, over which she throws a long black coat, every day to the office. Krebbs refuses to engage in any light chat or discussion with us. In the mornings she greets us, switches on her computer and types away furiously until her break. Any attempt to engage her in conversation chat is met with a distracted nod and a thin smile, all calculated to make us aware that she doesn't really think that it's a good idea to speak to her while she's working.

The police have handed us all the information that they had in their possession. There is a lot of material to go through. Fortunately, most of it is on computer disk and is very well organised. Too organised. Somebody at the cultural centre was in love with computers. Minutes of meetings, memos, an impressive record of all financial transactions are neatly catalogued and filed in the correct directories.

By the third day it is plain to see that the information is useless. The transcripts are an endless collection of trivia and very boring to read.

The business details are marginally more interesting but it's all legitimate as far as I can see. It is an impressive audit trail, so I pass it on to the accountants.

It is Benschop-Fehr who brings to my attention to the details concerning the murdered Tamils. She is going through the minutes of their meetings, which they held every Wednesday at 1 pm.

'It starts here, on the 8th of January,' she says, whistling in astonishment. 'That's *months* before we started on the case. There's a note here about other cases from the previous year.'

'Are you telling me that they kept *notes* of all the people they killed?'

'No, no, you don't understand,' she interrupts, 'they seemed to have had discussions *about* the killings. The dates of disappearances, names of people, police information. This is very bizarre. Why would they kill their own people and then keep track of it?'

'To prevent us from thinking they were the killers,' I answer.

'No. Too elaborate. The notes say that "Dayananda" to investigate further. This is a good enough reason to bring in Kadirgamer, don't you think? Find out who this "Dayananda" is.'

'Suits me fine. I'm getting bored doing this stuff.'

I take the notes that she offers to me. The last few entries I recognise. They consist of details of the bodies found in the Thames, as well as the murder of Sri Lankan attache's son. The rest of it is a depressing catalogue of killings. I count fifty-three of them.

*

The interview is scheduled for 10 am. Boehme and I have been granted observer status by the police. Legally we cannot actually question Kadirgamer. I have faxed my questions through as requested by the authorities. Boehme offers me a lift to the

Leeukop prison which is in the old garrison town of Naarden, to the north of Amsterdam. It is a cold, grey morning and the prison is the only substantial building on the landscape. There are a few low farmhouses scattered here and there. Leeukop is an old fortress, built during the latter part of the nineteenth century. The concrete ramparts where the prisoners were hanged are still standing a few metres away from the main walls. The doors and the interior have been modernised. Our credentials are checked against a computer and we're waved through.

Laxman Kadirgamer is dressed in the same shiny blue suit. He is puffing on a cigarette and staring into the two-way mirror, trying very hard to remain calm, but his eyes dart in all directions. It is almost as though he can see us, staring into individual faces with a mixture of cockiness and fear.

'Tell us about Dayananda and the killings.' The interrogation officer addresses Kadirgamer as if she were providing directions to a kindly old man. Whether this is for our benefit, or the normal way the police conduct their enquiries these days, I cannot tell. All I know is that when I was trundled into the back of a police van at seventeen for protesting against a multinational Dutch petroleum company selling its products in South Africa, we were handled with a lot less politeness.

Kadirgamer forgets that he has the cigarette in his mouth so when he starts to shout it flies out across the table. The police officer jumps back in alarm, before quickly regaining her composure.

'It's you bastards who are killing our people,' screams Kadirgamer.

He half stands, gripping the edge of the table. A trickle of spittle runs down the side of his mouth.

'What have you done with Dayananda? Have you murdered him like all the others? You bastards will pay for this. I will make sure that you hang.'

Boehme glances at me helplessly. Kadirgamer's anger looks very real.

Or he is a very good actor.

'Where is Dayananda?' persists the officer, with almost surreal calmness.

'How should I know!' He rages. 'He hasn't arrived back at the office for four days. Our people disappear all the time and you do nothing. You people are Nazis.'

He is practically foaming at the mouth, working himself into a frenzy.

The officer gets up slowly, studiously ignoring him.

In the empty tearoom festooned with pictures of windmills and dykes and farm girls with broad smiles, the police captain in charge of the operation hands us the paperwork. His subordinate who did the questioning is gulping down copious amounts of water at the dispenser.

'It appears that this Dayananda went to investigate the disappearance of a certain Ramakrishnan, whose body was found in Rotterdam. According to Kadirgamer he received assistance from a ...'

He consults his notes.

'A Miss Merijen. She works at the Dutch Centre for Displaced Citizens. She was helping him, with the police and so on. The place is in the "Old South".'

'Where else,' I say as a parting shot. The "Old South" is where most of the city's new arrivals gravitate to.

*

Miss Merijen is a tall, striking blonde woman attired in ostentatiously shabby second-hand clothes. Her lack of sartorial discrimination does not detract from her beauty. She carries herself like a model on a catwalk. Merijen wrinkles her perfectly formed nose in distaste when I hand her my card.

'So, this is where all our taxpayers money goes to. Don't you think we have enough police forces in the world without another one? It's like the Gestapo all over again. Spreading your tentacles. Grasping for more and more power. When will you people learn to give up?'

'The LTTE,' I say to her, 'are a bunch of terrorists who are not averse to killing anyone who stands in their way. And they're quite happy to use whatever assistance they can get. And if that means fooling gullible teenage westerners, then so be it.'

I take a deep breath.

'Now, what do you know about Dayananda?'

She glares at me, nostrils flaring like a thoroughbred horse.

'Firstly, I'm twenty years old, so that hardly makes me a teenager. I'd watch my language if I were you. He came here to get assistance on behalf of the family of Mr Ramakrishnan, who - as you probably know - was found "drowned" in the harbour.'

She snorts at me as though I personally had something to do with it. As if I'd held his head down until the last gasp expired from his lips.

'I know nothing about the LTTE,' she continues.

'Do you have an address for him?'

Her mouth opens and closes silently.

'I can always get a court order,' I pre-empt her.

Reluctantly, she pulls open a drawer from a steel cabinet behind her desk. She removes a card and hands it to me. His full name, Dayananda Kumaratunga, and address are on the card. His apartment is just around the corner, in De Pijp district.

'I know you,' she says suddenly, 'I know you.'

I stare at her blankly, wondering where our paths might have crossed. She's too young to have been at university with me. A party perhaps.

'You're that lawyer. We used to talk about you. What happened.' Her voice is dripping with sarcasm.

'Job security.' I answer.

Outside, I stuff a few Guilders down the collection box for Guatemalan refugees that is built into the front wall. It assuages my twin feelings of guilt and anger. PLEASE HELP!!! shriek the large red letters.

De Pijp is a ten minute walk away. It is called The Pipe because of the narrow streets that run between the long buildings that tower overhead, making you feel intensely claustrophobic. The apartments in the buildings are supposed to resemble pipe-drawers, but these days not many people know what pipe-drawers are. It is largely an immigrant area, the one place in Amsterdam that is truly a melting- pot. Refugees from Albania, Croatia and Cyprus live together with Eritreans, Kurds and Sikhs. It is the one place where separate cultures are highly visible, either by dress or physiognomically, but where the children have no problem playing with together other in the streets.

Poverty is a great equaliser. I walk past the daily market. It is the largest and one of the best in the city. My mother used to make occasional forays to the market, to assuage her cravings for carambolas, a South-East Asian fruit that she couldn't do without. She also used it for cooking, the one occasion that I didn't like her food.

Through the stalls I can see the light of the braziers, people standing around warming their hands. It is a very medieval scene. I resist the urge to make a detour. A trio of Arabic women come sashaying down the street, djebbellas swaying in the breeze, heads swathed in florid towels. They leave behind them a trail of ineffable freshness, of jasmine, saffron and citrus. The have been to a sauna or gym. The Arabic communal baths or hammam would be too exotic, even for this area. Soft Berber melodies float down from the apartments above my head.

The building is not easy to find. Most of the apartment blocks do not seem to have numbers. The people I ask either do not speak Dutch or English or pretend not to. Eventually a young girl shows me the way.

Number four is on the fourth floor of a dark, dank and dingy building.

It smells overwhelmingly of stale fried food. The few people that are hanging around outside their doors melt away. Only the children follow me upstairs. I knock on the door. There is no answer. I had passed a door on the ground floor that said "Caretaker". I try ringing the bell.

An old hag in hair curlers yanks the door open with a frown on her face. Before she can speak I flash my ID at her. I ask her for the keys to number four. She closes the door and comes back five minutes later with the keys.

'Don't steal anything,' she growls at me, 'and give me back the keys when you're done.'

'I promise,' I retort.

The apartment consists of a single room. There is a tiny sink and a two-plate stove that make up the kitchen. A door leads to a shower and toilet. The single bed has a grey blanket tucked neatly into it, army style. With the exception of the two LTTE posters that adorn the wall above the bed, it is very monastic. The room is also spotlessly clean, an air freshener on the kitchen windowsill masks the room's normal odours. Dayananda's few clothes are folded neatly on a chair at the foot of the bed. I start with them, checking the pockets of the two pairs of jeans and the two shirts. They are empty. I check under the bed. Nothing there except for a pair of large-sized sneakers. There is an old notebook and a short yellow pencil under the pillow. I leave it on the floor and remove the blanket to check the bed. My attempts to tuck the it back as it was are not very successful. The notebook and pencil I place in my handbag.

Downstairs, I give the keys back to the caretaker.

'I hope you didn't take anything,' she snarls at me before quickly slamming the door.

I knock on the door again. Another long wait before the door is opened, this time by a man. He is just as slovenly in appearance as his wife.

'Did the occupant of number four pay his rent?' I ask him, dispensing with any pleasantries. My patience is running out. He grunts and turns away. The hag returns, food sticking out of her mouth..

'Yes, he paid his rent for the next two months.' She slams the door again.

*

Back at the office, I flip through the pages of the book. It is a sad and fitful record of his existence in Amsterdam. Tram routes, the cost of basic groceries, amounts he has paid in rent, the pittance he receives as a wage or stipend. Here and there a few words of Dutch. *Goede morgen* [good morning]. *Dag* [hello]. *Ik begrijp het niet* [I do not understand]. He is also a compulsive scribbler of flowers, or rather the petals of flowers, and he has decorated all the pages with little florid designs.

On one of the pages there is what looks like a telephone number. I almost miss it as it seems to form the background for a series of elaborately executed curlicues. The number is not Dutch. I consult the phone books. It is not German or French either. Dutch directory enquiries tells me that the number is possibly English. She puts me through to the international section. The woman on the other end tells me that it is an English number and the code preceding it is for an area called Hertfordshire. Before I use my brain to think, I dial the number. A man answers. He sounds like a member of the servant classes.

'Dr Laville's residence,' he intones mournfully.

'Sorry, wrong number,' I reply.

'Thank you madam.' He puts the phone down. Even the click sounds polite.

'They found your Mr Dayananda.' Boehme pokes his head through my door.

'Oh good,' I answer.

'He's dead.'

Boehme relishes my shock and surprise with a ghoulish smile.

'He was found out the in countryside by a farmer, near Utrecht. In one of the canals. Shot. Hands intact, by the way. Has all the hallmarks of a professional execution. You won't be getting any information out of him.'

He withdraws just as abruptly. I fold my hands around my head.

*

I dial Scotland Yard to get Helm to check the number for me.

'Mmm...nice part of the world, Hertfordshire.'

'You sound like you know the place.'

'I do, or rather, I did. Haven't been back in years.'

He types furiously as he talks to me.

'Why's that?'

'I was sent there as a child to work. Cleaning out stables and so on. I hated it. All those horsey people and their horses. I have never understood the pleasures of horse-riding and never will.'

'It's all about sex,' I add.

'You're kidding?'

'No, I'm not. All that rubbing against the saddle provides a vicarious thrill. Not to mention the smell of leather, the sound of snorting.'

He laughs nervously, 'Eh, this is a joke, right?'

'Relax,' I laugh, 'I was only pulling your leg.'

'Phew! I thought it was something I said.'

'It's me, I'm in a strange mood.'

'La de da, here we are.' He hits the keys. 'Phone number belongs to one Toby Laville, doctor. Now there's a name that reeks of money and class. And Hertfordshire.'

'Tell me,' I venture, 'does it not bother you that we are able to do this?'

'Do what?'

'Well, tap a few words into a computer and get access to all this information. Pry into people's lives. Dig up information on whoever we want?'

'My, you are in a strange mood. To be honest, I don't actually think about it. I'm doing a job and I'm helping other people, protecting their lives, their property.'

'That's the difference between England and Europe,' I say. 'England has not lived under a modern fascist dictatorship.'

'Thanks for your help.'

'My pleasure.'

'One more thing,' I ask.

'Name it.'

'Can you find out Laville's international travel for the past few months.'

'Will do.'

The report I present to Boehme is as accurate as possible. The only thing I leave out is the phone call I made to Laville's residence. In the harsh light of day, it sounds silly. Boehme would only say 'That's something a woman would do.'

He scans the document. Boehme never offers a chair to anyone unless they are above him in rank. I pretend to look out of the window. Boehme has the lousiest view in the department. All you can see are the backs of buildings. Even the lowliest specimen who works here, ie Ilsa, has a sea-view. It is not even the biggest office. Perversely, he chose it himself. Boehme says this was because it is the only office with wall-to-wall bookshelves and a steel safe. That's Boehme, practicality above comfort at all times.

'Very interesting.'

Coming from Boehme, this is like a heartwarming message of affirmation in my abilities.

My fleeting joy must have shown on my face because he quickly reverts to his usual state of affected obduracy.

'You may pursue the line of investigation,' he continues, a touch imperiously, 'but I must ask you to carefully document all procedures, as well as follow the right channels. Remember our position as a tool of the law.'

'Yes, and I wish you'd remember that too,' I mumble to myself.

'What was that,' he says sharply.

'Nothing,' I answer, 'just talking to myself.'

Outside, I idly wonder what would happen if I went around Boehme's desk, put my arms around his neck and gave him a peck on the cheek. It's quite possible that he would burst into tears.

'Message for you from your London boyfriend.'Ilsa interrupts my thoughts.

'He says Laville left for Amsterdam this morning. He is staying at the Regency Hotel. Room 235.'

She gazes at me quizzically.

'What are you now, Van der Valk or Sherlock Holmes?'

This seems to exhaust her knowledge of famous fictional detective characters so I respond. 'Mind your own fucking business.'

She gapes at me in stunned silence. I leave her standing there with her mouth open.

*

Dr Laville is an impressive-looking man, tall, handsome. It makes the three-hour wait in the hotel almost worth it. He's in his late fifties, stomach bulging out slightly, but with the sure and confident gait that success brings. His hair is almost white, but it's also slightly wavy, giving him an uncanny likeness to a middle-aged Charlie Chaplin. His face is ruddy, as though he's just come out of the shower. Laville is dressed in a pair of dark green corduroy trousers and a vividly yellow jacket, the kind of outfit rich Germans wear on their days away from the office.

He strides out of the elevator and passes the reception as though the space was his personal domain. The concierge, in an impressive display of both sign language and pro-activeness, signals to the doorman, who snaps his fingers at one of the drivers lounging around outside. Laville acknowledges this with a polite but distant nod.

The professional photographer accompanying me gathers up his bags. They are empty suitcases, props to make it look like we're part of the background. He has a tiny camera built into a leather shoulder bag which he operates by pressing the straps at a certain point. He told me that in the US you can pick one of these up for about thirty dollars. Europol paid two hundred Deutschmarks for the one he's carrying. His name is Leo Raphorst, and if he weren't so determined to sleep with me, he'd be quite pleasant. If it wasn't for his hair, I would have been tempted too. It's blond, but this is not what worries me. It's the length. It reaches to below his shoulders and the thought of having that tangled mass on my pillow sends shudders of revulsion down my spine. To avoid hurting his feelings, I don't ell him this.

Raphorst has had a fascinating and eventful career working as a freelance photographer around the world. While we were waiting he had regaled me with tales of his adventures in Ethiopia, Chile Nicaragua and Kashmir. How much is fact and how much is fiction, is hard to tell, but I enjoyed them anyway.

Curious, I had asked him how he'd ended up working for Europol.

He doesn't look the type. Everything about him says "hippy", from his long hair to his cowboy boots to his Nepalese shirt. Money and the excitement were the reasons, it turns out. It all came about as a result of him sleeping with a Dutch NATO official in Addis Ababa three years ago. Hey presto, he was a spy, providing his source with whatever titbits he would stumble across in whatever country he happened to be in. If it was good, the Dutch kept it for themselves, otherwise it was shared with other NATO members, standard modus operandi for intelligence gathering and dissemination

I size him up again, marvelling at the human propensity for delusion and self-deception. You never can tell with people these days. What is even more scary is that he had related all this to me in a very matter-of-fact way, without a shred of moral or ethical ambiguity.

Laville is waiting for his car outside. It gives us enough time to get to mine. We catch up with him as he's pulling out of the hotel. He takes the motorway heading north. It's a long arterial road. If we keep going we could end up in the Frisian Islands. Fortunately for us, after thirty minutes he takes the off-ramp to Groningen. We arrive at the open space that is the town centre, the Grote Markt, a few minutes later. From there he takes a side road to the University of Groningen, my Alma Mater. His car pulls into one of the parking lots near the main entrance. It is a hive of activity, as befitting one of Holland's most prestigious universities. It's been eight years since my last visit, and all the memories involuntarily flood back. They were not bad years. As a matter of fact they were fun, carefree years. A time when the world seemed to offer so many endless possibilities. If someone had said to me then that I'd end up working for a quasi-police organisation, I would have hurt them. Badly.

We follow him through the winding corridors. The smell of the freshly polished wooden floors stirs more memories, this time of examinations, tutors and lectures.

Laville enters a new wing. It is across a wide courtyard, and was not there when I was around. There is a glass dome overhead, giving it a vaguely rococo feel. Although the building has been constructed with careful attention to the surroundings, it's clear that a lot of money has been spent. The air is redolent with the smell of hard cash. Near the revolving glass doors, I see the reason. A small plaque is embedded in the wall. It has on it the name of the large multinational corporation that donated the new wing. A debate my friends and I had a few years ago at this very institution come sto mind. We had been arguing the merits of businesses providing "donations" to universities, thereby holding the institutions to ransom. I wish I could remember the outcome.

Laville enters through a set of large wooden doors. We give him two minutes and then follow. Inside there is a small atrium with another set of doors. The walls are covered with laminated posters of gory looking body parts. To me they look like exploding blood vessels. It's hard to tell if the pictures are meant to be modern art or accurate representations of the human body. There is a desk in the middle, occupied by a young woman. She gazes at us expectantly, fingering the receipt book on her desk. The thought that we may have stumbled into a religious meeting crosses my mind. It is too late to turn back so we walk casually towards her.

'Name and institution please.' She gives the photographer a plastic smile.

'Are you students here?'

'Not any more.' I reply.

'I'm afraid you have to pay five Guilders each,' she says.

I write our names down while Raphorst takes out his wallet.

She hands us two pink slips.

'Thank you. You may enter.'

The room is packed with an eclectic mix of people of all ages and, it seems, backgrounds. Students, businessmen, lecturers, a smattering of retired academics. They are totally absorbed in the words of the man on the podium. Laville is being escorted to the bottom by some lackey. He takes his seat in the front row, obviously a favoured guest.

Even from where we are, and with my short-sightedness, it's possible to discern that, in addition to being good looking, the speaker has what you would call a magnetic presence. He is a tall, and lean, hawkishly handsome man in his early thirties. The scholarly slight stoop he is already developing balances the prettiness.

The audience is enraptured. They listen intently, laughing here and there at his self-deprecating jokes.

The photographer and I slip into one of the back rows. Gradually what he is saying begins to take form, not that I understand any of it. He has a voice worth listening to. The cadences rise and fall through the PA system like an actor's emollient tones. The end of the speech is greeted with loud applause, which he acknowledges with a slight bow and a timid wave, as if he is too afraid to believe in his powers.

The audience slowly filters out. There is a small crowd around the podium. Laville takes a few steps towards the speaker. He doesn't go all the way, aware of his own prestige. The lecturer bounds down towards him. They shake hands.

I grab a passing student and ask her who the lecturer is. She looks at me with something approaching scorn, as if Mick Jagger had been on the stage.

'That's Dr Lex Laurier of course. He's our new head of molecular medicine at the university.'

She shows me a leaflet with the good doctor's smiling face on it. When I attempt to have a closer look, she clings to it.

'I ONLY wish to read it,' I snap contemptuously to her.

She lets me have it reluctantly. Academic groupies are new to me.

I scan the leaflet quickly to see what we paid five Guilders for.

Dr Laurier has had a brilliant masters degree at twenty-one, significant research and medical breakthroughs at twenty-five. Now youngest head of department at thirty-one.

I hand it back to her and she scurries away, lost in the profundity of her own thoughts.

Dr Laville and Dr Laurier are still engrossed in each other. That the younger doctor defers to the older one is plain to see. The lecture room is emptying rapidly. In a short while the photographer and I are going to look conspicuous.

The two of them start to move slowly up the aisle, still talking animatedly. Raphorst and I pretend to be engaged in an intimate conversation. He uses the forced intimacy to ask me for a date. He doesn't have a hope in hell, I tell him. On the sheet of paper before us he sketches a crude broken heart.

We get up to follow the two doctors. It looks to me as if Laurier is signing autographs. I use the opportunity to ask the receptionist at the desk where I can get hold of him. By the look on her face, she's used to such enquires. Coolly, but with the slightest hint of disdain, she gives me a number for the department. Nothing more, she's sorry.

'You've got to keep him away from us girls,' I say to her.

*

After winding their way through the university's corridors, they enter a room. Dr Laurier's new office, according to the nameplate on the door.

I buy the photographer a mediocre lunch in the university canteen for his trouble. Squash, peas and steak. He accepts graciously, as though he was getting the consolation prize in a television game show.

Chapter 8

There is a message on my answering machine. It is from Benschop-Fehr. It's been a long time since I heard from her.

I call her back. She answers her phone.

'Nothing serious. Only wanted to know if you would like to have a drink after work some time?'

'Is this business or pleasure?'

She laughs in response to the wariness in my voice.

'Purely pleasure.'

We make arrangements to meet.

*

'Why', I ask Boehme, 'would someone with this kind of wealth be involved with a terrorist organisation?'

He has called me into his office and presented me with a package. The London people have done a thorough job. The documentation consists of bank statements, share portfolios, ownership deeds, offshore funds, Laville's entire financial history. It is an impressive list, and much more than I need to know.

'It is *precisely* the reason why he would. He's respectable, so he fits the profile of the kind of person that the LTTE uses. A pillar of society, as they say. This is all purely speculative, however. There could be a simple explanation why the doctor's name was in the book.'

'Yes, it is,' I concede, 'but my gut tells me otherwise. Could it be that he provides medical services to the LTTE, gunshot wounds, that sort of thing?'

'Possible,' mutters Boehme, 'but if you look at the dates here, all the activity starts from a period of ten years ago. He would have been fifty then. Where would a respectable doctor earning a respectable salary suddenly get so much of money to make so many investments? This kind of pattern is classic, for drug dealers, that is. But no doubt a lot of this money is tainted with drugs somewhere along the line. The LTTE gives him the money. He invests. Pays them the handsome dividends and keeps a decent sum for himself. It's quite possible that he doesn't even know that he's dealing with the LTTE. Oh, I'm sure he knows that it's not legal but he probably thinks it's drugs, a simple exercise in money laundering.'

He puts down the report. 'Now stop bothering me and let me eat my lunch.'

Lunch at his desk is Boehme's daily ritual. He has sandwiches sent up from a German delicatessen every day. He sits there, reading his copy of Time magazine to catch up on the latest world affairs and gulping down mineral water, his only concession to anything remotely healthy.

Helm phones again with more news.

'We did the local research on your Dr Laville. Definitely didn't inherit any wealth from rich aunts. His father was an administrative clerk at a hospital in London, mother, a nurse. He was an only child. They put him through medical school. Brilliant career, by the way. Lots of firsts for his degrees, groundbreaking research, that sort of stuff. I'll send you the paperwork.'

'He jeopardises all that to become a money-launderer?'

'Perhaps not,' remarks Helm. 'What if he'd won the lottery?'

'You're joking,' I answer.

'Only half. It's always a possibility, and in our jobs we're trained to examine all possibilities. It's something that we haven't thought about. It *is* possible to get wealthy suddenly these days. There's something else. You say that the LTTE is not averse to any means of making money. What if Laville was a potential target, say for extortion or kidnap? The LTTE doesn't go in for high-risk jobs like kidnap, but let's say they discovered something dirty on Laville, and they were planning to extract money from him?'

'It's a good scenario,' I answer.

'But you aren't convinced,' he replies, with a touch of asperity in his voice.

'Let's say I'm keeping all options open.'

*

Benschop-Fehr is already at the bar when I arrive. She looks like a regular, perched on her bar stool like an elfin midget, having a quiet chat to the barman. She sees me coming by looking in the mirror behind him. I know that she's seen me, but she doesn't turn around. To her credit she doesn't pretend not to see me either.

She waves in the direction of the chair next to her. Then she introduces me to the barman, Hendrik. He smiles as though he knows more than he ought to know about me. I give both of them quizzical looks.

'Barbs has just been telling me about your jobs,' says Hendrik, flicking back his hair from his eyes.

I raise my eyebrows at her, puzzled. As far as I know, both our organisations have sworn us to confidentiality on pain of dismissal, for our own good and theirs.

'Did you really?' he asks eagerly.

'Did I really what?' I purr politely.

'Barbs here says that you are her partner in crime. She was telling me about the fracas in Rio.'

'Oh that,' I answer. 'It was pretty exciting.'

He hands me my drink and moves away to another customer.

Benschop-Fehr's silent mirth could register on the Richter scale. I let her have her moment.

'When exactly were we in Rio?' I eventually ask.

'I've told him that I'm in the navy, and that we're fellow officers. It helps explain my erratic hours, my absences.'

'It's nice to know that you have a sense of humour,' I say.

'Yeah, I used to be a regular clown when I was at school, although it's hard to tell now,' she answers. 'Incidentally, if I were you, I would use the navy as an excuse. It's a pretty good one.'

'Are you instructing me in how to lie?'

'No, I'm instructing you in how to survive. I know that they teach you how to use guns, the ins and outs of electronic gadgets, but they don't teach you how to survive in an environment full of ruthless people. Quite ironic when you think that this is our raison d'etre. They're so wrapped up with technology and management they forget that what we're doing is still based on rules that are as old as civilisation itself.'

'Did I tell you about the first time I was shot? They taught me all about conflict resolution with terrorists, how to act, how to respond. But they didn't tell me about the man who followed me home, who tried to slit my throat as I was checking my mail. This is not the kind of job you leave at the office. I bet Boehme didn't tell you that.'

She touches the scar on her face.

'No,' I admit.

'Well, I am. We're dealing with people who don't play by any rules. It's like being a very careful driver, the most careful in the world, but getting hit by a drunken driver. Nothing prepares you for someone else's actions. Nothing.'

What do I do?

'Take the punches and roll with it. At the same time you've got to make sure that your knickers don't show.'

*

Ilsa hands me the fax from Walther Karcher, the Hamburg police captain.

'I was reading this during my lunch break,' she pronounces cheerfully.

'Do you mind.' I give her a glacial stare and grab the fax from her hand.

'I was doing my job,' She splutters.

'Clearing out your out tray, by the way,' she goes on. 'It's a mess. There are papers in there from three months ago.'

I wave my hand airily by way of apology. She is right after all.

'There's something you ought to know.'

I've never seen her look so serious.

'There's an anomaly in the toxicology reports.'

'Oh, and what's that.'

'Both victims have traces of something called ...' she looks at the sheets before her, 'Mescoan in their blood. Do you know what it is?'

'No,' I answer.

'Well, neither do I,' she smirks, before flouncing off in the direction of her desk.

'It could be a substance found in aspirin,' I snap back at her.

'Could be. Then again, it might not be. The question is, are you brave enough to find out?'

'How do you know all this stuff?' I shout after her.

'I used to work in a hospital. Until I got fired for stealing drugs,' she cackles without a hint of shame.

'You're a woman of many talents.'

'You have no idea how many,' she sneers from a safe distance.

I log on to the Internet and surf to the pharmacological database of one of the local hospitals. It provides a helpful guide to hundreds of drugs, both legal and illegal. The web site has achieved semi-cult status in Holland due to its even-handed description of illegal substances.

'Mescoan' is listed as an anti-coagulant. It prevents the blood from clotting and is one of many such drugs available on the market.

The manufacturers are a pharmaceutical company based in Oxford, England. I take their details down in my electronic diary.

In the related database, there's a description of anti-coagulants. They are used to treat blood clots which appear in the veins of susceptible patients. The drug therapy helps to reduce the risk of such clots reaching the heart, lungs or other organs.

I dig out the toxicology report from Ton van Kessel. There is no mention of any such drug in the report, and neither did I expect there to be. I call him back anyway and ask him to send the blood sample to one of the main pathology centres in Amsterdam. Then I get Boehme to phone the centre to request an urgent analysis.

I get the results fifteen hours later.

The victim from Rotterdam also had traces of Mescoan in his blood.

Exultant, I present my findings to Boehme.

'Interesting,' he concedes, rustling through the report in his usual semi-detached fashion. 'Find out more.'

'It would mean travelling,' I say to him.

'Why?' he snaps at me suspiciously.

'The company that makes Mescoan is based in England. I could also use the opportunity to make personal contact with Helm.'

'Okay, okay,' he shoos me out of his office. 'But don't spend too much of the taxpayer's money. We have a budget here.'

*

I take the ferry to London. It would have been quicker taking a plane, but I prefer the sea. The ferry is Swedish, and brand new. It promises all kinds of luxurious comforts, but ferries cannot escape their destiny.

They are used by people who do not have the money to fly, or those who want to take large quantities of alcohol back to England. Consequently, ferries are a people-watchers' paradise; impoverished students necking brazenly on the upper decks, sad couples acting as human mules, furtively tucking their parcels around them as they sit gazing blankly into the distance, dreaming of grubby pound notes, beery louts thrusting their distended bellies at passing girls. The odd drug user, so obviously carrying drugs that one feels a touch of sympathy for his inevitable fate at the hands of the sharp-eyed customs officials.

All is forgotten when the white cliffs of Dover loom into view. It is a thrilling sight and always will be. The first time I arrived in England on a school trip, somebody was playing We'll Meet Again, not the World War II version, but a rather odd cover by the Righteous Brothers. Nevertheless, it was so haunting that it made me want to weep. The ambience was assisted by the illicit consumption of cider, as well as me having just received my first proper kiss. It was behind a large red plastic water drum on the ferry, and the boy was English, returning to London after *his* first trip to Amsterdam. They say that our first kiss is one of the most memorable events of our lives, that it has a greater impact than losing one's virginity, or even the death of a family member. That's the way I'll always remember Dover, the kiss and the song.

I bypass London and drive directly to Oxford. After getting lost in the city centre I offer a lift to a student who's heading in the same direction. It is only a few minutes out of the city. She is a tiny girl with orange hair and multiple piercings on her face, the strangest budding astrophysicist I've ever seen. She is charming and bubbly, full of ambition. Her dream is to work at NASA. As I drop her off I warn her that the Americans are not so tolerant of eccentricity as they pretend to be.

'Eccentricity is a human indulgence,' she smiles beatifically at me and waves goodbye.

The building I drive up to looks like any of the old manor houses in the area. Only a discreet bronze plaque at the entrance gate states that it is Manning Pharmaceuticals. Inside it is different. The sprawling and well-maintained garden, and the attractive stone buildings covered with ivy creepers cannot disguise the institutional chill. I park my car and ask for the scientist Mary

Kebble at the reception desk. A few minutes later she hurries down the corridor, white coat flapping. She seems surprised and flustered to see me, even though I had made an appointment. Kebble is a mousy woman dressed in dull clothes. She's wearing a faded black jersey, jeans and a white blouse. Her red hair is tied in a loose knot, but most of it seems to fall across her face.

She's in dire need of a makeover.

I introduce myself. Recognition dawns on her face, although she doesn't look particularly thrilled to see me. She ushers me to the leather couch in the corner of the reception area, furtively glancing over her shoulder.

When I take out my tape-recorder she shrinks back violently, wringing her hands. The nervous tic on her left eyelid has become even more pronounced.

'No, no, I can't do that,' she jabbers.

'The tape recorder?' I say.

'Yes, you *positively* have to switch it off. I hate those things,' she mumbles.

I do as I'm told.

'You wanted to know about one of our drugs, Mescoan?'

'Yes.'

'It functions as an anti-coagulant in the blood and primarily by inhibiting the body's ability to manufacture prothrombin, a clot-forming substance...,' she fires rapidly.

'Woa, hang on a minute, take me back a few steps.'

She continues. 'Blood clotting occurs when blood coagulates to form clots. The way it works is that blood platelets or thrombocytes produce a substance in the blood called thromboplastin, which in turn converts the protein prothrombin into an enzyme called thrombin. Thrombin then converts fibrinogen, another protein, into a substance called fibrin. Fibrin forms an intricate network of structures called fibrils, which forms the clot. That is why you see the thickened clumps of blood when you cut yourself. Our anti-coagulant works by preventing the body from producing the protein prothrombin, after which the rest of the reactions cannot take place and therefore no clots will form. Simple.'

She pushes her thick glasses firmly back into place.

'Where would your drug be used?' I ask.

'Mescoan is slightly different. Most of the commercial anti-coagulants on the market are used to treat blood clotting which appear in the veins of people, especially in the leg areas. The drug help to reduce the risk of clots reaching the heart and lungs. Our drug works on the same principle, except that it is highly localised. It is not something that a patient would take intravenously. Rather, it is applied to the desired area as a solvent. What this means is that the wounds are normally open wounds, let's say in heart surgery, where you don't want the blood to start clotting, or even in blood a transfusion. There are people that are predisposed to rapid clotting. Mescoan helps in these cases.'

None of what she says makes any sense to me.

'One more thing,' she adds, ' Mescoan is not yet widely available. It has not been given FDA approval in the US, which is potentially our biggest market. Its effectiveness is dependent on a great deal of skill during application and there are not that many doctors around. This is primarily why we are waiting for FDA approval. Until it is more stable it needs a practised hand.'

'And a certain *sang-froid*,' I add.

'That would be correct.' For the first time there is a sliver of a smile playing on her lips. If she got rid of the bad glasses, had a decent haircut and invested in a new wardrobe, she'd be attractive.

'Why is it such a problem?' I ask.

'If it enters the blood stream in significant quantities it can destroy the blood's natural defences, which can result in organ damage and, ultimately, death.'

'And who would be the type of people who are skilled in administering Mescoan?'

'Hard to say. We are required by the BMA, the British Medical Association, to keep track of the hospitals that purchase the drug. The thing is, with enough practice, a lab technician can do it, as they frequently do in research institutions.'

'Do you have access to the names of the hospitals?'

'No, but the company does, probably the accounts department. You'll have to talk to the relevant manager.'

I say goodbye to her. She acknowledges my farewell with a raised eyebrow and a diffident shrug. I watch her scurrying down the corridor, tugging at the sleeves of her jersey.

One of the clerical lackeys promises to e-mail me the list of all the hospitals who are currently using Mescoan. I ask him to also fax it to Helm's office in London.

The mobile phone rings in the car. It is Helm, checking to confirm whether I'm still meeting him. He also gives me a new address where he'll be. I haul out my street index of London and pinpoint Wapping High Street. The name sounds vaguely familiar. As I get nearer the destination it all comes back to me.

After my courtroom debacle I had sought solace at a friend's house in Greenwich. The four weeks I had spent there consisted entirely of walking. The Thames encourages that. It is very different from the other European waterways. Hardly anyone ever seems to enjoy its pleasures.

It is not like the Seine in Paris or the Grand Canal in Venice.

True, the ads for apartments say "fantastic views of the Thames" but implicit in those messages is the fact that the river is far away, that one can see it glittering at night, but one needn't encounter it. I encountered it every day, wondering through the desolate buildings that make up the Isle of Dogs, the warehouses at the West India docks that still reeked of spices. My favourite was exploring - against the imploring of my host - the nooks and crannies of the river. Here, one encountered the flotsam of humanity, tramps jumping out of bushes, heartbroken men seeking solace by the river.

I used to walk all the way down past Wapping and onto London Bridge.

I'd get home dog-tired, my feet hurting, but the physical exhaustion helped me fall asleep instantly.

At the headquarters for Thames Division, I ask for Helm.

'Oh, he's with MIT,' says the woman at the desk. 'Hang on, I'll ring him up.'

With the sandwich still in her hand she attempts to turn the pages of her phone book, as well as dial the number, a marvel of legerdemain.

'Third floor, first office on yer left,' she instructs. 'He's expecting yer.'

I take the rickety old elevator to the third floor.

There's a man standing at the entrance with his arm outstretched.

'You ought to do something about the building,' I say to him.

'Are you referring to the elevator or to old Susie downstairs?' he says with a sly grin.

'Both,' I respond.

'Terence Helm. Nice meeting you at last.' He shakes my hand firmly.

'Barvalis de Hoop,' I answer.

'We've been here since 1798,' he continues, 'so the decrepitude comes with the package.'

'That's a long time,' I concur.

'Yup. Thames Division used to be called the Marine Police Establishment. It was set up to police the Thames. There used to be a lot of criminal activity in this area, river pirates, gangs, etc, preying on the hundreds of ships that came upriver.'

'See that?' He points to a building visible from the window. 'It was known as Execution Dock. Criminals were hanged from the scaffolds there. Then the bodies were chained to the river wall to be washed over by three tides, as a warning to others. Of course, this didn't deter anyone.'

Helm is about my height, a lean man in his late twenties.

He's wearing jeans and an old sweatshirt, not the sort of outfit one usually associates with the Metropolitan Police. That's not to say anyone would mistake his wiry frame for anything other than a member of Her Majesty's armed forces. It must be very difficult for him to go undercover. If I was a criminal, I'd have no problem singling him out. Helm's shaven head accentuates his high cheekbones. There's a twinkle in his eyes, but I suspect that it's not an everyday occurrence. He's doing the same to me, checking me out, seeing if his pre-constructed persona matches what's in front of him.

Helm shares an office with another officer who's not in at the moment.

He pulls a chair out for me.

'Tea?'

'Love some.'

'Sandwich?'

'Yes.'

He disappears. It gives me an opportunity to look around the office. On the wall behind his chair there's a large map of London which is adorned with multi-coloured pins. His desk is cluttered with papers and files. It is utterly devoid of any personal effects.

He returns a couple of minutes later bearing a cup of tea on a chipped saucer. The boiled-egg sandwich is stale.

'It comes from the vending machine down the passage.' He smiles apologetically.

'What's MIT?' I ask.

'Marine Intelligence Team. It's a specialised unit within Thames Division, set up in 1992 to address the problems of marine crime. We work with just about everybody; Customs and Excise, the Immigration Department, the Port of London Authority and the National Rivers

Authority. In addition there's the National Criminal Intelligence Service, Ministry of Defence Police, Interpol and, of course, Europol. Lately all we seem to do is pull bodies out of the water.'

'Help me and you'll get your fifteen minutes of fame,' I quip.

'Not for me, that fame malarky. All I want is a quiet life by the river, preferably with a fishing rod.'

'Bet you won't find any fish in this river.' I point to the Thames.

'Now that's where you're wrong. The river has seen some of the best fishing in over a hundred years. There's some good being done in this modern world of ours.'

He tugs at the reams of computer paper on his desk. 'Okay, let's see what we've got so far.'

'First, details of Laville's history as requested, direct from the BMA.

It's been an impressive career thus far. Scholarship to study medicine at Oxford. Gold medal in his class. Another scholarship, this time from a private company, for postgraduate studies in biochemistry. Groundbreaking research in cell division, whatever that is. Papers, fellowships and posts too numerous to mention. Current position is that of senior consultant at Guy's and St. Thomas Hospital. I took the liberty of ringing up the hospital to find out exactly what he's doing. No-one could tell me, so I'm willing to bet that a "consultant" is sort of like a non-executive director, that is, he gets paid lots of money to do nothing. He's not married, no relatives, owns a flat in a posh area of London, Mayfair, and a large house in St. Albans, Hertfordshire.'

Helm scratches around his desk for another printout.

'Oh, here's the trips abroad, courtesy of our friends at immigration. He's a busy man. Lots of trips around the world.'

'Anything to Sri Lanka?' I ask.

'Nope. Far East trips include Singapore and Malaysia, for medical conferences, but no Sri Lanka.'

'But he could have caught a short flight from one of those places to Sri Lanka?'

'Very possible, but we cannot track that. Why the interest in Sri Lanka?

I start to tell him what I know.

'Hey, hang on a minute. You've lost me,' he raises his hand.

'Don't worry, I'm pretty lost as well,' I smile.

'Okay, let's plot it out. I'm surprised that your superiors let you carry on in this fashion.'

'So am I,' I add wryly.

He moves to the white board next to his desk and draws blocks on it.

'You'd better start,' he says firmly.

'Dead bodies. Lots of them. Six in London. One in Rotterdam, one in Hamburg, and the other in Utrecht. All Tamil nationals. All sans hands. Tenuous link with the LTTE but no proof thus far. Two victims had traces of an unusual drug in their blood, Mescoan. Too strange to be a coincidence, therefore must be viewed as a vital clue. One promising lead. Dr Laville, of whom we know nothing. Could be the victim's doctor but highly unlikely. There's something that Sherlock Holmes said about all this - in the absence of further evidence, etc, etc - but for the life of me, I can't remember.'

'What you're saying is that we're clutching at straws?'

'Yup.'

'What about credit card information on Laville?' I ask.

'Sorry, this is England. We do not have access to company computers, and to get legal permission would take about six months. He's got to be a bona fide drug baron for us to get within sniffing distance of that sort of information.'

I make a mental note to ask Boehme how to circumvent this particular regulation.

'What are you doing later?' he asks suddenly.

Why, are you planning to buy me dinner?' I respond.

'No, no,' he blurts out, momentarily flustered. 'I thought we could take a drive out there. It's about an hour out of London. See the lay of the land, so to speak. Mind you, if you want dinner, it's on me.'

'Sounds good to me. What time should I come around?'

'About six. Need me to pick you up?'

'No,' I answer. I have other plans.

It is 4 pm. I leave Thames Division and walk down to the quay at the top of King Henry's steps. The air is cold, as it always is near the water. A few ancient craft chug serenely through the river. I start walking. In a short while there a distinctive change in the architectural landscape.

The buildings her are only sporadically maintained. There are gaping holes where the windows used to be. Unchecked vegetation obscures the names of the properties and the warning signs. Unseen dogs, sensing a human presence, unleash a cacophony of vicious barking.

Across the river the lights from the huge apartment blocks start twinkling in the darkening October sky. An old couple, on what looks like a floating junk shop, wave to me as they come perilously close to the water's edge. Nearer to me there are less friendly people. In the lengthening shadows of the dying day, the hobos lurking in the old buildings start coming out to scavenge in the dark. I turn back.

Helm is ready and waiting. We take the elevator down to the parking lot to my car.

'Go window shopping?' he asks.

'Nope. Went for a walk up the river.'

There is a look of horror on his face.

'Are you crazy? It's not a very safe place. The area is crawling with vagrants.'

'Relax. I'm a big girl. I can take care of myself,' I assert.

He shakes his head at me.

*

Hertfordshire is normally about a forty minute drive out of London. With the peak- hour traffic, it takes us twice the time. Once we reach the countryside, the traffic thins out but the makes of the cars take on a sleek uniformity, all four-wheel drives and expensive saloon vehicles.

Helm helps with the navigation. As we move further away from the town of St Albans, the houses become bigger as well. Eventually we are in mansion territory.

'Slow down,' urges Helm. 'This looks like it.'

We drive past a large brown Georgian house. Most of the property is obscured by gigantic oak trees layed out like sentinels around the edges. There is a solid wooden gate at the entrance. It is swung wide open. A few cars are bottlenecked at the entrance.

'Looks like your friend is having a dinner party,' observes Helm.

It must be very important. There are young men in uniform running around trying to direct the cars. The head honcho is on a two-way radio waving his arms around and trying to look important.

'Shall we gatecrash?'

'Not a good idea,' answers Helm. 'Let's have a drink instead.'

Back in the small town, things are livening up. It is after all Friday night. In the high street a group of youths are attacking a rubbish bin as if it had a life of its own. The police car that drives past only elicits a momentary pause from them. In a side street we catch a glimpse of a woman with her arms draped over a man who's vomiting into the gutter. No doubt similar scenes are being played out in small towns all over Europe. It is a depressing sight. Neither of us says a word, probably because nothing needs to be said.

Helm directs me to a car park in front of a pub. A group of young boys stand outside puffing self-consciously on cigarettes.

'Don't you know that smoking stunts your growth,' growls Helm at the nearest boy. They let rip a stream of foul-mouthed invective, but not before moving to a safe distance. Helm shakes his head at them.

The pub-cum-restaurant is a bit more sedate. Most of the crowd seem to be over forty. An old-fashioned jukebox is belting out Sixties songs. The restaurant section is empty, and the waiter looks at us as though he'd prefer it if we had a few more drinks at the bar first.

Over steaming duck and cherry pies, Helm starts to tell me about his working holidays in Hertfordshire. Before long he has me laughing. He's easy company so I don't feel the need to talk. It is 11:20 pm by the time we leave.

I have to catch the ferry back to Amsterdam at 8 am the next morning. For once, I don't feel like going back home.

Chapter 9

If ordinary European citizens were aware of the amount of power exercised by government they would revolt in droves. Barring a brief flirtation with anarchism in my teens, I have largely succumbed to the notion of good citizenship. In a way it is a form of brainwashing, but it has placed a system of checks and balances over the Dutch people that has largely had a positive influence. What concerns me however is how the idea of good governance has been subverted to make the large-scale invasion of privacy acceptable. Our daily passage through the city is tracked by thousands of cameras at strategic points; we leave glaring audit trails with practically every financial transaction we perform; even in the countryside, cameras disguised as disused beverage cans monitor our rural activities. After a while, a weariness infects the spirit. We simply accept things as they are, forgetting that information is power, and power is danger.

Which is why I feel the slightest regret in invading the privacy of Laurier. This naturally worries me but I will deal with this later. In my mind, it has become imperative that I find out what the link between Laurier and Laville is. Something about the way they interacted intrigues me, especially the familiarity between them, like father and son.

The Dutch policing system is different from the English one. The police and the various peripheral agencies do not have the authority to pick up the phone and request information on citizens. A commercial company on the other hand can request extensive credit information on anyone. It is highly ironic but Mammon rules these days. It takes me only a few phone calls to assemble a complete profile on Laurier. On many levels it is an ordinary profile, but what is fascinating is the extraordinary parallels between his life and that of Laville. They seem to be on the same trajectory, the master and the pupil. His mother is a supermarket supervisor and father is a minor functionary in the tax department. Very bright boy as well, and like Laville he did not have to fork out any money for his university education. It was all paid for by scholarships and bursaries.

Also unmarried like the doctor. Unlike the doctor, he is not wealthy. A small investment portfolio for the past year, monthly amount deducted directly from his salary and paid by debit order. The one anomaly is a fat chunk of shares valued at fifty thousand Euros. The shares are in a company called Biogen. My accounting skills are not very good but I cannot see references to the purchases in any of the documents. The name of the company seems familiar. I haul out the already bulging file on Laville. There it is in black and white.

Laville is listed as a non-executive director of a company called Biogen.

*

The secretary who looks after the five professors in the medical department is the same one who manned the reception desk at Laurier's inaugural lecture.

She recognises me.

'Dr Laurier isn't it?'

Her face has the kind of blank professionalism one would imagine nurses put on when they hand out sex aids to patients at those private sex clinics in the countryside. There is, however, a smidgen of smarminess in her voice.

'Yes.' I hand her my card.

'If he can't see me now, I would like to make an appointment to see him sometime soon. It is urgent.'

'What is it about?' She knows right away that she has asked me the wrong question. I can almost see her bite her lip.

I don't even bother answering.

'Dr Laurier does not have any lectures at the moment. He may be able to see you now. I will give him your card.'

Dr Laurier is sitting on the edge of his desk, making no effort to hide the bemused expression on his face. I am starting to recognise that look. It is the card that elicits it. Most people start to wonder what they've done wrong. At the same time they have no recollection of committing any criminal act. And yet they cannot be too sure. It is the look of the innocent plagued by self-doubt.

He does, however make an effort to stand up - too late, of course. In this feeble gesture he embodies everything that is screwed up about modern gender interaction. I would not have minded if he hadn't bothered standing in the first place, nor would it have made any difference to me if he had. It is an act conforming to an increasingly redundant set of rules. But the poor man is trapped between his ingrained habit and the knowledge that standing up in a woman's presence is irrelevant, unless of course she was a queen. The Dutch or the English one.

Close up his face is even more interesting. There are more lines of introspection that one would expect in someone so young. His eyes tell the tale of hard work and pain. Only the twisted curl of his full lips leaven his seriousness. His physiology is more Danish than Dutch as well, but then again, as we merge Fortress Europa, people are becoming more homogenous as well. If we ever reach the stage where citizens are bred from test tubes, this task will fall to the Scandinavians. After all, they have to do *something* in the new Europe.

I shake his proffered hand.

'First of all, I would like to say that under no circumstances are you allowed to discuss our conversation with anyone else. If you wish not to speak to me, that is your right, but under article 42 of the Europol Convention established by the European Union, if you wish to voluntarily engage in a discussion with me, you must agree to this regulation. If the party breaks the rules, they're liable to criminal prosecution.'

'Phew,' he whistles through his teeth. 'I had no idea I was in so much trouble. Do I need a lawyer?'

'No trouble at all,' I purr smoothly, embarrassed at my verbose speech.

Unfortunately, it was necessary.

'Think of it this way,' I improvise rapidly, 'I am your best friend and I'm about to tell you a great secret. All I'm asking you to do is swear to secrecy.

'Well, if you put it like that, how can I resist?' He smiles sweetly.

I start to weave the elaborate tale of lies that Boehme and I had agreed on in the office. How we were investigating the illegal trafficking of drugs by rogue elements within a company called Biogen. That all levels of staff, from distribution clerks to managers, were involved, hence the need for secrecy. It was my idea so Boehme had made the construction of a web of deceit my responsibility as well. I had checked out Biogen on the internet and found that it was some kind of drug manufacturing company. Then I had spent the best part of the previous day making up a range of false facts and figures. It was quite impressive.

The lies come easily as I consult my notes of false data. Fortunately he doesn't actually ask to see any of it. I am conscious too, of the fact that I am doing what he was doing in the lecture hall. Not merely presenting a story, but building a plausible story, with dramatis personae, a thrilling plot, and a denouement. Except that it wasn't all over, that it was both my and his duty to put an end to the crime. I get carried away, embellishing my imaginary set-up with information that is not in my notes. He listens intently, displays the right emotions and answers my questions.

When I leave he shakes my hand longer than necessary.

Not that I mind. He promises to think long and hard about what I've just said.

*

I have a dinner date with Boehme. It's at the hotel D' Alfonzo. That's in Paris. Very romantic.

Actually it's a briefing session by the Co-ordinator of Europol, but Boehme agrees to take me out for dinner beforehand.

The hotel is one of those places that seems to exist solely to host conventions and conferences. The food is thus accordingly bland and international. The menu says "Fusion cooking - combining the best of East and West" but never in my life have I had Thai prawn soup that tasted like tomato soup. Boehme pays the bill with his Europol credit card, so I don't feel too bad about complaining.

This place seems to have mastered the art of draping multicoloured posters in its foyer. The staff too, reflect a robotic professionalism, uniformed personnel scurrying around with notebooks in their hands.

After dinner we stroll around the bustling foyer. There is the heady smell of power in the air. I understand now why power is so sexual. It's both mental and physical. A shared sense of destiny, combined with physical proximity make for a dangerous cocktail of emotions. Even amidst all the bustling, strangers go out of their way to make eye contact, to indulge in little tactile gestures. There is also serious networking going on. Middle-ranking EU functionaries without their satrap bosses are suddenly in charge. Their middle-ranking secretaries scuttle around, performing their errands, and doing their own networking. Boehme seems to know a lot of people around us. It is like a gathering of old school friends. Most of them seem to be German. Two scenarios that come to mind; one, the Germans have a deep and abiding interest in ensuring that their liberties are not infringed on; and two, they simply enjoy being policemen. A large amount of floor space has been cordoned off for the Europol meeting. On the edges of the restricted area groups of people eye us as they walk past. Is it my imagination or do I detect the occasional glance of rancour in some of their eyes?

Outside in the rain there is an anti-police demonstration by a coalition of various organisations from across the continent. We had missed them as we had come in via aside entrance, a small precaution that Boehme took to avoid getting his photograph taken. The dim figures are barely visible from the hotel windows and the noise they make cannot be heard, but they are there.

I'm not sure why Boehme has asked me along. Perhaps it's because he feels that he needs to reinforce my beliefs, that I might be weakening. In a way it's like going to church. Sometimes solitary prayer is not enough. One needs the hallowed ground, the like-minded votaries and the holy sounds of worship.

Inside the main convention hall the lights have been dimmed and the gigantic screen in front flickers into life. The blue and white Euro-logo shimmers into view.

The Co-ordinator is up on the podium with his colleagues. The Co-ordinator, in his blue suit and black brogues is determinedly civilian - for a former member of the *Bundeskriminalamt*. Even in the office he exists only from newspaper cuttings, a man who might as well have been on the moon. The audience is a surprise. There are no uniforms in sight, apart from the waiters, that is. There are members of the continent's police forces present though, that much is easy to see. Big men looking ill at ease in suits, women dressed in power outfits that were in fashion ten years ago.

What is interesting, are the members of the other groups represented in the audience. There is a large contingent of journalists, social workers, academics and politicians, all bridling with barely concealed outrage.

For the first time I realise that I *am* afraid of having to explain what I do for a living. Boehme is cleverer than I thought. He has seen that I am weakening even before I noticed it, the bastard. He guides me, he shepherds me, right into the lion's den so that I may be confronted by all my fears at the same time. What will be clear then in both his mind and mine is whether I stay or leave. There will be no room for vacillation.

The Co-ordinator is on the podium, second from left. This is the first time that I have seen him in the flesh. He is a short, stocky man in his late fifties, with a rim of short hair around his bald pate. He looks like any of the hundreds of EU officials that flit regularly across our television screens every night. We have all been handed folders with papers inside. One of the sheets is a short CV of the Co-ordinator. Not surprisingly the details are exactly the same as what we were given in the office. Extensive police field experience to show that he's had his hands dirtied, plus a smattering of degrees along the way to show that he does have a brain. Likes fishing, reading and spending his spare time with his family. Appointed by the Council of Ministers to perform the proverbial cleaning out of the Aegean stables.

He's been described in the press by the head of the German Data Protection Association as an "absolute monarch" but right now he looks like a rabbit caught in the glare of powerful headlights. He is clearly not used to being scrutinized by so many people.

I do not envy him. Whatever his good intentions, the whole process around the formation of Europol has been marred by accusations of secrecy and the abuse of power, not to mention being a waste of taxpayers' money. This semi-public gathering is the first meeting since the Europol Convention was ratified by all the member states in 1998. Instead of getting some smooth PR person to front the questions, the head of the organisation has been thrust into the limelight.

It is unfortunate for him that his name has been invoked in the same breath as J Edgar Hoover's, much to his horror, said Boehme, who had worked with him in the BKA. It was not Hoover's cross-dressing habits that his detractors were trying to compare though. Rather it was the FBI head's unchecked power that lead him to accumulate interesting information on just about everybody for so many years.

Next to the Co-ordinator is a strange English member of the European Parliament. He stands up to speak with a sheaf of notes in his hands. After a cursory glance at them he puts them down, as if what he has to say transcends mere notes. The Englishman is a sight to behold; flaming red hair, freckles, bad teeth, and a dress sense distinctly at odds with the sleek Euro-MPs surrounding him. He has a voice though, that is by turns seductive, opprobrious, cajoling, hypnotic. He, on the other hand, relishes the attention. The audience pays attention.

It takes him only three minutes to compare the Co-ordinator with Hoover. He is starting to get carried away by his own enthusiasm, railing at the destruction of civil liberties and the privilegess of those in power. He stabs his finger in the air, constantly referring to "those outside". That's not to say what he says doesn't make sense. It is however, hard to look at people like Boehme, and even the Co-ordinator, whom I don't know, but who's exhibiting some distinctly non-megalomaniacal tendencies as he squirms on stage, and think of them as people who are out to destroy the freedoms of society. There is uncertainty and fear in the room, and he exploits it. He is a reader of situations. His name is Ambrose Runcie, I see from the notes, and as he sits down he quickly scans the room to gauge the reaction from the audience, professional that he is.

It's a hard act for the co-ordinator to follow, but he plods through doggedly in his business English.

I open the folder that we have been given. On the first page is the mission statement of the European Police Office. It is as vaguely worded as any corporate manifesto.

"Europol is the European Law Enforcement Organisation which aims at improving the effectiveness and co-operation of the competent authorities in the Member States in preventing and combating terrorism, unlawful drug trafficking and other serious forms of international organised crime. The mission of Europol is to make a significant contribution to the European Union's law enforcement action against organised crime with a particular emphasis on the criminal organisations involved."

I check the legs under the covered podium table. The Englishman is tapping his foot impatiently on the floor. My gut feeling about him is that he is not a very nice person to be around, no matter how passionately he feels about the rights of man.

After him the co-ordinator is merely prolix. He makes a valiant attempt to outline his policies, which are ultimately those that were approved by the Council of Ministers in the first place, but he has lost the battle. What has happened is that the numerous groupings have organised an effective campaign to highlight what they regard as the dangers of an unregulated police force. They have won the battle for the hearts and minds of the people.

That is when I make up my mind. I am a sucker for losers.

Outside, the protestors are still there, stoically maintaining their presence through the rain, although a few have broken away and are standing beneath the balconies of an apartment block next to the hotel. Two people with a Greenpeace banner are huddled near a shrub at the hotel entrance. It is an ineffectual barrier against the rain.

I turn my face away so that they don't see me. One can never be too sure. They might be people I have worked with in the past. My last encounter with the woman from the agency still hurts, like a sting.

'Christ,' I say to Boehme as we get into a taxi. 'I feel as though I've signed up with the Gestapo.'

Boehme doesn't say anything. He gazes thoughtfully out of the window at the grey Parisian skyline, slowly massaging his chin with his fingers. It is probably the wrong thing to say. He doesn't say another word to me.

His mood is infectious. I slump back into introspection. I want to tell Boehme that I am staying but his body language suggests that he's not in the mood for talking. Then again, if he's so smart he can figure it out for himself.

Only when we are ensconced in the aeroplane does Boehme finally deign to address me.

He tells me that Scotland Yard have authorised a phone tap on Laville. And the Dutch police on Laurier.

'Why Laurier?' I ask. 'He doesn't look like the criminal type to me.'

'Cast your net wide enough and you'll catch a few fish,' Boehme answers, doing his best Buddha act.

He explains how the two know each other.

'Laurier was a student of Laville's at Oxford University. Laville was Laurier's personal tutor. And then Laurier became a sort of underdog to Laville.'

I think he means understudy, but I don't contradict him.

'They must have liked each other very much.' I say to him.

Why do you say that?

'There's a photograph of the two of them on what looks like a holiday trip. Next to camel with the sphinx in the background.'

'Could have been one of those academic junkets that those sort of people go on.'

Boehme has a low regard for academics.

'Could be, but then there are only two people in the picture,' I point out.

Boehme has a thought that he doesn't know how to share with me. I can tell by the signs of internal struggle on his face.

There is an embarrassed pause before he blurts out, 'Do you think that Laurier and Laville are...er.'

'Do they sleep with each other?' I take away his pain.

'Yes,' he answers glumly, slumping over his drink like a defeated man.

'I have no idea. Possibly not. It's true that Laurier and Laville are single, but...'

It is difficult to articulate to Boehme the narcissism written all over Laville's face. The sense that he is incapable of loving anyone else, male or female, but himself.

Boehme can look at a face and decide whether the person is guilty of a crime or not, but when it comes to reading other signs he's hopeless. More than that, he's also blinkered. He has old-fashioned notions about character, ideals, honour and loyalty. Any straying from this righteous path incurs his wrath. And it's dangerous to incur Boehme's wrath.

Chapter 10

Boehme drops me off at home. He is now chatty and friendly, like he's had a good time. His demeanour is that of a boy scout returning from a weekend adventure in the forest. I stop trying to analyse him. It's driving me crazy.

The caretaker is standing at the door, watering his droopy pot plants that stand outside like two shabby sentries from a banana republic. They're tropical plants, not used to the cold.

'Hullo Ms De Hoop,' he coughs, 'the men you missed the last time have come to fix your floor.'

My heart stops beating and my blood freezes. I struggle to breathe in.

'Are you all right, miss? Are you all right?' The caretaker is touching my arm.

'I'm fine.' I breathe in deeply. 'I've just forgotten to bring something home from the office.'

I step outside and phone Boehme. Then I go back in and wait in the corridor, wondering if they will walk past me. The old man has gone back inside. I had pretended to walk up the stairs before doubling back to his door. I keep an eye on the entrance as well as the stairs. This way I would be able see and hear them.

The five minutes before Boehme bursts through the door seem like an eternity. He has a worried look on his face. I had only asked him to come back right away. My nails are pressed into the palms of my hands as I explain to him what the caretaker had told me.

He calls the bomb squad.

We await. Fortunately Boehme doesn't even bother making small talk. No emollient noises emerge from his mouth. He doesn't even bother looking at me. It does make me pause for thought though. I'm not sure how much of this I can actually take.

It is a grim, interminable wait.

They arrive after five minutes, sirens blaring loudly. It feels like five hours.

The sniffer dogs are causing a riot at the front door.

'Hullo *Choco*.' No-one's called me that since I was at school. I look up into the vulpine face of Jonny Wouters. Jonny is still the gum-chewing nerd he was when we were at school, although he's now decked out in the vestments of his profession.

I hate the nickname, but I had always liked him for his quirkiness and brilliance. He was the school maths whizzkid, always winning maths awards and getting his name mentioned at assembly. He was always a pain. The sight of his gangly frame mincing its way to the front of the class whenever no-one else could solve a problem, the way he did it in what seemed like five seconds, his gloating smile when he finished. And yet, none of us ever hated him. He always had friends.

'Still living dangerously, eh?' His grin is the same. So are his teeth.

'We have to go in from the back. There might be something in here that will go boom when you open the door.' He relishes my flinching.

'Window open by any chance?'

'I have no idea.'

'Never mind, we'll have a look.'

It's a couple of minutes before the fire engine arrives with the crane to hoist up Jonny and his colleague to the window. He chats amiably to me, at the same time keeping a wary eye out for Boehme. He thinks that we are together, his brain working out all the permutations of our relationship.

I try to deflect his questions by asking him about his life.

'Me, I'm a happily married man. Been married for eight years. Got twin girls. They're six years old, so they keep us busy.'

They have to break one of my windows to enter the flat. We stand across the road and watch the crane slowly arc its way up. It is a dark and gloomy late Sunday afternoon, with the threat of rain in the air. Nobody on the street shows the slightest interest in what's happening. Only the caretaker came out in response to the yelping of the dogs.

Jonny hops nimbly out of the crane box through the open window. The wait is nerve-wracking. I have visions of a violent explosion shattering all the windows, flames erupting forth.

Then Jonny's thin legs come out from the window, followed by the rest of him. Even from a distance he manages to look comical.

He jumps out of the crane beaming, like he's just delivered a healthy baby.

'Yup. Very interesting gizmo. We'll take it to the lab.'

In his hands he has a package wrapped in brown paper. It is about the size of a hardback book. We keep our distance until he places it into the reinforced van that his companion arrived in.

'How come you've got no pictures on your walls,' he asks me as he turns to leave.

'I'm an iconophobe,' I answer.

My mobile phone rings. It's Benschop-Fehr. She's already heard. She asks if I'm all right and then offers me a place to stay. Out of the corner of my eye, Jonny waves cheerily at me and opens the door to his large off-road leisure vehicle. It is only then that I notice the children in the back seat, playing with each other's hair. His wife is in the front, waiting patiently. They must have been on their way home from a family day out.

I drop the phone and run to him.

'My car!' My voice strangulated and hoarse. It does not sound like me.

Jonny freezes. At another time the sight of his buttocks frozen in mid-air over his car seat might have been funny.

'My car!' I shout again and wave to him frantically across the road. The others have turned to look at me.

He gets out and walks towards me in bewilderment. I point to the car. The dog handler releases the dogs and they race to it. They are in a frenzy again, excitedly prancing around as if they were performing some sort of Dionysian ritual.

Johhny turns back and returns to his car for his bag of tools. His assistant hauls out what look like a gigantic skateboard. Jonny lies on it on his back and rolls under my car.

Time stands still all over again.

Only his legs are visible. They shake. It is not fear. They constantly drum against the ground. He's always been the edgy, nervous sort.

This time when he walks away, he doesn't look so chirpy. He's very careful with the small package in his hand.

*

My room in the hotel that I'm staying at has almost the same view that I have from the office, except that I'm on a higher floor and I have bigger windows so I get a panoramic view of the ships entering the harbour. There is an added bonus. A full moon rises up from the horizon and casts a yellow glow over the sea. It is a deep and rich yellow but as it ascends into the sky it gradually becomes silver.

Finally, it keeps a cold and distant eye on the planet from high in the heavens.

Part of me wants to sit in the hotel room and spend the next few days watching satellite television. To order room service and dull the brain with food and noise until it becomes aware of nothing. But it is the coward's way out, so on Monday morning I force myself to get out of bed. To bathe, to change and to put make-up on. Downstairs I say goodbye to the two policemen who look as though they'd spent the night in the foyer. I tell them that they can have breakfast on me, signing the restaurant bills for them. They beam broadly like two schoolboys.

It is a fifteen minute walk from the hotel to the office. I take a detour. One that takes me past the boats in front of Centraal Station. The morning is the same as most days, shards of mist, and an occasional gust of light rain, so ephemeral, caressing the skin.

Amsterdammers are late risers, especially on Mondays. The streets are devoid of people. The only people out are miserable-looking backpackers just off the train and a few bedraggled prostitutes desperately attempting to slow down the traffic of vans and trucks.

A soggy American youth in a yellow anorak tries to ask me directions to a boat that's been converted to a floating hostel. I think I know the one he is referring to. He is very grateful.

It is only 7:30 am. I beg the Turkish owner of a café sweeping away last night's rubbish to sell me two croissants, offering to pay double the amount. He takes the money grumpily and points to the paper bags on his counter. Then he watches me to make sure I only take two.

· The office has that freshly cleaned smell of having being thoroughly scrubbed over the weekend. I make the coffee, the first time I have done so. The secretary has expensive tastes. In her filing cabinet she has a packet of Italian Lilley coffee hidden away. She usually serves us the rubbish, but my nose has occasionally told me otherwise. I put the pot on. Then I sit at my desk and read the morning papers.

Surprisingly, Ilsa is the first to arrive. I can see by the look on her face that she knows what has happened. It is an osmotic process, telephone calls being made, discussions in hushed tones, tales of my ordeal spreading like electronic wildfire.

'I see you found the coffee.' There is a muted tone in her voice, as if she is trying to offer her sympathies doesn't know what to say. It has to be taken for what it's worth. I offer her the other croissant as a peace offering. The hesitant way she accepts it tells me that she avoids them, no doubt to keep her slim body in the shape that it is, but she bites into it anyway. Either that or she thinks it's been poisoned.

We sit in silence, pretending to be absorbed in the morning papers.

Boehme comes into the office at 9:30 with Benschop-Fehr. I had no knowledge that she was coming over. I feel a twinge of irrational panic. She murmurs her commiserations and goes back to being her professional self. I apologise for not taking up her offer of a place to stay the night. Boehme had made me the same offer and when I had refused he'd booked the hotel room. And paid for two extra breakfasts.

Benschop-Fehr is in working mode. Her folder is held tightly to her chest and she impatiently and irritatingly clicks the pen in her hand.

Boehme, too, tries to behave as though we're about to settle down to our normal Monday morning meeting.

Ilsa brings the coffee into the conference room. She quickly appraises Benschop-Fehr when she's not looking.

Benschop-Fehr gets right down to business.

'We have an inside man in the LTTE. Unfortunately he's not very high up in the echelon, so we're not privy to all the really important decisions. We do however generally know what they're up to. So far they have not committed any acts of terrorism on European soil. They do have some sympathy for their cause here and they wouldn't want to jeopardise that. They also know that we will come down very hard on them. So far they've had it easy precisely for the reasons I've mentioned. There has been the odd deportation from our side but nothing else. The bottom line is they wouldn't dare. It's too risky. They would lose a large chunk of their finances overnight. The attack on De Hoop is inexplicable.'

'So are you saying that someone out there doesn't like my face?' I respond.

Benschop-Fehr permits herself a wintry smile.

'No, what I'm saying is that we don't know. It's quite possible that there's some kind of internal struggle going on within the LTTE but it is highly unlikely it would have remained hidden for so long. I don't know what else to say. Forensics are examining the bomb for any signatures. We have to wait for their report. I have also been instructed to set up measures to ensure your safety. We are treating this as a grade I terrorist incident.'

'What exactly do you mean by "measures"?' I ask.

'It means that we will set up security nets that we deem appropriate to ensure your safety. We will also pro-actively attempt to find out who is behind this.'

Boehme has risen from his chair. His face is an impassive block but his lips are tightly pressed together. You don't need to be very perceptive to see the anger in him.

'We appreciate your help but we have the structures in place to sort this out,' he intones. 'This is an act perpetrated against a member of Europol.'

Benschop-Fehr consults her notes.

'With all due respect to the extraordinary powers of Europol, you happen to be on Dutch soil. You have no jurisdiction here except those that are defined within the Europol mandate, which is in article 30 of the Amsterdam Treaty. The document states that your organisation, inter alia, "aims at improving the effectiveness and co-operation of the competent authorities in the Member States in preventing and combating terrorism, unlawful drug trafficking and other serious forms of international organised crime". Are you suggesting that we are incompetent?'

She slips two sheets of paper in our direction. I pick one up.

OBJECTIVES AND MANDATE

THE OBJECTIVE OF EUROPOL IS TO IMPROVE THE EFFECTIVENESS AND CO-OPERATION OF THE COMPETENT AUTHORITIES BETWEEN THE MEMBER STATES IN PREVENTING AND COMBATTING TERRORISM, UNLAWFUL DRUG TRAFFICKING AND OTHER SERIOUS FORMS OF INTERNATIONAL CRIME WHERE THERE ARE FACTUAL INDICATIONS THAT AN ORGANISED CRIMINAL

STRUCTURE IS INVOLVED AND TWO OR MORE MEMBER STATES ARE AFFECTED.

She knows what she's talking about. She's also come well-prepared. The only reason she consults her notes is to avoid looking at us.

Boehme doesn't answer her question. He is aware that she's right. Naturally he does not admit defeat. He simply stands up to indicate that the meeting is over. I avoid looking at either of them. What they have done is place me in a position that makes me feel very guilty, that all the squabbling is my fault.

Outside I say a quick goodbye to Benschop-Fehr lest Boehme thinks that I'm fraternising with the enemy. He doesn't give me time to chat anyway, beckoning with his finger to follow him into his office.

Once he's closed the door, he glances at his message pad.

'Phone Wouters at the bomb squad. He'd like to talk to you.'

'Is that all?' I ask.

'That is all,' Boehme answers.

*

Jonny has a desk that looks like a fourteen year old's with a passion for electronics. Dismembered circuit boards, bits of multi-coloured wire and switches are strewn all over the place. On a side table he has an assortment of chemicals in test tubes bubbling away like a witch's brew. It is not what I imagined a bomb disposal centre to be like.

'How did you get into the bomb squad? I thought you'd end up as a mathematics professor or a computer tycoon,' I ask him.

'I was recruited at university. Maybe "recruited" is the wrong word. They offered me a job, subject to my passing an aptitude test. They were a bit worried about my behaviour at school, believe it or not. Basically, they were looking for an electronic whiz-kid, like in the same way they recruit spies. I was a bit taken aback, but the more I thought about it, the more I liked the idea. It sounded better than working in a laboratory for the rest of my life. I would not have fitted into the corporate life anyway.

'You know me, always wanted a life of danger and excitement,' he adds with a touch of drollery.

The funny thing is, he's not being ironic. At school, Jonny, nerd that he was, was still always getting into trouble. He once climbed the school posts and hung a huge banner at the entrance. It said, "ABANDON ALL HOPE YE WHO ENTER HERE".

To make matters worse, it was also during the visit of a team of school inspectors. His reprimand was mild though, seeing that he was the school's only hope in the annual Dutch mathematics olympiad. The principal did go around to his house talk to his parents. It was a good move. They cut off his pocket money. Jonny, of course, showed them all by winning the olympiad.

He sweeps aside some of the junk on his table and removes a tray from underneath, like a proud baker about to present fresh bread.

'Here's your bomb,' he announces with a flourish.

On the table it doesn't look so remarkable. No clocks. No sticks of dynamite. Just little bits of wire and a two phials, one containing a red and the other a blue liquid.

'Workmanlike quality but made very professionally. Almost as if it had rolled off an assembly line, God forbid. Whoever made this bomb is capable of a lot better. This was just a quickie job. Door opens. Bhoof! Car ignition, bhoof!'

'How can you tell?' I ask.

'The chap who made this used quality materials. He knows where to source them. But it was put together in a hurry. Didn't shave the wires to the right length, etc.'

'How powerful?' I persist stupidly, as if it would have made any difference to whether I had lived, or half lived.

'Oh, enough to have blown you to kingdom come.

'I must check my little black book,' he continues. 'All bombers have their signature. It's a work of art to most of them. The power of human vanity often transcends the need to not get caught.'

'Who does this belong to?'

'No idea, but give me a few days. Then again, it could have been made by a chemistry student who downloaded the instructions from the Internet. There's a lot of that floating around. Bloody amateurs.'

Jonny offers me a chocolate bar from his pocket. It must be the source of all his nervous energy. Even at school his mouth seemed to be perpetually crammed with chocolate. On reflection he was the one who gave me that darn nickname in the first place.

Outside the office there's a small concrete enclosure. It's meant to be some sort of rest area, but it looks like the courtyard of a prison. A few concrete benches, straggly plants in ugly square concrete blocks, and lots of cigarette buts. There's a view of lots of tall buildings. They obviously don't have much of an opinion of the recreational needs of the staff.

'So what have you been up, Choco?'

I raise my hand at him. 'Jonny, please don't call me that.'

At school Jonny and I had a relationship that could only be described as friendly-but-distant. He used to joke with me, and I used to retort back wittily. One miserable morning, we had a conversation about Descarte. This was during my philosophical period so naturally I was impressed by his erudition. We were both prefects huddled alone together in a corner of one of the buildings. I found him interesting and looked at him in a new light but to my shame he was too nerdy to hang out with. The closest we ever got together again was when we happened to be seated next to each other in a cinema. It was one of those end-of-term social rampages and we were in a group. Again, we joked and laughed in the dark, but in the harsh daylight I melted away from him to hang out with the cool kids. Teenagers can be cruel. I wonder if he remembers.

We talk about the old days, flitting from face to face. He tells me about his wife and family. She's been a terrific mother, and is also a nuclear physicist at CERN in Switzerland. His twin girls are in a special school for accelerated learning. There's no braggadocio in his voice though. He's still the same twitchy teenager, with only his thinning hair to differentiate him from the Jonny I used to know. All he succeeds in doing this time is make me feel very empty and despondent. My biological clock is ticking away *and* I don't even have a lover.'

'What about you,' he asks. 'Biological clock ticking away and all that.'

My slightly hysterical laugher causes him to cock his head at me.

'Nothing,' I choke. 'Private joke.'

'I see. No man in your life, heh?'

'No.'

'Well, you must come to dinner sometime. I might be able to fix you up.'

'Thanks.' I smile wanly.

'My pleasure.' He pats me on the shoulder.

*

'We've had a tip-off about the bomber from the LTTE.' Benschop-Fehr can barely contain her excitement over the telephone.

'He's a fifty year old South African, now resident in Amsterdam. Name's Dawie Louw. A former member of that country's BOSS intelligence agency, that's Bureau of State Security. They were a pretty dirty bunch, acting mostly against opponents of apartheid. Used every thing from poison to bullets, but their speciality was blowing up people, mostly in neighbouring African states where anti-apartheid activists sought refuge. They were active on European soil as well, where sadly, the intelligence services of some countries provided them with information. Things did cool off somewhat after BOSS was reputed to be behind the bombing of the ANC's offices in Paris.'

'How do we find him?'

'We're going round to his flat.' She cannot resist the smirk I detect in her voice. I allow her to savour her moment of triumph.

'What exactly is he doing in Holland?'

'As far as I know, the South African government has made no attempt to have him extradited. He has a long Dutch lineage, like so many Afrikaners,' she comments.

'Which might explain why 'Dutchman' is a derogatory term for an Afrikaner,' I add spitefully.

'Yes, indeed.' She's determined not to be riled by me and my stringy petulance.

Five hours later Benschop-Fehr arrives at the office with a video tape tucked under her arm. Boehme fortunately is out. She seems a bit disappointed when Ilsa tells her this.

I put the tape into the video machine in the conference room and we all gather round. Ilsa is there as well but I decide against exerting my authority.

It's Jonny pretending that he's an uninvited guest in a stranger's house. Same old Jonny, cocky, jokey, silly. I get him on the phone while I watch him look into the cistern, go through the cupboards, and generally monkey around imitating the police officers who are conducting the search.

They add his computer and disk to the list of impounded articles.

'The computer contained the memoirs he was writing,' interrupts Jonny over the phone.

'Are you joking or are you serious?' I admonish.

'I'm deadly serious. Ask the coppers. I sneaked a look. It's just like the Bible. Full of murder, torture and mayhem.'

Dawie Louw's flat is as clean as a whistle, no half-made bombs lying about. His bank statement shows that he has about 20 000 Guilders in his account. Large sums had been deposited into his account about five months before South Africa's first democratic elections in 1994, but no further amounts were paid in. Since then he has steadily used up his income. It looks like he's down to the last bit of cash.

'He did it.' Jonny's voice is urgent. 'His glasses.'

'What are you going on about?' I ask, concerned that he might about to launch into another one of his surrealistic ramblings.

'The beer glasses in the kitchen.'

I groan silently.

'They're from a small East German glass factory called Schmittel, from the town of Schmittel,' he continues. 'They used to make fine glassware up until the war. During the communist era they branched out into industrial manufacturing, including really good test tubes that they supplied to laboratories all over Eastern Europe. They've now gone back to making glassware. There was a set of beer glasses in his cupboard. It could be just coincidence, but they're from the same factory. He couldn't really have picked them up from his corner supermarket.'

'But he could have picked them up, say on holiday in Prague, or Budapest, or East Berlin.'

'Very possible, except for one other thing.'

'What's that?' I ask.

'The scissors.'

'Scissors?'

'Yup. We took the bombs apart. The chemicals were a dead end. None of them contained trace markers - these are chemical bonds that manufacturers place in explosives for the purpose of identification - but we did find striations on the wires that matched the pattern you'd get from using the pair of scissors we found in his bathroom. He got careless.'

'Amazing,' I say, 'I thought you could do that only with guns.'

'It's brilliant what you can do with computers these days.'

There's Jonny in the video again, putting the two round beer glasses to his eyes and pretending that they're binoculars. In the background, I can hear the raucous cackle of the cameraman and see two of the police officers doubling up with laughter. His corniness is infectious.

Chapter 11

As I open the door to my local organic greengrocer, a man stumbles into my arms. We apologise profusely to each other and I help him pick up his vegetables. He doesn't look like the clumsy type. As a matter of fact he looks very much like my type. He's in his forties, but his body is lean and trim, all the curves subtly accentuated by the black T- shirt and faded black jeans, both well-worn and not too tight. His thinning hair is cropped very short. His face is sharp and intelligent, but there is a mournfulness in his eyes. He has very hairy arms, like a gorilla. It is difficult to tell whether he is a millionaire businessman on his day off, or a painter.

'I'm very sorry honey.' He says "honey" as though I was a ten year old, so I'm not as offended as I ought to be. He also has a very disarming smile.

'Jesus, did I hurt you? I lost my feet there for a moment.'

'I'm fine,' I answer, 'just fine. If you take that loaf of bread out of my eye, I'll be even better.'

He squirms in embarrassment.

'Man, this gets worse and worse. I'm like an elephant on a ballroom floor.

'Can I buy you a drink?'

I'm a bit taken aback. 'What? Just for bumping into me?'

He laughs at my indignation, which is tinged with such coquettishness that even I feel embarrassed.

'Why not?'

There's something about his smile that makes me think that he doesn't do it very often. Not that it's forced in any way, or that he's not the kind of man who smiles. It's simply that he's probably careful about who he smiles at, and for how long. In other words, he rations it out very carefully.

'Next thing I know you'll be asking me to dinner,' I say.

He gazes mournfully at his groceries and shakes his head.

'Tell me,' I continue, 'is this a well-practised routine. You hanging around shops waiting to bump into women that you can chat up. Is this another variation on the old supermarket routine?'

This hits a nerve. He is contrite, lifting up his arms abjectly. It is not a good idea as they are full of carrots, leeks and a battered French loaf.

'No, I swear. Absolutely not. I happen to live around the corner. Just moved here. Temporarily that is.'

He tells me the address. It is the block of flats opposite mine. He is a neighbour so I attempt a little friendliness.

'Are you vegetarian?' I ask, looking at the foliage in his arms.

'Mostly yeah, although I am occasionally tempted by a Texas steak.'

The shopkeeper hands me my litre of milk. He has a smirk on his face which I pretend not to notice. We walk down the road in the same direction. It is a pleasant evening, coldly crisp with not a hint of moisture in the air. I don't have the time to join him for coffee, I explain to him. It is news that he greets with a philosophical shrug.

He tells me that he's an information technology consultant, in Amsterdam on contract for a few months.

I ask him to elaborate.

'I deal in information. It's a very expensive commodity these days.'

'Yes, but what do you actually *do*?' I persist.

'I assist companies in trafficking, massaging, disseminating and protecting information. Being the period that we live in, it's mostly done via computers.'

'I presume this also means hiding information?'

He stops and turns his head in my direction. 'I'll be honest with you. This is exactly what most companies want. Even if they don't say so upfront, they get around to it eventually.'

'Thank you,' I say.

'What for?'

'You've just added another bit of validation to support my lack of respect for corporate culture. So what do you peddle, ideas or technology?'

'A mixture of both. In my line of business, the one can't do without the other.'

'Who are you consulting for now?'

'Davids & Mckie. It's a global management consultancy. Offices all over the world so I get to see the sights.'

The name doesn't mean anything to me.

I tell him what I do for a living. The only thing is, it is another lie. I tell him that I work for a travel magazine. My job is to manage a pool of writers as well as travel myself. Since it is indeed a recurring fantasy of mine, the embellishments come easily. I make a mental note to ask Boehme what the policy is regarding divulging job descriptions to total strangers. My immediate concern however is the frightening ease with which lies seem to emanate from me of late.

'Fascinating,' is his noncommittal reply. 'What's your favourite destination?'

'Hanoi.' I answer.

'Haven't been there myself. My brother has, during the Vietnam War.'

'I'm sorry,' I say.

'No need to be. He came back alive. Heard it's changed quite a bit. We have planeloads of Americans going there now to do business.'

We reach the stretch of road outside both our buildings.

'Well, it was nice meeting you, miss er ...'

'Barvalis de Hoop.'

'I have a confession to make,' he blurts out.

'Oh no, it was all an act after all.'

'No, no, nothing of the sort. What I wanted to say was that I *have* seen you before. Outside the apartment block, going to your car.'

'What's the big deal? I'm sure that you've seen the grocer more than once.'

'Well, what I'm trying to say to you is that you were in my consciousness, my line of vision so to speak. The memory lingered after the picture faded. I don't remember the grocer after I come out of the shop.'

'That's very sweet,' I acknowledge politely.

It suddenly occurs to me that I've seen him too, a distant figure from my window, jogging in the park. There aren't many joggers in Amsterdam, at least not in my area. Most of the city's dwellers prefer stately strolls through the parks when they're not riding bicycles.

'Ciao. Hope to see you around.' He gives me a wink and turns to walk towards his building.

'What's your name?' I shout after him.

'Marlon Woods.' He yells back.

'Did they call you 'Manny' at school?'
'Nah, they used to call me 'Woody'!'

*

'How ', I ask Benschop-Fehr over the phone, 'did the LTTE come to get hold of Louw in the first place. Isn't this all a little too convenient, the way his name suddenly popped up?'

'He worked for them for a long time. In the old days he supplied them with weapons from the South African government arms corporation that manufactured that country's excellent weaponry. As you know they sold to anybody who could pay them in dollars or oil. Then when things starting changing politically he left the country to become a mercenary, first in Mozambique, then around the world as a roving gunman for hire. Age has crept up on him so he found a job as an advisor to the LTTE in Sri Lanka. Taught them how to make bombs, at least that's what they say.'

'So now they're conveniently selling him down the river?'

'Like I've said before, they don't want to jeopardise their position on European soil. They're desperate for us not to hassle them anymore. It will cost them millions of dollars as well as an established base in the West. They certainly can't go to the US. The Americans are a lot less tolerant of other people's freedom fighters these days. So, it looks like they've been doing some research of their own.'

'Well, they've had better luck than us,' I add acidly.

She doesn't answer.

'Your informer in the LTTE,' I continue, 'what's he getting out of this?'

'A Dutch passport,' she answers.

'He knows that any lies would negate his chances of getting one,' she adds defensively.

'Louw's payments for helping them. Where did they pay him?'

'We don't know.' She pauses, as if contemplating the issue for the first time.

'Why do you ask?'

'Well, his Dutch account doesn't have much money in it. Presumably if he acted as a middleman in arms dealing he would have got something for it. As well as for his work in Sri Lanka, not to mention his fee for his last act of terror. Unless he did it for free.'

'Good question. We'll follow it up.'

*

In the apartment next to me lives a professional conspiracy theorist . Everybody in the block gives him a wide berth on account of the rubbish he puts under our doors; pamphlets about aliens living amongst us, strange substances in the water that we drink, the government's plans to brainwash the entire population of Holland. It's difficult to imagine anyone believing in the stuff but he always has friends around so there must be a group of people out there who do. All this is photocopied and regularly shoved in our post-boxes as well. Fortunately he's not a total crackpot because he has organised funds for earthquake disaster relief in Mexico, blankets for the children of Kosovo and other such humanitarian efforts. I therefore have a soft spot for him.

Somewhere along the way he must be earning a good salary because the rents in the block are not cheap. Kaauw had helped me sort out my home modem once, and in the process had given me some very detailed instructions on how to fiddle my telephone bills. He lives and breathes computers and spends all day trawling the Internet in search of ever-increasingly fantastical conspiracies, but he's a damned good hacker, unless he's lying to me. He also has a crush on me. But he's so physically repulsive that I don't think I'd even be able to give him a full mouth penetrative tongue kiss, which is as far as I'd go in terms of handing out sexual favours.

Not that he's particularly ugly. He just doesn't care about his appearance. He has pimples, greasy ginger hair and, worst of all, a pathetic, scraggly unkempt beard. Every time I see him, I long to hand him shampoo, decent shaving blades and moisturiser. I've walked past him in the corridors a few times and caught the whiff of his unwashed body and stale deodorant.

When I knock on his door, the look of surprise on his face is such that you'd think he'd seen one of his aliens.

'Need help with your computer?' he enquires eagerly.

'No.' I smile at him. There is, in his eyes, a flicker of hope, but it dies just as quickly as it rises.

Caricature exists, one suspects, because so many people attempt to force themselves into self-defined roles. The urge to carve a uniqueness for oneself is overwhelmingly strong in mankind, be it the rural, xenophobic farmer who lives his life railing against everybody else, or the young raver with pierced nipples and silver clothing. At the same time we all desperately try to fit in. The computer nerd is only the latest in a long line of incarnations.

Kaauw's flat is littered with the detritus of his calling. The centre of the room is occupied by two computers linked to a massive printer. Together the lumbering equipment looks like a family of sleeping dinosaurs.

'You can print dollar notes on that,' he points confidently to the printer, as if he had already done so.

A long trestle-like table runs along the length of his walls, right around the flat. In addition to the innards of computers, he has tons of books, magazines, comics and piles of computer printouts on the tables. Here and there are Aztec artefacts, voodoo dolls, and ceramic Roman fertility symbols. I sneak a look at the book titles. Nothing there surprises me. It's the usual litany of CIA plots, unknown beasts and distant civilisations.

I take out a copy of Benschop-Fehr's fax from my briefcase. It has on it the details of Louw's Swiss bank account. It was my brilliant idea to have the financial auditors at Europol check the meticulous records kept by the LTTE's office. Sure enough, there were details of payments to Louw into a Swiss bank account going all the way back to 1988. The problem is that although the Swiss have, in the face of considerable international pressure, opened up their banks to scrutiny, getting them to provide us with details on Louw would take a good few months, even with the legal juggernaut at our disposal. I cannot afford to wait that long.

Kaauw utters a low whistle when I tell him my problem. He is unable to keep his hands still. They're constantly fluttering around, as if he's typing on an imaginary computer keyboard. In a previous lifetime he was probably a mad pianist.

'I knew there was something about you. You have that air about you.'

Exactly what sort of air I don't dare ask, for fear of him comparing me to a Druid high priestess. Instead I give him a mysterious smile. He likes that.

'This could take a good couple of hours, maybe a day,' he says, looking at me worriedly, as if I would turn him down and go somewhere else.

'I'll wait.' I stress.

'Okayyyy.' He rubs his hands in glee. I give him the details.

He glances at it. 'Good. They have an Internet address. I can trace the DNS address and go in via the back door. Got to find the right protocols.'

I cook supper for him. He's a meat and potatoes man. He asks politely if I could do the cooking in his flat, so I go next door to my place and pack a box with pans, cutlery, vegetables and remove the pastry from the deep freezer. I also scan through some of my old cookbooks to make sure that I know what I'm doing.

It's a meagre supply. I plonk it all down in his flat and walk to the supermarket to get the mutton, and a blueberry cheesecake. On the way back, I get a bottle of wine and a six-pack of beer from the off-license, just in case he doesn't drink wine.

In my absence, he has turned on the music, a film soundtrack. It's probably the only album he has with slow songs on it.

His gas stove is encrusted with soup stains and other unidentifiable blobs of muck. Inside his cupboard, there's a year's supply of cheap instant soup packets. The oven, fortunately, is clean, probably because it has never been used.

He does drink wine, but he has no glasses, so I make another trip to my flat. Served with Ciabbatta bread, the meal is a bit of a culinary mishmash, but he doesn't seem to mind.

It's been a long time since I have cooked for anyone. The experience is a slightly unnerving one, like riding a bicycle again after a long absence.

Kaauw is making strange low sounds to himself. Grunts of pleasure and disappointment emanate from his direction. In the three hours that it takes to get supper ready, he talks to me intermittently. Mostly I remain in the kitchen making sure that the pie doesn't collapse in the middle. He's a network engineer for a software company, which explains how he can afford his extra-curricular indulgences.

I place the plates alongside him and watch him take frantic, wolfish mouthfuls, as if he hadn't eaten for a while. Then he wipes the plate in broad strokes with the bread. He doesn't pay much attention to me surfing his own particular wave of enthusiasm. There is the sporadic glance, a mingling of shyness and something close to lust. In between he makes phone calls to his friends around the world. talking in strangulated yelps in a patois so esoteric that bits of it might as well be another language.

'I'll pay for the phone calls,' I say.

'Don't worry, it's free,' he grins.

There is nothing much for me to do but sit around. My feeling is that his enthusiasm would wane considerably if I left the room, so I keep him company, volunteering information about myself that might be of interest to him. Our relationship is that of a dentist to a patient in the chair. I'm the dentist.

In between making coffee, I indulge in more furtive perusals of his bookshelves, and sneak off to my flat for a gasps of sanity.

At around midnight, there is a knock on his door. He looks at me incomprehendingly. I shrug my shoulders. Then the light dawns, but he doesn't look so happy. His girlfriend has arrived. They whisper in the passageway. We can both see each other and I smile weakly at her. She doesn't smile back. Their conversation becomes heated in that way that couples have when they fight but don't want others to hear. His whispered entreaties are audible. Eventually she leaves, slamming the door violently behind her. He comes back, hunched in embarrassment.

'We had planned to see a band at a club tonight. I completely forgot.'

'Hope I didn't cause any problems,' I mutter, not too convincingly.

It is 3 am when the harsh grinding of the printer shatters the hypnotic clatter of the keyboard. At the back of my mind, there is a nagging suspicion that he has taken longer than necessary, that he has prolonged his hacking so that I could sit next to him while he soared into the heavens. I am, however, willing to forgive him. To see the look of glee on his face as he brandishes the piece of paper is to see the holy light of passion for one's work.

'Hot chocolate,' he pipes enthusiastically.

What can I say?

*

When I arrive at the office late, Ilsa makes a point of looking at the clock on the wall. I ignore her.

Settling down, I study the report. The details of the financial transactions are erratic but this would be in keeping with the nature of his job. He is like a predator, one big hunting expedition, a large sum of money and then nothing for a while. The total sum that he has is seven hundred and fifty thousand dollars. This is not what I'm interested in. The last transaction is what I want, a deposit of fifty thousand dollars paid in five weeks previously.

The rest of the printouts looks mind-blowingly complex but then numbers were never my forte. My eyes tend to glaze over from barely looking at my salary slip each month. Then I notice the cherry on the top, a very big cherry. Kaauw has crossed-referenced the last deposit to a bank in Germany. It is the only deposit initiated from a European country. The previous ones are from the US, the Far East and the Middle East. The account belongs to a Frau Martha Bollomberg, who looks very rich. She has almost three million Deutschmarks in her bank account. Her entire banking details are on the printout, including date of birth, her address in Cologne and occupation. She's the managing director of a construction company, Merkelbach, in the city. I stare at it for a good five minutes, unable to believe my luck.

My next dilemma is presenting all this to Boehme. There is no way of knowing how he will react to my illegal activities. He might fire me. Then again, he might not.

There is only one way to find out.

Chapter 12

He phones me at home just after 10 pm. I am sitting in my pyjamas eating soup and watching television.
Waiting for his phone call.
I can tell from his voice that he has been drinking. Boehme went out for lunch at 1 pm. The documents in my possession stayed well-hidden under my files as I debated with myself what to do with them.
When I left at five that evening, he still hadn't returned. That's when I had resolved to leave them on his desk with a note about my transgressions.
'You are a coward,' he whispers to me. Boehme is under the misconception that if he lowers his voice and adapts a Clint Eastwoodish timbre no-one will be able to pick up the fact that he's been drinking rather heavily.
He's almost right. Generally they don't, but I know him well enough to know better.
There is no menace in his voice and for this I am pathetically grateful.
There is something else, a hint of admiration perhaps. I can only hope that this is what it is and not a product of my fervid imagination.
'Why?' I ask innocently.
'You know why. Leaving that file on my desk after checking with Ilsa that I wouldn't be back in the office. Don't worry, you still have your job. I have spoken to my contacts in Germany to find out who this Frau Bollomberg is. We should have results on Monday.'
I cradle the phone to my chest and say a silent prayer.
That's Boehme. Even when he is so drunk that he can barely stand, he still does his job.
I wish him pleasant dreams.
On Sunday afternoon I stop by the office to pick up some paperwork. There's a note on my desk as well as pages of a handwritten fax, scrawled in precise German. Beside it, a translation. Boehme must have come in over the weekend and worked on it. Then I look at the tiny phone numbers at the very top of the page, the area where no-one bothers looking. The fax had

been sent to Boehme's private number at his flat on Sunday morning. It is typical of him, being careful, covering his tracks by having the fax sent to his home.

According to her official records the real Martha Bollomberg was a former East German citizen who died in a car accident in Magdeburg in 1990. Her photocopied, faxed photograph bares a slight resemblance to the woman who is now using her identity. On closer examination, she bares no physical resemblance at all. The mind's eye sees what it chooses to see. The resemblance is in the hairstyle, in the sour mouth and in the air of suffocating, middle-class mediocrity. It's amazing what a grainy passport-sized photo can reveal.

Needless to say, the construction company doesn't exist either.

'East Germany is a good place to choose a dead person from.' Boehme is standing at my door, acutely aware that he's making a rare stab at levity. He is wearing an old shirt and trousers and he is unshaven. His eyes are bloodshot, possibly from Friday's drinking session.

'What are you doing here on a Sunday?' I ask startled.

'Same as you are,' he grunts.

'You were making a profound statement about East Germany?' I continue.

'After unification all the records were a bit of a dog's breakfast. They still are. It's an easy place to get lost in. The federal government is busy planning a consolidation of all the records, but it's going to take a long time. I wouldn't want to guess how many files have been "lost".'

'How do we find the woman in the picture.'

'Publish her picture in all the German newspapers. As a Red Brigade terrorist.'

He's on a role. This must be his weekend mode, which I have not been privy to witness before. I'm not sure if I like it.

'What I have done is pass the original photo to the European Liaison Bureau,' he chortles. 'They are in touch with all the European police forces. You'll be surprised at what comes out. Criminals are like movie stars. They don't become big overnight. Dig into their pasts and you'll find a trail of small, petty jobs to progressively larger ones. But we have no idea who she is.'

'What's the Liaison Bureau. *Another* police force?' I ask.

'It's a liaison unit within the European Secretariat of Interpol. Set up specifically to deal with the problems of the European member states. It's a clearing house, nothing more.'

'Where have I heard those words before,' I say.

'There is no need to be so cynical,' answers Boehme. 'In this business it helps having the right contacts.'

It's hard to argue with this, so I shut up.

*

'Her name', grunts Boehme, 'is Charlotta Gattschalk. But we are not certain. I received an e-mail from a *Bundeskriminalamt* officer in Karlsruhe. Says he thinks it might be someone he came across in the Eighties.'

'Long criminal record.' I say.

'Nothing of the sort. She was in the Stasi, according to him. The police officer is ex-Stasi. Like I said, he's not certain. Could be anyone. Let's phone and find out.'

Boehme dials the number on his screen.

He asks me to listen in but my German is limited to about thirty words.

The two of them chat for about ten minutes. The only thing I pick up is the tone of deference in the voice of the officer. He is obviously in awe of Boehme. From the way Boehme addresses the officer, he enjoys his role as heroic cop. Most of the time I study my nails. Boehme knows that I don't speak German.

He puts the phone down with an emphatic clunk.

'What do you think of that, heh?'

'I don't speak German,' I snap.

He pauses, his face so comically wracked by internal struggle that I could easily go over and hug him. He articulates an apology in his mind, but somehow it doesn't come out.

'It's okay,' I say to him to ease his burden.

'He says he can't be too sure, but he was stationed in East Berlin until the fall of the wall. He saw Gattschalk about twice a year for about two years. She was in charge of the munitions depot in the city. He was a a transport co-ordinator. He never dealt directly with her so he can't be sure, but she was in charge. Says he remembered her because of her ugliness.'

I role my eyes at Boehme.

'Better phone Gauck,' says Boehme.

'Who the hell is Gauck?' I ask.

'Joachim Gauck, but it's not him that you need to speak to. The Gauck Authority is the German government organisation that oversees all the Stasi records. Only they have the power to check the files. They are the people that are going through all the records at the moment.

'Looking for all the juicy bits,' he adds bitterly.

'You'd better phone,' I demur, 'seeing that you know who they are.'

'Besides, you speak German.' I add nastily.

It is not often that I have had the chance to see Boehme squirm.

*

The package arrives by late afternoon. The people at the Gauck Authority are very efficient. I untie the neat blue ribbon holding the file and groan at the mass of photocopied documents. The photographs are also photocopies but there is no doubt that it is the same person

On his way out, Boehme sees me contemplating the package.

'It won't help if you stare at it.'

I show the picture to him.

He studies it thoughtfully. 'Ja, it is her.'

'Come.' He beckons to me with his finger. 'Bring a pen and a notebook.'

We walk two blocks down the street. The board swinging in the breeze says "TRADITIONAL DUTCH FARE" in English. To my surprise we enter the restaurant.

'It's very good,' opines Boehme. 'I eat here often.'

I remain noncommittal.

Inside there are a number of tourists tucking into their traditional Dutch fare.

Boehme leads the way to a booth at the back of the restaurant. It is big enough for six people. Restaurants with booths immediately endear themselves to me. Booths provide a false sense of security and comfort.

'Good evening, Herr Boehme,' smiles the waitress as she presents us with the clumsy, wooden menus. The waitresses conform to the Dutch stereotype. They are all blonde with heaving bosoms, attired in Dutch national costume, or parts of it.

Boehme unwraps the package delicately. He shuffles the documents and starts to read.

Two beers later he's still at it.

'Okay,' he says finally, just as our food arrives. 'Let's get writing.'

'Charlotta Gattschalk. Born 1945. Resident of Berlin, Moscow and then Berlin again. She was a supplies manager, grade seven. It's a non-military position, so that's like a middle-ranking manager.'

I write furiously while Boehme feeds me chunks of information.

It is Gattschalk's recent past that concerns me. From 1979 to 1989 she was head of munitions in Berlin. Her job was to manage the supply and distribution of small arms and ammunition in the city. Nothing big, as most of the weapons were for the police and paramilitary units. Most of the equipment was manufactured in the East, either in the former Soviet Union, or in Czechoslovakia or Poland. A small quantity came from China.

She has the usual smattering of inflated communist rewards, an Order of Lenin (5th class) in 1985 . She was also allowed to acquire a holiday flat in the German coastal city of Rostok. Naturally this had to be shared with two other comrades. Interestingly, Gattschalk studied chemistry at Moscow University in the Sixties. Then again, the former citizens of the Eastern Bloc countries never had much say in their career development. She was also recruited by the Stasi when she was seventeen. Her place of residence was the Stasi barracks in Berlin, which Boehme says has been turned into a recreation centre.

'We Germans are very thorough,' says Bohme. 'All the paperwork is here.'

He pats the file. 'Birth certificate. School certificates. Membership lists. Her entire career with the Stasi. She was an apparatchik, nothing less nothing more. And then it was all finished in 1989.'

'Just like that.' He snaps his fingers.

'You sound almost as though you wish you were.' I say.

'No. I am glad I was born in the Allied Occupation Zone, but she is the same age as me. It was fate that decided for us.'

'You'd better check it out,' he adds.

'You mean you actually want me to go to Germany,' I answer. 'Are you sure you don't want to go yourself?'

Boehme gives me one of those indulgent looks, like I was a favoured - but slow, child. He can be quite adorable at times.

In the end, the evening has largely been a pointless exercise. Boehme has merely corroborated what I had already guessed from her photograph and her endless list of certificates. It seems that her life has been a passage from one official document to another. Thus far, there are only two important facts; the details of her mother and that of the holiday apartment in Rostok. Both of which Boehme has kindly allowed me to investigate.

*

Germany from the air always looks so square. The squareness of the fields, the squareness of the traffic junctions, the squareness of the man sitting next to me. Even his red-framed glasses, retro Fifties haircut and loud pin-striped suit can't hide his squareness. I offer him my dinky bottle of red wine, as I don't drink red, but he refuses with such shocked politeness that I might as well have offered to give him a blow job in full view of all the passengers.

There is a woman waiting for me at Tegel airport. A tall, glacial Viking princess whose short-cropped haircut is jarringly at odds with her angelic face, like one of those Manga heroines with idealised Caucasian features that the Japanese draw. It's hard to tell whether she's the secretary sent out on an errand to pick me up or my Berlin counterpart.

Fortunately for me, I treat everyone equally.

She introduces herself carefully, 'Anna Diehm, Berlin ELO.'

I reflect bitterly that it's only a matter of time before the newspapers start calling us ELOs instead of European Liaison Officers. We're an elite force - there are only forty-four ELOs out of a total of two hundred Europol personnel - so it's inevitable that we will get singled out for attention.

'I run the office here. If there is anything I can help you with, please do not hesitate to ask me.

'Herr Boehme has briefed me,' she adds.

In the taxi into the city she maintains a polite and steady monologue, telling me what they've been up to at the office and doing a sales pitch for Europol, almost as if she was planning to offer me a job.

I make suitably polite noises in return.

'What do you think about Berlin being the new capital of Germany?' I ask her suddenly.

The poor girl almost breaks her slender neck by jerking it back in surprise. She marshals her thoughts for an inordinately long period of time before giving me a appropriately measured response. 'You must remember that the vote in the Bundestag to move was very narrow. Most of the deputies from the west voted against. Without the *ostlaenders* the seat of government would have remained in Bonn.'

I decide not to pursue the line of conversation.

The Berlin branch is a satellite office. The main Europol centre is in Wiesbaden. They share office space there with the *Bundeskriminalamt.*

In keeping with the frenetic rush to Berlin by government and quasi-government organisations it was felt that a presence was needed in the city. Although small the office is much glitzier than ours, with a range of Ikea-styled furniture that lends it a minimalist-but-warm look. It looks like the offices of a fashion magazine run by three people.

I have a tiny cubicle with a computer and a telephone. There is no room for my own notebook computer. The three agents nod to me. They barely seem to communicate with each other, talking in some sort of verbal shorthand when they need to. Diehm introduces me distractedly and then fusses with hotel bookings and taxi requisition slips. Ludwig has the air of a browbeaten accountant and the junior member Tina, attired head to toe in black Prada, is suitably morose. She looks as though she is having a spot of boyfriend trouble.

With an apologetic shrug Diehm asks me for my Europol identification number which she checks via the computer.

I have a phone call to make. To one Karl Teschler. He is a close friend of Boehme. It is to a mobile phone number. Before I can indulge in polite niceties he asks me where I am.

'I'll be right over,' he interjects urgently. 'Wait for me downstairs in ten minutes.'

The others stare at me in consternation when I get up to leave.

'I have ordered you coffee and sandwiches,' mutters Anna Diehm so mournfully that I almost ask if I can take the sandwiches with me.

When the car hoots, I take a tentative step forward, trying to make sure that the occupant not another flabby fifty year old mistaking me for a prostitute. I hear my name being called and the side door is pushed open. I don't turn around but I'm sure the girls in the office are gazing in perplexity through their expensive Swedish blinds.

The smell of garlic sausages and wet dog inside the car is overpowering. It's hard to tell if it's emanating from him or if it's the natural smell of the car.

There's also a large amount of scraps of paper on the floor, which I try, not very successfully, to avoid.

Karl Teschler looks very scruffy, as if he has been sleeping in the park.

'You have to excuse me,' he coughs ruefully. 'My wife. She locked the door last night, so I slept in the office.'

I wonder what he has done to earn his wife's wrath. It would be too impolite to ask. Not right now anyway.

'So you work for Boehme, eh?' He glances at me appraisingly, as if it was beyond Boehme's normal powers to employee someone like me. His English is deeply accented, unlike the American-tinged gutturals that most Germans, and Dutch, have when they converse in the language. He has a bad haircut, a short back and sides, as though someone had placed a bowl over his head and cut along the edges. He must have trouble convincing people that he's not an *Ossie*, as the East Germans are derogatorily referred to.

'Are we going to your headquarters?' I ask.

He grinds the gears of his old Mercedes, looking perplexed.

'Headquarters? I do not understand.'

'Where you work?'

'Oh no. I work for myself.'

'You work for yourself?' The puzzled look on my face ignites a spark in his brain. He slaps the dashboard.

'Ha. Boehme did not tell you?'

'Tell me what?'

'I am not a policeman anymore. I am a freelancer...' Another spark flares up in his head. 'I am a PI. A private investigator.'

The dubious look on my face must have worried him. He tries his best to mollify me.

'Boehme and I, we go back a long way. Thirty years in the police. And before that we were school buddies. We come from the same town, Tubingen. I have been a police consultant for two years now.'

'So what are you, a freelancer, a private investigator, or a consultant?' I interrupt.

He doesn't seem to understand. 'You make fun of me, jah? It's okay.'

Although he is sitting next to me, and his voice is loud and booming, I have to really pay attention to what he's saying. It's like one of those PA systems at the airport, or in the supermarket. Sounds issue forth but you're not exactly sure what's being said.

'We have a drink, *jawohl.*'

'Yes.'

'We don't go to my usual *kaffeehaus*. A pretty girl like you will upset all my friends. We go somewhere nice.'

"Nice" to Teschler is the Hotel Adlon on the busy, frenetic Unter den Linden. The thoroughfare is starting to resemble London's Oxford Street, with its proliferation of tacky shops and hordes of tourists trawling the area looking for a good time. It is a crisp clear Berlin morning and for a moment I almost envy those people who are already starting to wander around in blissful aimlessness. Only the Russian Embassy slumbers away like a dinosaur next to the Adlon. At ten in the morning the hotel foyer is quietly seething with wealth and status. The city's bankers, industrialists, corporate raiders and politicians are leaving after their 7:30 am power breakfasts. Their wives are taking over, to chat over mid-morning tea. The way they are dressed you'd think they had businesses to attend to as well. The waitress who serves us in the lounge turns her nose up at Teschler, as if he was something that should be banned from five star hotel lounges. Sitting face to face affords me the opportunity to study him properly.

Even if he hadn't spent the night in his office, Karl Teschler would have still looked an unprepossessing specimen. Unlike

Boehme, he has not made any effort - however sporadic - to keep in shape. His stomach reflects too many beers and too much sauerkraut. His thinning, greasy, long hair falls in a flop over his right eye, which he keeps brushing away with a strangely effete gesture. There is a dark smear of five o clock shadow on his jowls. The excellent standard of German dental hygiene seems to have passed him by as well. His teeth are stained brown, and some are crooked. He has Boehme's intelligent eyes though. They are constantly watchful, taking in and analysing everything. The teacup in his hand is grotesquely dwarfed by his large ham-sized fists.

'So,' he puts down his cup as if he means business, 'Boehme tells me that you're his prodigy.'

Whether he actually means prodigy, or meant to say protege, it's hard to say. In any case, it doesn't sound like something Boehme would discuss.

The only thing for me to do is laugh it off in a vaguely embarrassed sort of way.

'Who do you work for?' I enquire quickly, hoping to deflect more personal questions.

'Who do I work for?' He pauses and stares at me, as if impressed by the profundity of my question.

'Everyone. Companies and government departments mostly. I don't do missing persons. Mostly I assist the police.'

'As consultant?'

'As a consultant.'

'Tell me about Boehme,' I say.

His gaze meets mine. I can see the questions in his eyes.

'Boehme is the best policeman that there is. He is a very brave man and he has the brains. We used to be joined at the hip, Boehme and I.'

Teschler rummages through his wallet. He hands me a tattered photograph. The two of them used to be much slimmer in the old days.

'Did I tell you that Boehme saved my life?'

'We've only just met,' I answer.

'It was in 1973. There were terrorists all over Germany then. This was the PLO. They had robbed a bank in Bonn. We managed to get inside the building, but I was shot in the leg. I couldn't move. The bastards had taped a grenade to my body and pulled the pin.

Instead of running away Boehme walked up to me and placed his hand over the spring. Three seconds later and I would have been blown into pieces.'

'Very brave of him,' I comment.

'Boehme tells me that you're looking for a woman, Charlotta Gattschalk, who was in the Stasi.' The notebook appears in his palm as if by sleight of hand. 'Along with her two former associates and her mother?'

'Yes,' I say.

'Well, the mother is dead, so you can forget about her.'

He grins in response to my gasp of surprise.

'She died in an old age home two years ago. Ninety-two years she was.

'Now, about the other two. They show up in the old Stasi records as well. Like Gattschalk, they had long service records with the Stasi, but nothing very exciting. One, Eva Nabering, was in personnel, the other, Johanna Paffhausen, was in administration. Both senior positions but like I said nothing exciting.'

'Where are they now?'

'No idea. I have started looking. Everything is computerised nowadays and nobody gives you the information if you do not have the authority. With the Stasi records it is even worse. There are a lot of people in high places, both from the East and West, who worked for the Stasi and everybody is trying all kinds of tricks to get their hands on the files.

'But I have my contacts,' he adds with a wink.

'Why the interest in the Stasi?' he asks.

'Purely incidental to what I'm investigating,' I answer.

'Which is .....?'

- I decide to take a chance. He is after all Boehme's bosom buddy.

I narrate the long and convoluted series of events that has brought me to Berlin. The discovery of the bodies without the hands. The bomb in my flat, and how our main suspects, the LTTE, kindly dropped the bomber into our laps. I also explain to him, the other puzzling aspects - which seem to have no relation to the case. Mescoan in the blood of two of the suspects, and how Laville and Laurier seems to linger around like a bad smell.

And now Gattschalk. Another puzzling dimension to a case that seems to be unravelling like the universe. The further we go into it, the further it moves away.

He whistles softly. 'You don't think that the LTTE were so desperate to get you off their backs that they sacrificed the bomber?'

'No, why would they. *If* he did the contract for them, he would have been in a position to spill the beans, which would have meant us shutting down their operations in Europe. Doesn't make sense.'

'It doesn't,' he admits. 'Sounds like you've got a case and half on your hands.'

'How often do you see Boehme?' I ask.

He shrugs. 'Every time he is in Germany, I guess. We have fun together, Boehme and I.'

'And you both get gloriously drunk,' I remark.

'How did you know that?' he says in surprise. 'Did Boehme mention me?'

'Educated guess,' I reply.

I realise how alike the two of them are. Cloddish yes, never, never doltish.

'First we start at the property records office. Find out who owns the flat in Rostok. I have asked someone to check it out for me. I will be able to find out this morning. As a matter of fact, I can check now.'

He whips out his mobile phone, dials a number, and chats for a few moments. His phone is an extension of his personality. It is chunky and unwieldy but it does the job.

'My contact says that there is a fax waiting for me at my office. He sent it through this morning.'

I am most impressed at the speed and efficacy of the man and wonder aloud what I have done to deserve such service.

'Any friend of Boehme's is a friend of mine,' he answers with a hideous grin. 'Come, let's go to my office.'

Teschler must have been aware of the snootiness of the waitress because he leaves her an insulting one shilling tip. Unfortunately I don't get to see her face when she picks it up as she is at the other end of the lounge, fawning over a few rich old ladies in revolting hats.

Teschler's office is in one of the narrow streets of Berlin's hip Mitte district. The area is packed with bars, clubs and coffeeshops. It is Berlin's Greenwich Village, the trendiest spot in the city. Its denizens are only just stirring into life. Across the street a couple is walking their dogs. In addition to being almost half naked, both of them have pink hair. What is most striking however are the pink poodles. Teschler shakes his head in disgust.

At this time of day, the streets are mostly occupied by numerous beer trucks refuelling the cellars. The ground floor of Teschler's office block is occupied by a cyber-cafe. We climb up the narrow stairs of the solid stone building. It is three storeys high and does not have an elevator.

There are old-fashioned gas lamps embedded in the walls and they give off a faint light.

'I love this new government,' wheezes Teschler. 'They are offering tax concessions and low rentals to anyone who will start a small business in this part of town. I have taken up the offer. It is better than working from home.'

'I would hardly call your operation a small business.' I reply.

He chuckles, 'I work very hard and I pay my taxes.'

His office is not as dingy as I had expected it to be. The windows glint in the sunlight. The carpeted floor is slightly threadbare, but well-brushed. In the centre there is an enormous old-fashioned desk that looks like it was chucked out of one of the Reichstag offices. Perched somewhat incongruously on it is a new computer. The space smells of pine forest air freshener. Teschler flops into a large, luxurious, but very battered leather chair and gestures for me to sit down in another one. It almost swallows me.

He swivels around to face the computer.

'I love modern technology. With the fax-modem inside my computer, I don't even need to buy a fax machine. But I still don't know how to use the Internet. I have Boehme's e-mail address but I have not been able to send him a message. I asked those kids downstairs but they said I had to use one of their computers. Can you show me how?'

I show him how to create an electronic address book with Boehme's name in it. Then we send Boehme a silly message, wishing him all the best from sunny Berlin.

Teschler prints out the fax from his friend. He stands very close to me as we study it, but not so close as to be obtrusive. He smells of old-fashioned hair oil, mingled with a sour body odour. It is not entirely unpleasant, evoking nebulous memories that I cannot place. It is said that we have the will to create our own memories, that what we sense as real may not necessarily have existed, such is the power of the human mind.

The property ownership documents show an interesting change. Up until 1992 it was in Gattschalk's name, then it was to changed Eva Nabering.

'You want to visit?'

'How about a telephone call?'

'I can get you the telephone number, if she has one, but I think a visit is better.'

'Why's that?'

He's at a loss for words. He gapes at me for a moment, as if I had asked him why humans need to breathe.

'It rattles people. Makes them nervous. You can see if they're lying, or afraid, or got something to hide. Is this not what you want?'

'Do you think perhaps we should go at 3 am, wake them up?'

He raises his arms in indignant protest. 'I am not a fascist. I am a policeman.'

'I have to be satisfied with that,' I concede.

'We have to go by train,' says Teschler. His battered Mercedes is going in for a service.

I haven't used a train since I was at boarding school. A train journey sounds good. It will give me time to think.

'Okay,' I say.

'Good, but I have to tell my wife.'

He phones the station. There is a train leaving for Rostok in an hour and a half.

I go back to the office and tell the girls. Diehm has a fax for me. It has details of the transfer of the Rostok apartment from Gattschalk's name to Nabering's. To avoid hurting her feelings I pretend that I don't already know. I thank her profusely and share a quick cup of coffee.

*

The 12:30 pm IR - the InterRegio train - is discreetly packed, as only German trains are, that is, everyone is in their place and all the seats are taken. Teschler is seated opposite me. It is difficult to maintain a conversation without everybody listening, so he promptly goes to sleep after voicing a few vaguely solicitous concerns about my comfort. I pass the time by reading and gazing at the German countryside. It's a three and a half hour trip to Rostok.

Travelling at just over 125mph the train reaches Rostok at 4 pm. We then catch the S-Bahn to the seaside suburb of Warnemunde. A former popular holiday destination for the patriotic workers of the German Democratic Republic, the town is slowly being tarted up to its former pre-World War II glory. While Rostok itself suffers from its image as a neo-Nazi haven, Warnemunde is all about sandy beaches and quaint fishermen's cottages. The unseasonably warm Berlin weather has not touched this part of the world. There is a cold wind blowing from the sea. Teschler offers me his coat but I'm sure it's the same one he slept in.

There are still relics of the old order around though, like the low apartment block we are about to enter. It is a squat, ugly building, badly whitewashed. It does have a nice view. The intercom system for the apartments is new. There is a remote security camera mounted on the wall, but even an untrained eye like mine can see that it's fake. There is no lens behind the glass.

Teschler presses the buzzer to apartment 104. A distant, barely intelligible voice answers. They didn't spend too much money on the upgraded system.

Teschler's voice changes. He becomes harder, more official. He talks to the person at the other end in harsh German.

There is a buzz and the door clicks. He pushes the gate and I follow after him. Apartment 104 is on the first floor. The staircase smells of stale urine, and the corridors of burnt cabbage. Teschler knocks on the door. We hear the metallic grind of chain locks.

The woman who stares suspiciously at us is in her late fifties. Her greying hair is severely scraped into a bun at the back of her head. She has the air of a retired school matron, or head nurse. Her clothes consist of a grey blouse and a skirt. The blouse is of a slightly darker shade of grey than her skirt. It looks like a uniform with all the insignia ripped off. She gives me a withering stare, one that looks harsher than the one she gives Teschler. I don't know if it's because I don't conform to her standards of womanhood or because I'm not Aryan enough.

'*Ausweis,*' she barks.

'ID,' whispers Teschler behind my back.

I can see why Teschler has pushed me in front. I have a Europol card. He's only a retired policeman.

She examines my card with punctilious attention and hands it back to me, beckoning us with a jerk of her head to enter. She doesn't turn her back to us.

The flat inside is furnished with an eclectic mishmash of bric-a-brac.

Most of the heavy furniture is from the Thirties but there are a couple of red lava lamps scattered around. The walls are adorned with prints of German castles. Thick brown curtains keep the light out. The air smells of cigarette smoke, like someone has smoked in there for twenty years without opening the windows. There are two ashtrays on the table and both of them contain cigarette stubs. There are also two sets of slippers next to two lounge chairs. There is another person in the apartment. A woman enters the room carrying a tray with two cups on it. She is startled to see us.

'I am Eva Nabering,' says the virago who opened the door, 'and this is Johanna Paffhausen.'

Frau Paffhausen attempts a cold smile to hide her bewilderment and puts the tray down.

The only difference between the two of them is that Nabering is blonde going grey, whereas Paffhausen is a brunette going grey. She also wears glasses. Her outfit is exactly the same as Nabering's except that it is beige. Otherwise, they are twins.

'What is your business here?' Nabering is not letting any hospitality get in the way of our visit.

I get to the point. 'We're looking for Charlotta Gattschalk.'

Nabering directs a look at me of such savagery that I almost wither away on the spot. Almost.

Somewhere inside me there is a little seed of determination and I carry on. 'This is the last known address we have for her and...' I pause and gaze meaningfully at the two of them, 'you and Frau Paffhausen were her nearest acquaintances.'

Paffhausen sits down next to Nabering. She takes a sip from one of the cups. They're both perched on the edge of their seats, eyeing us like two unfriendly eagles. Paffhausen has her hands clasped tightly in front of her. She is the nervous one, the weak link.

'We have not seen Frau Gattschalk since 1992, ' says Nabering finally. 'We bought out her share of the apartment and she moved to Hamburg. That is all we can tell you. She has a job in an insurance company. I do not know which.'

'It is a criminal offence not to tell us the truth,' persists Teschler.

'Do I look senile?' barks Nabering. 'I have told you, we have not seen Frau Gattschalk since we got the apartment. That is it. If you have no further questions you must leave.' She stands up abruptly.

As we leave, Teschler turns to Paffhausen. 'You say that you have not *seen* Frau Gattschalk in three years, have you had contact in any other way, phone calls, letters?'

Paffhausen hesitates for a spilt second, enough for Teschler's wolfish senses to make him step forward sharply and glare at her. The tactic works. She cannot turn to look at Nabering as she is standing behind us.

'We received a postcard about 18 months ago.'

'Where is it?' snaps Teschler sharply.

'I will fetch it,' growls Nabering from the back. She stomps off down a passage, her arms swinging at her sides.

Paffhausen tries not to look at us. Her hands are trembling. She notices and tries to stop them by clasping them even tighter. I feel a twinge of pity for her.

Nabering returns and thrusts a postcard violently into Teschler's hand, even though I am closer and standing with an outstretched hand. She glares suspiciously at Paffhausen. Teschler flips it over, glances at it briefly and gives it to me.

It is a postcard from Sri Lanka. An island scene, the sun setting over the palm trees, a silhouetted couple strolling hand-in-hand on the beach.

'What is this Europol? I have never heard of it,' says Nabering sharply, as if remembering something.

'We're here to make sure you don't get murdered in bed by Nigerians, or have your neighbourhood taken over by illegal Moroccan immigrants,' I answer.

'What was that?' She glares at me.

'Nothing,' I answer.

'Are you Mohammedan?' snaps Nabering at me.

'No,' I answer, taken aback this time.

'Catholic,' I lie. In her books, it's probably just as bad.

Teschler touches me on the arm. We say our goodbyes. Nabering practically shoos us out the door. On the sofa, I catch a glimpse of Paffhausen tensing up to face a tongue-lashing. She must put up with the hectoring and bullying every day. I wonder if it's worth doing a bit of meddling of my own and getting a social worker to pay them a visit, on the grounds of suspected mental torture.

On the stairs I ask Teschler what was written on the card.

'Nothing much. Holiday stuff. Having a good time, that sort of thing.'

'Where to now?' Teschler asks me the question as if he already knows the answer.

'Absolutely no bloody idea,' I smile at him.

'The nursing home here. We can check the files.'

We walk to a public phone booth. Teschler flips the pages looking for the name of the nursing home. He writes it down in his grubby notebook.

'Want an ice-cream?' he asks, pointing to a kiosk on the promenade.

'I'm freezing,' I say.

We hail a cab to take us to the nursing home. It is away from the sea, in one of the dull middle-class suburbs that ring Rostok. It is a depressing sight, street after street of neat little houses with neat front lawns. The only thing that punctuates the flow of residences is the occasional church, school or hall. The streets are completely deserted. The taxi pulls up alongside the old-age home. It is the only property that we have passed with a fence around it.

Once again, he uses me to flash my ID card at the authorities. The senior nurse in charge, Frau Rudel, is horribly obsequious, which makes me wonder what they have to hide. They probably starve and beat the old people.

'Do you still have the files for the deceased?' asks Teschler.

She escorts us to a musty strongroom piled high with racks of cardboard files. Computers don't seem to have reached this part of the world yet.

It doesn't take her long to find Gattschalk in section G. She hands it to Teschler.

'I will leave you alone,' she half-bows and leaves the room. Teschler and both look at each other and giggle.

He translates haphazardly from the notes, 'diet, toiletry habits, meal requirements. *Mein Gott*, they even write down what time they have to go to bed every night.'

It is a sad litany of life in a nursing home, and as he reads it out I see a shadow pass over his face, a glimpse of the terror at what the future holds. It is a revelatory moment for both of us. No matter how much we may proclaim our independence, or cherish our aloneness, it is merely illusory. Our fates are the same in the end.

A few pieces of yellowed paper flutter to the ground. I pick them up. They are old cheques dating from ten years ago.

'Lets go,' I say.

I am cold, tired and hungry and the place feels like a gloomy Sunday afternoon in hell.

Teschler takes the cheques from me. He says something in German to the nurse. She nods her head and shrugs her shoulders as if she couldn't care less. Teschler stuffs the cheques into his pocket.

On the way out, he dials a number on his phone. He reads out the cheque details. As the taxi pulls up he clicks the phone cover shut.

'Dead end,' he sighs. 'The address for the bank account is the same as the Warnemunde flat. The account is also dormant, no transactions in the past four years. She has covered her tracks well.'

The train back to Berlin is an hour away. There is an Italian restaurant near the railway station. Inside, a few early diners are scattered around. They have the look of people who want to eat in a hurry and leave. There's a couple who look like they have just quarrelled. A young man glances up expectantly as we enter. In a corner sits a young girl dragging on a cigarette, newspaper in her hands. She radiates peace and calm.

'Oh well, it's better than sitting on one of those stools at the kebab place,' jokes Teschler trying to lift my spirits.

The only other travellers going back to Berlin are groups of teenagers. At every stop they board the train in desultory units. They're all dressed in standard rave uniform, silver trousers, boots, shiny black jackets. There's obviously a party in the city, but the would-be revellers are so lacking in any ebullience that they might as well be on their way to a funeral. In my day we knew how to cause a riot on trains.

One of party animals, an ugly, mean-looking girl, starts to write on the wall near us. She doesn't even attempt any furtiveness, and neither, it seems, with any sense of passion. Teschler stands up, walks over to her, and whispers something in her ear. She desists immediately and sits down, giving him a hateful glance.

Naturally I'm curious. 'What did you say to her?'

'Told her if she didn't stop writing I'd throw her off the train. By pulling the ring in her nose.'

Chapter 13

The shrill ringing of the phone jolts me awake and shatters my dream. I bang my head on one of those stupidly trendy wooden headboards that interior designers think add character to beds.

It is Teschler. 'I may have got something. I will pick you up in ten minutes.'

Before I can protest that I have to follow procedure and check in at the office, he has rung off. With a touch of unfounded trepidation I dial the office and tell Diehm I won't be coming after all. Her disapproval is palpable over the phone. I grab whatever I can put on quickly and rush downstairs.

'We have a meeting with someone.' He looks me up and down.

'What?' I snap. 'Are my trouser buttons undone?'

Poor Teschler actually blushes.

'I didn't ask you to get me out at such short notice,' I say.

He puts his hands up in surrender. Then he opens the door for me.

'I have new information. One of my contacts has heard that I was making enquiries about Fraulein Gattschalk, and has volunteered information.'

There is the slightest hint of irony around the way he says 'volunteered'. It is, I suppose, an elemental Teutonic humour.

The man we meet is sheltering from the rain outside the Adlon Hotel. He is a member of the staff, judging from his uniform. He is over six feet tall, and he looks very imposing in the long, grey buttoned coat that he wears. His hair is cut short and there is a scar on his face. He has the bearing of an ex-soldier. A defeated ex-soldier.

'Same hotel,' I comment.

'Berlin is a small town,' grunts Teschler.

He shakes my hand vigorously. 'I have just gotten off duty. All night long.'

He aims his thumb contemptuously at the hotel.

'Felix Quetscher is a security officer at the hotel,' interrupts Teschler, 'and ex-Stasi. He used to work with Gattschalk.'

It is a cue for Quetscher. 'Ja. Tough woman that. But I saw her last year when I was taking my hiking holiday in Lausitz. She was buying food in Spitzen, the local village. I said hullo. First, she looked at the people that she was with and then greeted me. I have been in the police long enough to know when someone is hiding something, behaving suspiciously. I come across it all the time, they come through the door - the *Informelle Mitarbeiter* - but they pretend that they don't know me now.'

'The *Informelle Mitarbeiter* were unofficial Stasi employees, those good people who spied on their neighbours for the Stasi. All two million of them,' adds Teschler bitterly.

'She was caught off-guard, believe me,' continues Quetscher. 'They were all carrying shopping bags. Three of them altogether. Two of them had white coats on, like doctors.'

'Did you talk to her, tell her that you were on holiday, etc?' I ask.

'No chance to,' replies Quetscher. 'They all left in a hurry. I bet they didn't finish their shopping.'

'Would you recognise any of them again?'

He looks at me as if I'd just insulted his intelligence.

'Ja, definitely. The fact that they were behaving so suspiciously made me look at them even harder.'

'Thanks,' I say.

'Where are we going?' I ask Teschler.

'Nowhere. We're only dropping Herr Quetscher off at his flat.'

Herr Quetscher's block of flats is in a different world from his glamorous work environment. It is in a shabby sector of the former East Berlin, with old Communist monstrosities that the developers haven't as yet reached. Quetscher is looking out of the window.

'See that bridge over there.' He points to the Bornholmer Bridge intermittently visible through the high-rise buildings. 'That's where I crossed the line on November 9th 1989. I was working the night-shift, so I left my house in the evening to go to work. On the radio I heard all these stories saying that you only needed to show your personal identity document to leave East Germany. I was driving past here anyway and I saw this crowd near the bridge and I stopped. They were laughing and singing and dancing. There was a white line in the middle of the bridge and people were crossing over and then back again. So I drove my Trabi over the bridge to visit my sister. She was shocked when I arrived at her place in the middle of the night! When I told my wife in the morning where I'd been she accused me of drinking. When I gave her the American coffee and the English biscuits that I'd bought in a West Berlin supermarket, she knew.

'Now that man has become a star, while I cannot even afford a car anymore.'

He's referring to General Markus Wolf, the former Stasi spy chief who has become a celebrity as a result of the publication of his memoirs and, bizarrely, a German cookbook.

'They are talking about the "new Berlin". What is this "new Berlin"?

All they are doing is coming back to occupy the old Nazi haunts. The Reichstag, the War Ministry, the Propaganda Ministry. They're taking over all those buildings again. We should have razed them to the ground. Do they not understand that the spirit of war is in those buildings. Know what the funny thing is? I used to be a Communist.

'There is an old German proverb,' he says to no-one in particular, '*Frei sein ist nicht,* to be free is to be a vassal.'

He is embarrassed, but we pretend not to notice.

'If you see Gattschalk, tell the bitch I said hullo,' is his parting shot as he gets out the car. He stands and waves, a tall yet forlorn figure. There is something noble and heroic about him. Like a defeated soldier back from the front.

'Did we need to give him something?' I ask.

'Not to worry,' assures Teschler, 'I have already paid him.'

'How much do I owe you?'

Teschler waves my protestations away. 'Don't worry, Boehme has bought me plenty of dinners.'

'Poor Quetscher, he has problems adjusting to the new Germany,' he adds.

'Life is full of bruises,' I reply.

Teschler rolls his eyeballs in agreement.

'See that.' He points to the new glass dome on top of the Reichstag.

'They think by covering it with glass, they will erase all the memories.'

He shakes his head in disbelief, turning the ignition to his car. It grumbles to a start.

'Lausitz,' he says, 'is a wasteland. It is like the surface of the moon, but with water. The area was used for lignite mining by the

East Germans. They stripped the land bare and destroyed everything, the land the villages, so that they could feed the power plants. After unification, most of the mines were shut down because of the pollution and the cheap quality of the output. Many miners were laid off and it was in all the papers.'

It's hard to decide what to do so I throw the ball in Teschler's court. 'Are we going there?'

'If you like. The Lausitz area is south east of Berlin, approximately two hundred kilometres. We can go in my car this time.'

'Do you need to check with Boehme?' he asks.

'No. It will be a recon trip. I'm sure they're long gone anyway.' I answer.

Teschler swings his car around. Like him, it is surprisingly agile for its size and age.

'First we head east,' he says, 'down Frankfurter Allee. It used to be called Stalin Allee in the old days. We have a joke. Who succeeded Stalin?'

'No idea,' I answer.

'Frankfurter of course.' He wheezes with laughter, his body shaking so hard that I can feel the car quivering.

*

Spitzen is in a slight hollow, surrounded by straggly bits of forest. We cross a wooden bridge, under which runs a brown river, to get to the village. Most of the trees are long gone and the grass grows only fitfully around the town. The Germans call it *Waldsterben* - "dying forest syndrome", the result of pollution and other forms of environmental degradation. At one time it must have been a beautiful part of Germany. It will take years to recover, if ever.

The village of Spitzen wears its hardship like a battered and abused housewife. Many of the houses seem to be boarded up. Things don't look so desperate in the main street. At least there are people walking around, although most of them seem to be over sixty. They look heavily burdened, as if World War II ended the year before. There is a conspicuous absence of children and teenagers.

Teschler parks his car outside the general store. It ambitiously calls itself a supermarket. Inside, he shows a photograph of Gattschalk to the owner. He's a round, friendly man with a mustache like a walrus. He even wears an old-fashioned striped blue and white apron.

'Yes, she's been here a few times, maybe once a month for the last seven, eight months. Always pays cash. Unlike the other government people.'

'What government people?' Teschler is leaning casually over the counter, pretending to be fascinated by the packs of cigarettes on display behind the storekeeper.

'The research people who work in the mine fields. They come from all over Germany. Geologists, geochemists, hydrologists, microbiologists, even businessmen. Not that I'm complaining. It's good for business.

The government has a new plan now. They want to flood the area with water from the Spree, the Schwarze Elster and the Neisse rivers. Then they want to build a Wild West theme park with a western town and an Indian village.'

He shakes his head in disbelief. So do we.

'But,' he adds, 'it will be good for business.

'My son Werner works there. That's how I know so much. Maybe he can show you around. He might know where your friend is.' He taps the photograph.

'What does your son do?' I ask.

'He is a post-graduate student from the department for Land Preservation and Recultivation at the University of Cottbus. Studying to be a scientist, although I think he thinks that he already is one. The house is like a laboratory, full of bottles of water and soil samples. And they all look the same. He will be back home from the university this afternoon. About four thirty.'

I buy a couple of chocolate bars and a newspaper to make him happy.

There is a small tea shop across the road. We ensconce ourselves there for a stodgy lunch and tea. It also provides a good view of the general stores. There is nothing else to do. The owner of the supermarket says he will send his son over when he arrives.

The tea shop remains empty except for two old ladies who run it.

They ply us with sweet cakes and cups of tea. Teschler is having a good time. It's obvious that he doesn't get spoilt very often.

'Why did your wife kick you out?' I feel brave enough to ask, seeing the blissful expression on his face.

A dark shadow crosses it. 'She was always complaining about me working late. This week I was following someone around and I didn't call for two days. That was the straw that broke the camel's back. Enough is enough, she said. She told me not to come home until I found a regular job. She doesn't complain about the money though.'

His face brightens suddenly.

'Ha, that's what I'll do,' he beams. 'Tell her that if I do get a regular job, the money won't be as good.'

The son crosses the street at exactly 4:30 pm. He is tall and gangly and walks like a cowboy. His white coat flaps in the breeze. Inside the shop he makes straight for us. Werner has long lank hair and looks like he spends too much time in his laboratory. His skin is pallid and spotty. A chain-smoker, too, I would guess, on the strength of his breath.

A broad smile is on his face. He has his father's warmth and humour.

'My dad told me you wanted a tour,' he says, arm outstretched to me.

'Welcome to hell.'

His battered old US army jeep is around the back of the store. We drive bumpily over a series of badly eroded hillocks. The lack of trees has caused the soil to leach, creating gullies and holes. Teschler and I are in the back, hanging on for our lives.

After an hour of bumps and grinds we stop near a clump of trees that look as though they have had acid poured all over them.

The sun is setting behind us, casting long shadows. What lies in front of us is stranger than the moon. It is more like one of the moons of Jupiter, so utterly alien is the landscape. At first glance it doesn't even look man made. Dunes of sand shaped by the winds, the way deserts are,

Deeply rutted valleys tinged blueish by lignite rock from the bowels of the earth. Rivulets weave through the landscape connecting to the still pools of water that eerily reflect the light of the setting sun.

Then there is the smell. It is harsh and noxious. A sulphurous mixture that burns the nostrils at every breath. It is hard to imagine such a landscape existing in western Europe. Teschler and I are dumfounded.

'I have heard about this place, but I never thought it would be like this,' he finally mutters.

'Be careful!' Werner shouts at Teschler, who has taken a few steps forward.

'There are sinkholes everywhere. One false step and you could disappear forever. There are landslides too.'

'Probably better off on a boat,' grumbles Teschler.

'That won't help,' smiles Werner, a touch too ghoulishly. 'Landslides create huge waves that travel at fast speeds across the lakes. They are like miniature Tsunamis. You would get sucked under.'

'You're making this up,' snaps Teschler irritably.

'I'm not. There have been quite a few deaths here. Welcome to Lausitz. The most unique place in the world.'

Werner waves his hand extravagantly over the landscape, as if it all belongs to him.

'During the 1970s and 1980s the former East Germany dug up about 300 million tons of lignite every year from this area. They strip-mined this place. This is what we get for it. Total destruction.'

'What do you do here?' I ask him.

'The University of Cottbus has created a special unit for the study of this region. The government is planning on spending millions of Deutschmarks to get this area productive again, so they have all sorts of people advising them. Ideally, they would like to flood these areas with water from the Spree, the Schwarze Elster, and the Neisse rivers to make this into a pretty lake district.'

'The locals must be happy,' adds Teschler.

'That depends. The main plan so far is to build a Wild West theme park - with a "town" and an "Indian village", with theme evenings, etc.'

He wrinkles his nose in disgust.

'Some people - including me - are not too happy with this.'

'What would you like to see?' I ask.

'Well, it's hard to believe, but this place is not as barren as it looks. What has evolved here is a unique European ecosystem. A treasure of nature. There are strange microscopic forms of life that have evolved in the lakes, often quite separately from each other. There are also large numbers of insects, birds and flowers that are rare elsewhere in the country. What we have here gives an indication of how life evolves on this - and possibly other - planets. But of course a theme park would bring in more money than a conservation area.'

'Who works here?' asks Teschler.

'There's an army of people out here. Scientists mostly, with the occasional businessman dropping by to see how things are going. Did I tell you that the envisaged theme park includes a five-star hotel? No? Well, it does. Better a *rastplatz* [picnic area] than a *naturpark* [protected countryside].'

'Have you seen this woman around?' Teschler shows him a photograph of Gattschalk.

He glances at it briefly. 'Ja. At my father's store. You get to see more people there than here. Scientists are not as open as they pretend to be. Everybody here is really precious about their research. So they tend keep to themselves. I suppose at the back of their minds is the thought that they might discover something new, a new sub-species, a new bacteria.'

'Where is she?'

'No idea. Most of the researchers have got their own compounds or mobile units. Nobody trespasses. There is a common security operation in place. The government pays half and the private companies pay the other half.

'She's private, and they're even worse than the government when it comes to security. I've seen her go into the compound. Sym-Tech I think it was called. You can check with my dad. They used a company registered credit card for payments at the shop. No idea what they do but there are lots of private people here who have permission from the government.

'As I've said, people have died out here over the years. Children mostly. You can't keep them away. They already think it's one big playground. Also hikers and the odd person who works here. The death rate when this area was part of the GDR was even greater. We have a good rescue system in place, dogs, boats and sometimes the use of a helicopter from Cottbus.'

We follow the signposts to the main guard house. The barking from the three German Shepherds increases as we get closer. The compound consists of three caravans surrounded by a ring of barbed wire.

Eventually the door opens and a large grubby man, equally large sandwich in hand, sloshes over through the mud. I am not dressed for the occasion. My flat shoes and the lower half of my jeans are already splattered with mud.

His demeanor is not very friendly.

'What do you people want?'

Werner steps forward and explains who we are.

'Unit 7 behind hill 3,' he shouts and marches back to his caravan.

'Follow me,' says Werner. He has a computer-generated map of the area which shows the topography of the landscape as well as some of the station units.

The sand is soft beneath my feet and I struggle to maintain my balance.

Snowshoes would have been better. Now and then there are ominous grumblings from beneath the ground, like the rumble of a far-away train.

'Earth tremors,' says Werner. 'A serious one can cause tidal waves.'

'What's with the numbers?' asks Teschler, pointing to the map.

'Every research centre or mobile unit has to be registered. Some of the hills are mapped, and they've been given numbers. It makes it easier if something goes wrong.'

'Typical bloody German efficiency,' groans Teschler as he struggles to avoid getting water into his newish brogues.

'I'm sorry,' apologises Werner, 'if you had phoned first I would have told you what to wear.'

'How the hell were we supposed to know in the first place,' curses Teschler.

Werner drops to the ground.

There is a soft gurgle from his throat. Then a trickle of blood dribbles down the side of his mouth. For a moment, we all gaze in incomprehension at the body on the ground. There is an unnatural stillness in the air. It occurs to me that Werner may have suffered some kind of medical attack. Epilepsy, a stroke.

I move instinctively towards him, but Teschler pushes me roughly to the ground and falls down beside me. He rolls over twice, surprisingly agile for his size. Only then do I notice the gun in his hand. He is now behind a mound of earth, so he's able to raise his head. Werner gurgles quietly, one hand clutching his throat and the other clawing futilely at the sand. A dark stain of blood is spreading on the front of his shirt. At the back of my mind I remember the faint crack, like the distant snap of a whip.

He has been shot.

Chapter 14

There is a thunderous roar and a ball of flame shoots up into the sky, illuminating the surroundings in an orange glow. The landscape is harsh and alien, unfamiliar flows of terrain that belong to another planet.

The ground trembles beneath me. Every fibre of my body quivers. Even my teeth rattle. The others are flat on the ground, hands protectively over their heads. A blast of warm air wafts over us, like a summer breeze.

It is aftermath of the heatwave created by the powerful blast.

Teschler carefully raises himself on his knees attempting to spot the source of the shooting. I crawl clumsily towards Werner. There is a hole in his right side, somewhere near the lungs, which is why he cannot breathe.

Blood gushes out. If I attempt to staunch the flow, the blood will pour into his lungs, choking him to death. If I leave it, he will bleed to death.

His fingers bite into my arm, his face twisted in a grimace. I stroke his face.

Teschler is beside me. 'We have to get him into the sitting position, that will slow the flow of blood through the arteries. Then you can put your finger in the hole.'

The security man is rushing wildly towards us in his green dune buggy, dogs yelping beside him. It all seems to be in slow motion, a disembodied experience. I am an observer not a participant. The sounds fade away in the background. A moment of silence.

The buggy crashes to a halt, spraying us with mud. The security guard attempts to stand up but Teschler grabs him unceremoniously and hurls him to the ground. The dogs go crazy. One of them sinks its teeth into Teschlers' ankle. He kicks out at it viciously. The guard shouts them down, arms flailing madly. They slink away behind the buggy. I can hear Teschler's screams. He curses bitterly and shakes his fist at the helicopter sheering away into the darkening sky.

We help Werner into the buggy. There is a pool of blood on the ground as we lift him up. His clothing is completely covered in blood. He is as white as a sheet, head lolling to one side, eyes dead.

My fingers are sticky. I try to wipe them on my jacket but it only seems to make it worse. There is blood all over me.

I glance at Teschler and see the despair in his eyes.

Poor Werner. In a couple of hours his idyllic, scholarly life has been turned into a nightmare.

The ride back to Spitzen is a nightmare. After the first couple of bumps, Werner slumps into unconsciousness. Teschler presses my thumb against the bullet wound and asks me to hold it there.

Teschler leans forward suddenly. 'Do you have a ...?'

'A what?' I ask, puzzled.

'A woman's thing... a ...tampon?'

'No.' I answer.

'Pity. It would have been ideal for the wound.'

He wraps torn fragments of his coat around Werner's upper and lower body to function as a crude tourniquet and ease the pressure. I cradle Werner's head in my lap.

The local doctor does what he can to help Werner. There is an emergency vehicle on its way from Cottbus. He says that Werner has a punctured lung, but that the serious problem is loss of blood.

Werner's father is surprisingly calm. He doesn't exactly throw his arms around us, but he accepts my apologies with a graciousness quietness.

I phone Anna Diehm in Berlin and tell her the story. She listens in shocked silence. I tell her to do the necessary paperwork to get a forensics team sent over.

They arrive in two helicopters at the outskirts of the town. It is 2 in the morning. The guard from the compound is still hanging around with his dogs. We have to ask him to direct us back to the compound in the helicopter. The dogs are tied up at the doctor's premises.

The guard is nervous. He has never been in a helicopter before. Teschler says a few reassuring words to him.

It is a five minute trip this time. From the air the scattered pinpricks of light from the different units are easily visible. The area looks even more desolate and lonely. I wonder if anybody out there even noticed the explosion.

We land. The stillness descends, enveloping us like a gigantic blanket. The members of the team are awed by their environment, and they can't even see much. Somewhere somebody is playing heavy metal music, the muffled sound travelling across the landscape. Out in the distance there are eerie green and yellow spots of light. Some of the lights move, drifting slowly across the landscape. Looking at them it's easy to see why people believe in alien visitations. They are gas bubbles, their colouring caused by refracted light.

They had a helicopter. That is how they made their escape. The crude helipad is a few metres away from the scorched circle of earth. One of the investigators points to the neat circle.

'Planned, controlled explosion,' he says. 'They had it all set up. It was not done in a hurry. Either they were waiting for you, or it was sheer coincidence.'

'I don't think that bullet was sheer coincidence,' I say.

'Kamov-32, Russian military transport helicopter,' interrupts Teschler who is the only one who had seen the helicopter.

The investigating team cordon off the area. They have big torches but not big enough to light up the whole space so we decide to wait until morning. They warn us about moving around and contaminating the area. They also warn us about booby traps.

The guard offers us his caravan. They settle down to play cards. The guard is in his element, a big change from his earlier attitude. He plays the host, digging up three bottles of Schnapps and a packet of cheese crackers from his cupboard. I fool around with the remaining dog outside, as even Teschler has deserted me for the card game. The guard offers me his bed, but I decline. Being infested by bed-bugs doesn't sound like my idea of comfort.

The dog soon tires of fetching bits of wood that I throw and goes inside for a bit of warmth and company. It is old, which is why it didn't come bounding over with the rest earlier in the evening.

It sounds like they are having fun inside, lots of raucous male laughter. Someone is singing in a gruff baritone. It is probably some lush romantic song but it sounds very Martian, like they're about to cross the Oder-Neisse line. That's the problem with German songs. They all end up sounding like the Horst Wessel Lied. It's probably the way they're sung.

I step forward, a few feet away from the cabin.

Out here in the country there are stars to be seen. It is a shock to gaze at such a large expanse of sky. I cannot remember the last time I did it.

Life in the city has a way of robbing you of distance, of vision. Mostly it's physical, being blocked by buildings. You cannot see into the distance when all you see around you are concrete buildings.

I look out into the sky at our expanding cosmos. Astronomers say the universe is expanding like a giant balloon, that all the galaxies are rushing away from each other at tremendous speeds. The rate of expansion, what astronomers call the Hubble Constant, is subject to dispute, but all scientists are in basic agreement with the one salient fact - the further out you look, the faster the universe is expanding. To look up at the night sky is to see our own galaxy spinning away deeper and deeper into space, carrying us with it, like a ball caught in a wave. Not that we notice much these days. Very soon the stars over Europe will be dimmed, anaemic pinpricks of light hardly visible from the ground, the result of our desire for lights in our streets and homes. It is called progress. As Cicero once said, *'The contemplation of celestial things will make a man both speak and think more sublimely and magnificently when he descends to human affairs.'*

A loud grunt.

I scream.

The caravan door is flung open and the others come bolting out.

'What's going on?' shouts Teschler.

'I heard a noise,' I answer sheepishly.

'It's only a frog,' says the guard, shining his torch on the ground and highlighting a big ugly creature staring lugubriously at us. 'What are you doing out here anyway?'

'I was taking a piss.'

'There's a portable toilet inside,' he grunts lewdly.

'I didn't want to disturb your damned card game,' I yell after him.

In the small hours of the morning the guard makes coffee. Very strong and very black. He serves it in chipped tin mugs, with powdered milk.

It's amazing how fastidiousness vanishes in the face of real need. The others stumble out of the cabin, stretching their arms.

The more active ones fling their limbs about and do a bit of on-the-spot jogging. It is very cold and my toes are starting to go numb. The hours before dawn are always the worst.

The three forensics people get to work. First they gingerly check around for booby traps.

'They have these little plastic things, the size of your palm. You can practically buy them off the shelf in Moscow these days. Step on them and you lose both legs,' grins Johannes, one of the funnier members of the team.

They put on their gloves and carry their little black boxes with them.

Around their waists they have leather belts with pouches and compartments for carrying tools.

The bomb has obliterated everything in a very neat circle. The explosion is also quite deep, going down to a depth of about seven metres.

'Looks exactly like a meteorite site,' comments Johannes. 'They had some sort of underground structure in place. Judging from the height, I would say part of the site was beneath ground level. Offhand, I would guess that the explosive devices were a delicate mixture of deflagrating and detonating explosive. The first one creates high combustibility and the second a big bang.'

They are on their hands and knees, sifting through the meagre evidence and putting little bits into their black boxes.

The charred bits of paper they are extra careful with, gingerly sliding wafer-thin plastic sheets under them, then placing them on trays.

'What's that for?' I ask one of the team members, an elderly man who looks long past retirement age. 'It's burnt to a crisp anyway.'

'Crispy is fine. As long as it hasn't crumbled we can do something with it. It may be burnt, but because it's still intact it means that the degree of heat wasn't that high. That's why it is not ash. As long as it's not ash, we can analyse.'

'Can you do same with the charred computer disks?' I ask.

'Yup. Depends on the state of pyrolysis though - that's chemical decomposition by means of heat. Criminals haven't cottoned on to the fact that we can put together the damaged disks. Otherwise they would make sure the incriminating stuff was obliterated in the first place. Intense magnetisation would do the trick.'

There's nothing for Teschler and I to do but watch the professionals at work. They are a well co-ordinated team moving in ever increasing concentric rings outwards, methodically examining the ground.

A dark green van chugs its way slowly through the mud. It is Werner's father. He greets us, almost shyly, and opens up the back of his van. He has flasks of coffee and a ton of sandwiches. Beef on rye, cheese and tomato, and cold roast chicken. In addition, there are fresh rolls and a small box of *Buchteln*, dumplings with plum jam. The smell is intoxicating. I could hug him, but he doesn't look as though he wants to come too close to us. Werner will be okay, he says. The doctors in Cottbus have managed to drain his lungs and perform a minor blood transfusion. He'll be home in two weeks.

The forensics team have picked up the aroma. They make an undignified scramble towards us. The storekeeper beams happily, handing out the food and pouring the coffee. He has also brought the other two dogs back with him.

For the next couple of minutes there's silence, punctuated by groans of ecstasy as we attack the food.

At 10 am Boehme arrives with Anna Diehm. I watch them stride across the dunes, deriving a mean-spirited frisson of pleasure at the sight of Diehm tottering through the mud in her flimsy city shoes. Boehme is sturdy and sure-footed. There's a strange grace to the way he nimbly picks his way over the ground. As if he knows every step of the way.

He must have left Amsterdam on a very early flight.

He greets Teschler and I. Anna gives me what I can only describe as a chastising look.

'I didn't give you permission to destroy the German countryside,' says Boehme.

'From what I've heard, you did a fair bit of that yourself,' I reply, glancing at Teschler, who is grinning broadly.

'It was all my idea,' protests Teschler.

'I have difficulty believing that,' says Boehme waving to the old scientist I had spoken to earlier. There doesn't seem to be anyone he doesn't know in the BKA.

'There's nothing else to do here. Forensics will forward the reports to the police and to us. It's best you go back to Amsterdam.'

We get a quick helicopter ride back to Spitzen to pick up Teschler's car.

Boehme decides to come back with us.

On the way back to Berlin I insist that we stop at the Cottbus hospital to say goodbye to Werner.

He is alone and sitting up in bed, reading a chemistry textbook. It's amazing that he has managed to stay so thin, judging from the amount of food his parents foist on him. There are piles of fruit, cakes and sweets at his bedside.

'It's a good opportunity to get my studies done,' he grins at me, putting down his book.

I apologise again for all the trouble we have caused him and his family.

He brushes it away. 'I haven't had this much fun since I went camping in the Alps and got lost in the mountains when I was twelve.'

*

Back in Berlin, I harass the forensics team for the reports. They live in an ugly, grey building that has probably spent all of its existence housing government employees, way back to the days of Bismarck.

The first port of call is Johannes, the explosives expert with a sense of humour.

'I was right.' He's busy mixing a range of powders on a steel table. They erupt in little puffs of smoke. 'Fill your handbag with this stuff and you could bring down this entire building.'

'I don't carry a handbag,' I answer. 'What were you right about?'

'The explosion. We found traces of a crystalline compound, Trinitrotoluene, a high explosive which is prepared by the nitration of toluene. We also detected signs of ammonium nitrate in the soil samples. It is prepared commercially by the reaction of nitric acid and ammonia, a highly flammable substance. Mix the two together and you get amatol. You also get a big bang and a big fire. Pretty basic stuff.'

'How do you do this?' I ask.

'Gas Liquid Chromatography is the most widely used laboratory instrument for analysing compounds because of its ability to detect and identify trace amounts. A sample of the compound extracted from the debris is taken and introduced into the instrument where it is volatilised and swept by a gas stream through a long tubular column towards a detector. As the sample moves through the column the various components will separate so that the compound with the lowest boiling point will emerge from the column first, followed by the other components in order of their boiling points. By measuring the time from injection at which the individual components emerge from the column it is possible to positively identify each component. The entire analysis is recorded on a chart called a chromatogram where each component of the sample is represented by a peak and the overall pattern is essentially a fingerprint for each compound.

'Simple,' he grins.

'Are you saying that anybody could do it?'

'Nope. The secret is in the mixture, like a good cake recipe. Get the mixture wrong and you get an unstable compound. It is equivalent to sitting on an unexploded bomb. No, whoever did this knew what they were doing.'

The old man in charge of the team, Gleichman, *is* past retirement age.

He is seventy, although he is in good shape, tall but slightly stooped, with a full head of white hair. He also has a taste for bright, garish ties.

There must be a case for staying alone after all. He has been a forensic scientist for forty years and tells me that the department keeps him on because they can't find skilled personnel. 'Besides, what would I be doing? I have no wife, no hobbies. My work is my hobby.'

I begin to regret turning on the charm.

He points to the books that he has written on forensics, as well as the stack of journals that he's been published in. On the walls he has photographs of the numerous conventions that he's attended around the world. Always smiling, always with groups of happy men, Orientals, Blacks, Indians, Americans.

He's not so bad, a bit lonely and a bit regretful about the direction his life has taken, but then so are we all.

The computer printouts slowly dribble through. They are methodically catalogued, right down to the time each individual scrap of paper was picked up and by whom. It does seem a bit excessive, but it is the only way to identify the bits and pieces. At first glance they look like gibberish. The research assistants who have assembled the bits have simply attempted to decipher whatever characters they could work out on the paper and on the disks, without any extrapolation as their meaning. Some can be identified as fragments of letters and memos:

12th Jul

ATT:

Au |C |

'These letters here, with the lines,' says Gleichman, 'I would say that they are parts of a computer spreadsheet. Elements of the periodic table. Au is gold and C is carbon. Common elements. They look like clinical trial reports to me.'

'Think Gattschalk was out digging for gold?'

'Not unless she knew something the metallurgical engineers didn't. That area has been extensively analysed like no other region in this country. These elements are very common. They could be found in the human body, a lump of rock, a plastic toy.'

'Didn't know there was gold in our bodies,' I say.

'Oh yes, trace amounts, that is, very small amounts.'

Then we strike gold. A watermark on one of the pieces of paper. To me it looks like a burnt document but the spectrographic analysis shows a graphic.

'They're doing an enhancement at the moment,' says Gleichman.

'Don't get too excited,' he adds, noticing the gleam in my eyes. 'Pseudo watermarks are very common these days. You can buy pre-printed stationery from supermarkets with all sorts of fancy watermarks.'

The technician rushes over with the printout. I practically wrench it out of his hands.

It consists of two interweaving vertical lines with horizontal lines meeting each side. The letter B is superimposed on the picture in Arial font.

'What is it?' I ask.

'The spiral staircase,' answers Gleichman. 'The double helix structure made famous by Watson and Crick, the two scientists who discovered the genetic structure. It is only a segment of DNA. It is quite a common image. Anybody with scientific pretensions would use something like this.'

'I have seen it before,' I add, wracking my brain to remember.

'Got it,' I shout so loudly that heads turn in our direction.

'It was at the Groningen University. The molecular medicine lecture.'

Gleichman raises his eyebrow at me. 'Well, you would, *liebling*, seeing that it is closely related to molecular medicine. As a matter of fact it would be *hard* not to see something like this.'

'No, no,' I answer. 'It is the way it's drawn, with the B in the middle like that.'

Gleichman shrugs his shoulders. 'You're the detective. Go find out.'

'Thanks,' I say.

'My pleasure. Next time you're in Berlin, give me a ring. We can go and paint the town red.'

Back at the office I start to go through my rubbish. Piles of paper, brochures, and sundry documents waiting to be swept into the bin.

It is on the front page of the Biogen brochure, discreetly placed, but not so discreet that you wouldn't notice it. A silver and glass plaque, about 20 by 30 centimetres, in sleek modern design on the wall as you move through the revolving doors. The same double helix structure, this one etched in glass and inlaid with silver. The B over it. The inscription says that the new wing of the university was donated by Biogen - Opening the Future.

I show it to Boehme.

'This gets more and more bizarre,' moans Boehme, putting his hands on his head. 'What does Gattschalk have to do with Biogen?'

I shrug my shoulders. The fax from the environmental agency has also arrived. It states that, for an annual fee of 100 000 Deutschmarks, Sym-Tech has been permitted to carry out research on micro-organism strains in the Lausitz region.

'Waste of time, this Biogen link,' grunts Boehme. 'Find out more about Gattschalk and the Stasi. It's probably some old Russian vendetta carried over from the Cold War.'

First I have a hunch to satisfy. I transmit photographs of Laville, Laurier and a few other people to Teschler. Ask him to get them to Felix Quetscher to see if he can identify any of them as the visitors he'd seen in Spitzen.

Then I do a search for Biogen again on the Internet. It has an English-registered web address. The site consists of the usual bland corporate nonsense. It manages to say a lot without actually describing what it does, "committed to research excellence", "high standards", "superior staffing", etc. I wish someone would tell me what these phrases actually mean. They roll so easily off the tongue, honeyed words that no-one has the slightest idea of honouring, specially when companies lay off hundreds of workers at the slightest dip in profits.

Under the "Partnership Program" section of the company's prospectus for the year there's an extensive list of Biogen's partner's. A lot of the names are recognisable. Giant multinational corporations that spew out a myriad range of chemical cocktails that we cannot do without. Makers of cough mixture, aspirin, uppers, downers, any drug you could possibly think of. Open any bathroom cabinet in Europe and there it will it be, staring you in the face. All of them "forming exciting new partnerships to remain at the cutting edge of medical research by developing innovative ways to cure diseases. Forging ahead into the 21st century..." Blah, blah, blah.

Is there any corporate organisation that is not "forging ahead into the 21st century", I wonder.

The public relations woman at Biogen Pharmaceuticals in Amsterdam speaks to me as if I'm requesting a state secret. Not that she's anything less than polite. She smothers me in politeness. She promises to send me a fax outlining the company's business with Sym-Tech. I ask her to tell me briefly but she pretends not to hear me, and promises the fax as soon as possible.

The fax is about as informative as Biogen's web site.

Dear Mrs De Hoop (I don't know why she's assumed I am married)

Further to your telephonic enquiry today, and following consultation with the relevant departments, I have pleasure in providing you with the information you requested.

Biogen has been conducting exciting new research on our behalf for the manufacture of new medicines.

We have a number of excellent research organisations and companies worldwide which conduct research and product development for new drugs.

All companies adhere to a stringent set of regulations to maintain our high standards. These include unscheduled visits and auditing. In addition we work closely with independent regulatory bodies in all countries to ensure that all local regulations are strictly adhered to.

We are also sending you, by special courier, material on our company which you may find useful.

Thank you for your interest in Biogen Pharmaceuticals.

Yours sincerely

Sophia Hausenpfeff

Head of Public Relations

I phone her back.

'You don't say what research Biogen was doing with Sym-Tech?'

'I'm sorry but I'm not at liberty to say.'

There is a long pause from both sides. It does occur to me that bluster and aggression will get me nowhere. Sophia Hausenpfeff is much too refined for that sort of approach. I try the coldly polite method.

'You do of course understand that I'm calling from the office of the directorate of Europol.'

'Yes madam. I'm sorry, but our policy forbids the handing out of company information concerning current research projects. As a matter of protocol you have to apply directly to the company itself, in this case Biogen, who will then use their discretion, or get in touch with us. It has to be a decision taken in unison, whether the response is a negative or positive one.'

'And how long will this take?'

'A few weeks at the most.'

I say goodbye. It's not really her fault. She's only following orders.

I have another note from Admin on the second floor. It confirms that the Sym-Tech credit card used in the shop in Cottbus was a company card made out to a Swiss-registered company of the same name. The managing director is listed as a "Herr K Gattschalk". She obviously didn't use her imagination too much this time round.

There is an address too, in Zurich, but the Swiss police say that it is merely an office that provides business services to other companies, one of hundreds in the city.

Boehme calls me into his office. He doesn't look very happy.

'I received a phone call from the Co-ordinator's office in Paris. Apparently you've been impersonating a member of their staff.'

There are times when it's best to say nothing.

'They have tape recorders. They tape conversations. "In order to continuously improve their service to customers."' He closes the door behind him.

'I was only trying to get one step ahead,' I mumble.

'Don't bother. They are already one step ahead of us. This afternoon a letter was couriered to the Co-ordinator's office. It was from their legal team. A mere formality. All it said was that they wished to know the the reason *we* were making enquiries about them. In the business world it's called "pre-emptive action". This organisation has survived the Nazis. We are nothing but a bureaucratic nuisance, a little bug to be swatted away.

'That's my first question. My second is why are you chasing after Biogen? You don't think that they are in bed with Tamil terrorists and bombers?'

'Herr Boehme, you've heard of the expression "Where there's smoke there's fire",' I answer mischievously.

'Don't get your fingers burnt,' Boehme warns.

'No, I don't think Biogen are consorting with those people that you mentioned. Not right now anyway. I do understand one thing: there is a reason.'

'Sit down.'

I stare at him.

'Sit down,' commands Boehme again.

I do as I'm told.

'De Hoop,' he begins, 'not every big company is full of evil people just waiting to set machinery in motion to destroy you. If you carry on thinking this way you will destroy yourself. You have a job to do, which you have to perform to the best of your ability. If you cannot do this, let me know now so that I can relieve you of your duty. Please do not go around looking for monoliths to topple.'

'Boehme, I respond weakly, 'how can I be against big companies?

I buy my bread from Hoffnung.'

Hoffnung is a German-based bakery with tentacles reaching all over Europe.

Boehme smiles. 'Get out, De Hoop.'

Outside his office I take deep breaths.

'Having a bad day,' grins Ilsa maliciously. I had not noticed her lurking around the corner.

'Yes, especially when the boss demands sexual favours in his office. You know how it is.'

That shuts her up.

The fax that Boehme had handed me is no different in tone from the earlier one, but there is more information. Slightly more. There is a method to how Biogen works. At the same time that they sent the threatening letter they also sent through a document giving us slightly more information on their organisation. This makes them look like very reasonable people - we are the ones causing all the trouble.

Sym-Tech was doing research for a biotechnology component of Biogen. There is a broad outline of the kind of work. Nothing too specific. Below, in big letters, a warning to us of what would happen if any of the information was leaked out. There is nothing to leak out in the first place. Very, very clever.

*

It is good to be home again. To walk in my own space. Not just indoors but outside as well. We are all territorial animals, liking nothing better than the sights, sounds and smells of our little worlds.

It is noon. I go to the cinema and watch Jacques Tati being romantic and silly. I am one of three people in the cinema. When we exit, it feels like we are all friends. There is an unspoken camaraderie in the air. Deep down inside I recognise the emotion for what it is, a cannibalisation of the sensitivities of the artist. It is a disease of the lonely and the alone.

But what the hell, it still feels good.

The grocer has a note for me. He hands it over with a dirty wink. It is from the American. It is his business card with a work number. There is no message.

At home I call him up. The receptionist at Davids & Mckie asks me to hold on and then puts me through.

He answers the phone with a confident grunt.

'Sorry I didn't write a message, but I felt kinda silly. And the old man was looking at me with that smart-ass grin on his face.'

I tell him that I've been in Berlin. It is the only truth that I tell him. I can hear frenetic voices in the background, so I keep the conversation short. We make plans to meet, neither of us committing to anything.

Before we say goodbye, I tell him that I work for a government agency.

He laughs it away, as though I had confessed to a silly white lie.

Boehme was quite indignant when I had told him about my trail of deceit.

We are not spies, he had said. After all, policemen don't lie about being policemen. I was both relieved and disappointed. Some of the mystique had eroded somehow. Perceptively, he had also warned me about listening to Benschop-Fehr.

'That woman fills your head with rubbish,' were his exact words.

I log on to my mailbox to check my e-mail. There is a message from Teschler. He is very chatty and excited about finally using the system. At the end of his message he tells me that Quetscher identified Laville from the pictures.

I phone Boehme and tell him. He seems miffed that Teschler had mailed me first.

There is more person to call. The snooty secretary answers the phone again. This time she puts me through to the doctor right away.

'I knew that I'd be hearing from you,' he says.

'Oh? Why?'

'Gut feeling. Us scientists have those too.'

I make an appointment to see him.

'After lectures? This afternoon?'

'That's fine by me,' I say.

*

At 6 pm it is fairly deserted on his floor. The students have long since retired to the pubs and bars around town.

He is wearing a white cotton shirt and combat trousers, lurking around the secretary's printer as though he was waiting for something to come out of it. What he doesn't realise is that we all have these tricks up our sleeves.

He is very nervous this time, lost some of his superciliousness. To give him breathing space, I accept his offer of coffee. I do like him.

Once seated, I remind him again about Europol's paranoid obsession with confidentiality. This time his laughter is muted.

I have two pages of typed notes which I place in front of myself on the table, very businesslike.

'Any questions you don't feel like asking, please feel free to say so,' I start.

'I may feel free to say so, but why do I get the feeling that it will be held against me?'

'Guilty conscience?'

'Ha, ha, ha.'

'What exactly is your relationship with Biogen?'

There is brief flash of anger in his eyes.

'I think you already know, so why bother asking? I don't have a relationship with Biogen. I simply have shares in the company.'

He pauses for breath. 'And if you must know, they were given to me by a good friend, Professor Laville. It was on the occasion of me achieving my doctorate and the publication of a bit of research that we had worked on together. As you probably already know, I am not wealthy enough to have purchased them.'

'I'm not ...'

'No, no, please. If you wish to ask me a question, please go ahead. There is no need to beat around the bush. By your own admission you wish me to be honest.'

'Yes,' I concede.

'What about Sym-Tech?' It is a wild shot but I take it.

'Sym-Tech? All I know about Sym-Tech is what's in the annual report.

Small biotechnology company. Swiss-based. They are one of about five independent companies that do research for Biogen, which in turn does work for a range of international companies.'

'That is the nature of research these days. It's about fluid partnerships. You use the best people in the best companies.'

'What exactly are you doing anyway,' he adds sharply. 'It's not about drug smuggling is it? Is it one of those Euro-scandals to do with graft or corruption in the medical world perhaps?'

'You ought to stop reading the tabloids,' I say to him.

'Miss De Hoop,' he ventures seriously, 'the reason I am giving you my time is that I know all about you.

'Don't look so surprised. You have quite a reputation in intellectual or should I say, university circles. I checked up.'

'I had no idea,' I answer ironically.

'You talk about a scandal as if you almost expect it to be that. Do you know something that you're not telling?'

'It almost always is, judging from what I read. We live in a very corrupt world and Europe is no less corrupt than Africa, Asia or South America. We like to pretend that we're civilised and above that sort of thing, that it only happens "over there", but that is a delusion. I have no illusions about big business. Their tentacles extend all over the world these days.'

'Would your anger extend to murder?'

There are times when one must act with the flow that swells inside the chest, a gut feeling, instinct, call it what you want, but it sweeps up, presents itself, and demands attention. And my feeling about him is that he is inherently honest. I could be wrong. But I doubt it.

Besides, he has a nice face.

I tell him what has happened. All the details, starting with the discovery of the dead Tamils, of Laville's name in the notebook, hinting at a connection to the LTTE, as well as a confirmed link with Charlotta Gattschalk, a woman who has hired a professional hitman to do her dirty work. Altogether it adds up to a nasty racket. True, its precise nature is undefined, but we aim to get to the bottom of it. Then there are the two companies that seem to be so inextricably intertwined. Whatever the relationship is, we aim to find out. He is dumbfounded. 'I cannot believe it. This is way over my head.'

'I'm not saying I believe it either,' I answer. 'All I'm presenting to you is a series of scenarios. Take your pick.'

'Laville, mixed up in international terrorism? Are you sure he's not being set up in some sort of elaborate scam? These things happen don't they?'

He looks to me for affirmation.

'Anything is possible,' I reassure him. 'Like I said, we don't know the precise nature of what we're working on.'

He nods his head in understanding.

I glance at my notes. 'Let me ask you this. What knowledge do you have of Laville's wealth? What were you told? Or what did you infer?'

'I didn't ask.

'Please.' He rubs his hands over his face. 'It's not the sort of topic one discusses in normal conversation. I had always assumed that he had inherited a modest amount of money and through wise investments had managed to make a lot more. I knew that he wasn't born rich. Everybody seems to be doing it these days. Laville is always talking about the stock market, reading the Financial Times. Being a director of a couple of companies. As a matter of fact, we used to joke that he was paying more attention to the markets than he was to science. It seemed to have gotten under his skin, like gambling. I must admit it made me feel uneasy that the line between science and business was becoming increasingly blurred.

I'm an old-fashioned romantic. Dr Laville and I used to talk late into the night about it. He firmly believed that business was there to help science. He always used to tell me about the way the Medicis kept culture alive. I didn't buy it. I've never been a dedicated capitalist. We agreed to disagree.'

He sweeps his hand through his hair in that gesture that only boys do so well.

He looks at me as though he's had a brilliant thought. 'Maybe he got involved with these people once he started running out of money gambling on the stock market,' he says eagerly.

'What about blackmail?' he adds hopefully.

'I don't think so. Anyway I don't think that would in any way negate the facts at hand,' I say. 'You also understand that nothing of this has to leak out to him.'

'I suppose you have ways and means of making me disappear,' he responds bitterly.

'We do.'

His expression shows that he actually believes me.

'What do you want from me? More importantly, why have you told me?'

'Just wanted to see if you were involved.'

'And are convinced that I'm not?'

'I am.'

'Why? What makes you think that this is not a grand acting job on my part, that I'm not up to my eyeballs in this heinous racket, that I'm not going to pick up the phone to Laville as soon as you leave?'

'You don't look like the acting type to me,' I answer.

He slumps back into his chair. 'I've always heard things about him.'

I prick up my ears.

'No, it's not what you think. People at the London hospital where we worked used to try to run him down, saying that he gave himself airs and graces. Drove a Jaguar, Thatcherite lackey and all that. The thing is, he didn't really have an air of self-importance. He enjoyed wealth and luxury, restaurants, flying first class, holidays and all that, but he never pretended to be something he was not. I used to defend him, telling his detractors that if they bothered to ask, he would tell them exactly what his roots were. I wouldn't say that he went around boasting about the fact that he came from a middle-class background, but then neither did he hide it. He was that he worked himself up. You know what the English are like, always petulant and spiteful in the face of success. I never listened to them. It's also one of the reasons I work here in Holland.'

It's interesting news to me. I have always thought that the Dutch, of all the European nations, were the least ambitious, preferring to wallow in a state of permanent lethargy.

'What's the deal?' he asks me suddenly, catching me off-guard. 'Do you wish for me to be an informer?'

He says it in pedantic and precise phrase. It sounds almost comical, like a line from a bad film.

'No, I wish for you to keep things as they are. To pretend that everything is normal.'

'It's going to be difficult. I don't see him often - he's not some sort of surrogate family member - but what happens when I do? He is what he is. Somebody that I'm immensely fond of. Somebody that has been very, very kind to me.'

The enormity of what I've done sinks in. It is too late to turn back. I can only hope that his nerve doesn't fail. I also hope that Boehme never hears of this. It is not a very professional thing to have done.

'Have you ever seen this woman?'

Oddly, he turns the picture sideways, as if hoping to see her better.

'Nope. She looks like Brezhnev's sister.'

'She was. In spirit anyway.'

'I've had dinner at his house. Same sort of people as him. Medical specialists, people who ran hospitals and clinics, the odd stockbroker. No-one remotely like this.'

'Laville likes to surround himself with beautiful women,' he smiles.

'Is it possible,' I say to him very carefully, 'to let me know when he next arrives in Amsterdam, or in Europe? If you know.'

'Surely you have ways of tracking people?'

'We do, but we have nothing against false passports, which are as easy to get as takeaway chicken, if you move in the right circles.'

'You're not trying to crucify him, are you?'

'No. Merely trying to establish if he is without sin.'

'Nobody is without sin.'

'True,' I concede, 'but I want to find out if Laville's sin is mortal, or merely venal.'

*

There's a fax on my desk. It is a police report from London. Ringed in red by some smart-arse in the office, as if I wouldn't notice it.

It details an explosion that occurred in the underground parking of Guy's and St. Thomas Hospital in London. A car bomb. One person killed. The car was a red Jaguar.

It belonged to Dr Laville.

The person killed was a client services man who had arranged to collect the car for servicing at 4:15 pm. Mikale Yegev, a Russian financier believed to have links to the Russian Mafia, was in the same hospital for heart surgery.

The package from Biogen has also arrived. It consists of a couple of glossy brochures with pictures of smiling staff members, their philanthropic efforts in Third World countries, and how their drugs are improving the quality of our lives.

I phone Helm as I flip through the pages.

'What car does Yegev have?'

'A black chauffeur-driven Mercedes.'

'Are you telling me that the bombers were so inept as to confuse a red Jaguar with a black Mercedes?'

Dr Laville must be breathing heavily, a very confused man. By a stroke of luck he does not have to explain the attempt on his life to the police. Yegev's stay at the hospital is a fortuitous coincidence. He has become the victim of misidentification. He and his colleagues can shake their heads at the parlous state of world affairs. Even London is not safe from Russian riff-raff.

Inside, he must be wondering why there is a contract on his life. Unless he knows the reason.

Laurier is on the phone. 'He called to tell me about the bomb blast. Something about a Russian Mafia assassination and his car getting blown up by mistake. Up until now I was prepared to give him the benefit of the doubt.'

I heave a sigh of relief.

The phone doesn't stop ringing.

It's Helm again. 'He's disappeared.'

'Who's disappeared?'

'Laville. He knew he was being followed. Booked a first-class ticket to the Bahamas. Duly arrived at the airport in a chauffer-driven courtesy car. Waited in the executive lounge. Had his complimentary drink. Read his newspaper. Went to the washrooms. Never came out. Or he came out in disguise. We found out that he left on a chartered jet. He had made two reservations. Tricky bastard. Must have known that his phone was being tapped.'

'Where did the plane go to?'

'The pilot says Prague. That's all he knows. He says it was a normal business flight. He does two a day.'

'And there's more news, I'm afraid. Picked this up off Reuters, the financial news service. Financial scandal this time. I'll explain as best as I can:

It seems that Biogen has recently come under investigation by the American Securities and Exchange Commission - the body that regulates dealings on the American stock market - about some share-dealing. Biogen as a company seems to exist on paper only. And an expensive piece of paper it is. Since its formation five years ago, it has neither produced nor sold any goods. Rather, it seems that the directors managed to get enormous sums of money into the company solely on test trials conducted by Sym-Tech. The tests were for an eye disease called CMV retinitis. It is caused by the cytomegalo-virus, a herpes virus. The drugs block the production of a protein - via genetic manipulation - that the virus needs to replicate. The drugs were supposed to go on the market next year, and were expected to net the company something like 100 million dollars per year in the US alone, hence the mad rush by investors into the company. Well, it seems that the tests were either forged or didn't happen and the US Food and Drug Administration is very, very unhappy. No drugs are forthcoming, nor are any expected. The consequences of which is that shares in the company that were once worth about thirty pounds are now worth about fifty pence.'

It's all a bit too much for me.

'What,' I ask, 'has the LTTE to do with all this?'

'I think it might be beginning to make sense to me actually,' answers Helm confidently. 'Perhaps the LTTE invested a large sum of their money in this venture and it's now all gone down the drain. As I told you earlier, they have a very sophisticated investment arm, and lots of prominent investors were taken in by Biogen. Biotechnology is one of the hot markets at the moment. We currently have a group of people working through the list of investors. See if anything comes up. There's not much hope there though. Chances are the money was funnelled into Biogen via any one of the hundreds of investment brokers in New York or London. It's pretty easy to buy shares.'

*

At 2 am my phone rings. I stumble out of bed, once again cursing my pathetic ability to organise a phone line into my bedroom.

'He arrived at my flat,' says Laurier.

Oh, Christ, he's blown it. Blown, blown, blown. Signed his own death warrant. Whoever is after Laville must know of their friendship. Tapped his phone.

Then I hear his nervous laughter and the rumble of a truck in the background.

'I'm calling from a payphone,' he says, almost as if he's reading my mind. Huge silent sigh of relief from me. I could kiss him.

'What did he say?'

'Not much. A story about embezzlement in Biogen and how he was being set up. I almost believed him. That he's on the run from Interpol, trying to clear his name. Made a joke about that doctor from the American TV series. The one that was supposed to have murdered his wife.'

'*The Fugitive*,' I say. 'What does he want from you?'

'Moral support, he says. Wants to know that at least someone believes in his innocence. He's in a terrible way. Very frightened.

Grown a beard and wearing jeans and a khaki jacket. I've never seen him like that before.'

'Did he say where he was staying?'

'No, he wouldn't say. He did tell me that he had caught busses from Prague to Amsterdam.'

It must have been difficult for him, after all the first-class travelling, sitting in a bus with tourists and itinerant workers. Getting sweaty and dirty, washing in toilets, eating greasy food.

'Did he say where he was going next?'

'Slovak Republic. He has money there.'

'He's using you,' I say. 'He knows that you know.'

Laurier is silent. I can feel him being torn apart and I regret my brutality.

'Anything else?'

'Yes. He apologised for the shares that he had given me.'

I give him Benschop-Fehr's telephone number. She has the resources for any rapid-response action should he be in any trouble.

'Get some sleep,' I say gently.

I debate whether I ought to call and wake her up. I do. And I'm glad.

She unhesitatingly promises to send someone around to watch Laurier's apartment. She also promises to organise a phone tap on his phone.

Chapter 15

Boehme is in the conference room. He asks me to enter.

'Got this morning,' he says, waving a video tape at me. 'Surveillance tape from the German side of the border post.'

'Why', I ask him sourly, irritated from the previous night's disturbed sleep, 'do we still have border posts?'

'There will *always* be border posts,' he grunts emphatically.

He switches the video on. 'This was filmed at 3:30 yesterday morning.'

Even on tape the harshness of the place sparkles through. The harsh neon lights, hard benches, and the vaporous cold air. Then there are the guards, miserable bitter men, as most of us would be if we had to stand in the open at the three in the morning, day after day.

I can see why Boehme says that they will always exist. How else are we going to torture our fellow man so subtly?

The man on the tape is a sad and pathetic figure. Nothing at all like assassins in the movies. He has a skinny frame with a prominent paunch, a sign of excessive alcohol consumption. His straggly blond hair is thinning in the centre and he attempts to hide the bald spot by sweeping long strands of hair across it. When the camera is high up on the wall, you notice these things.

He also chain-smokes, nervously clinging to the packet as though it was the most valuable object in the world. On the table there is a tattered old bag with bits of grubby clothing sticking out. It's all in real-time so we get to see it exactly as it happened. The look of surprise on the face of one of the guards as he gingerly removes a rifle from the bag. The way their stance changes from a sort of swaggering bravado to military precision. The speed at which they snap the handcuffs on him, how he collapses back into his chair. It is sordid and pathetic.

Watching it so dispassionately it is easy to see how the soldiering instinct is triggered by fear rather than by discipline.

'Terrible weapon,' says Boehme. 'American. Barrett Model 90 bolt- action sniper rifle, used in the Gulf War. Get shot by one of those in the upper body and you're dead from internal injuries. It shatters everything inside you. Body armour is useless as well. It's a good thing he decided to blow you up instead.'

'Thanks Boehme,' I say. 'Does Benschop-Fehr know about this?'

'Not yet,' he snorts.

'Did I mention he was caught on the German side,' he adds sarcastically.

'There's no need for such childish behaviour,' I chide him, mentioning her offer to help Laurier. Boehme knows that we do not have the power to send armed guards to homes, or organise phone-taps so quickly.

'Okay, I'll phone her.'

'Good,' I answer, wishing my unspoken reasoning could have had its basis in charity rather than mere expediency.

*

Boehme and I drive to the small German village of Monchenberg, on the outskirts of Aachen. It is at the intersection of Germany, Holland and Belgium. It is not a very busy border crossing, used mainly by nature-loving tourists who visit the three countries. There are a lot of hills to climb nearby.

It is one of Louw's two fatal mistakes. He does not look like a tourist.

He should have used one of the busier posts further north that have a lot of traffic. Secondly, he crossed over at 3 in the morning. Guards are restless and bored at that time, seeking any diversion. He should have known. It is almost as if he wanted to get caught.

About half way to our destination Boehme phones Benschop-Fehr.

He hadn't forgotten. He's just making sure that we get there before she does.

'She has the use of a helicopter,' I say slyly.

He just clenches his jaw and keeps his eyes on the road.

In the interview room Louw is even more desperate. He begs for another cigarette but the officer conducting the interview points surlily to a sign on the wall that says NO SMOKING. I feel a twinge of sadness for him, for this man who tried to blow me up and who is now grovelling so pathetically in front of us. Boehme and I watch through the two-way mirror.

This is my first interview. The banality of it shocks. Instead of a cast of eccentric characters shadowboxing words at each other, there is, in front of us, a sad man and a disinterested bureaucrat going through the motions. The officer is from Bonn. He reads questions from a notebook at his elbow. His party trick must be to wear people down by sheer boredom. It must be the worst kind of torture.

It is quite possible that he may be a consummate liar but to me it is clear that Louw knows nothing. He looks like he simply wants to curl up and go to sleep. For a moment he lifts his head up and stares directly at me. He's simply looking in our direction, but there is so much misery in his eyes. It is almost as if he is asking me for atonement.

I step back.

He planted both the bombs, he confesses. The one in my flat as well as the one in Laville's car. Knows nothing. Money paid into his account. Received instructions via e-mail. He has an account at the local cyber cafe. He did it for the money.

Then he starts to weep.

I cannot take it anymore.

*

'Louw's e-mail account is a dead end. It came from another cybercafe in Amsterdam.' I announce to everyone.

I don't tell them that the information was provided by my good neighbour, who unfortunately is displaying latent signs of turning into a pest.

Boehme, Benschop-Fehr and I are sitting in Boehme's office. Boehme stands up and starts to pace. It is a sign that he has some serious thinking to do.

We wait.

He goes to the flip-chart on his wall and draws a big circle on it.

'What we have here,' he stops to stare at Benschop-Fehr for a second, as if seeing her for the first time, 'looks increasingly complex.'

It's hard to tell if she's forgiven him for his hard-headedness. She meets his glance with an admirable impassiveness.

'This link.' He draws another circle, then an arrow from left to right, touching both circles. One has Laville's name in it and the other Gattschalk's. In the centre, above the two circles, he puts a cross.

'Connects Gattschalk with Laville.'

He taps the cross. 'And this connects the LTTE to Laville.

'The question is: do we connect all three?'

'Perhaps it is the other way around.' Benschop-Fehr twirls her pencil in the air in front of her face, as if it could somehow deflect the intensity of Boehme's glare.

'What do you mean?'

'Our informants within the LTTE are not sophisticated enough to gauge opinion, feel the pulse of an organisation, but my gut feeling is that the LTTE has nothing to do with this. I get the impression that there is an air of angry puzzlement inside the LTTE - that they feel we are harassing them as a prelude to setting them up for something else.

We know that on the surface they seem to be just as puzzled about the deaths of the Tamil nationals as we are. The link between the LTTE and Laville is tenuous at best. All we have is a telephone number in a book. I don't think that it's all a big act on their part. What would their motive be?'

'Very interesting,' smiles Boehme. It is his killer smile. It is not without charm. It is also not necessarily a prelude to devastating sarcasm or a put-down. Boehme is much too complex for that. He knows how to give and take, that wars are sometimes won by stretching the elasticity of the front.

'Perhaps *they* know who *your* informants are. Perhaps they are one step ahead of us.'

Benschop-Fehr nods her head, as if agreeing with Boehme. Her eyes tell another story.

'Perhaps there is another possibility we ought to examine,' I interrupt quickly, lest they start a cat-fight in front of me.

I tell them about Helm's hypothesis, that the LTTE had invested large sums of money in Biogen and it had all evaporated, hence the possibility of the organisation carrying out some sort of revenge attack on Gattschalk and Laville.

It is a weak argument, full of holes, but it's better than nothing.

'What do we know about Gattschalk's company, Sym-Tech?' responds Boehme.

'Not much,' I answer. 'It's German-registered, for the purposes of setting up base in Lausitz. That's all, no office, no phone number. It's a phantom company.'

'All I am saying is that we have to make room for other possibilities in our plans,' persists Benschop-Fehr.

'I agree with you one hundred percent. But I would like to know what the basis for your reasoning is?'

'I think I already told you that.'

Boehme pauses. It is as if I am not in the room. It is not so much hostility as so much highly energised tension emanating from both parties. Flowing, crackling, sparkling.

'All possibilities will be given thorough consideration,' answers Boehme pedantically. 'We will leave no stone unturned in our pursuit for the truth.'

'Golem,' she mutters under her breath.

Benschop-Fehr is dawdling outside the office. She stops me as I leave

'Need to talk to you about your boyfriend,' she grimaces at me as if about to give me mildly unpleasant news.

'What boyfriend?'

'The American.'

'What about him?' The anger rises inside me. She has no right to meddle. More importantly, they have no right to follow me around without my permission. Even if it is for my own good.

'He's ex-CIA. Thought you ought to know.'

'What's he doing now?'

'Don't know. We haven't checked that far yet, but he is listed as a code Z-256.'

'What does that mean?'

'He's in the private sector.'

I heave a sigh of relief. He hasn't exactly lied to me.

I tell her what I know about him, and the company he works for, or claims to work for.

'We weren't spying on you, in case you were wondering,' she says.

'Oh?'

'We get a regular list of all foreign operatives on Dutch soil, active or inactive. What intrigued me was the fact that his address was in the same street as yours. Even more fascinating is that he rents an apartment in a building so close to you.'

'Did he travel to Amsterdam on a false passport?' I ask.

'No.'

'Good,' I answer. I don't wish to know anything further.

'What's with all the paranoia anyway? I thought we were all on the same side?'

She laughs sardonically and walks away.

*

He has left a message for me on my answering-machine. I phone him back. We meet in neutral territory, on the stretch of road outside our apartments. It is 5:30 pm, my favourite time for walking, other than early in the mornings. Autumn is almost over. It will be winter soon. Contemplating winter always gives a warm glow. Of course, when the cold comes around I hate it. Anticipation is so much better than reality. It's all those other images that float around in my head - Christmas, shopping, fires, not doing much.

I introduce him to the joys of *vlaamse frites,* with mayonnaise. As we stand at the kiosk I say casually, to him, 'By the way, I hear that you used to work for the CIA.'

There's a look of mock horror on his face. 'Does that mean that you won't sleep with me?'

'What makes you think...' I splutter.

He puts his hand lightly across my mouth, his eyes twinkling. It's a playful gesture. But it's also a very intimate gesture. I feel his fingers burn into my skin. I remove his hand from my face. Gently, as if I would give him offence, instead of the other way around. I can smell his hands. They smell of wood, as if he'd been chopping trees.

'Relax, I was only kidding. I thought you Europeans were a lot more easygoing than us Americans.'

'We generally are,' I answer.

'Yeah, I did work for the CIA. I quit five years ago. As your records will show,' he adds with a touch of bitterness.

'I'm sorry,' I say.

'Why did *you* join Europol?'

'Gives me an opportunity to travel,' I answer.

Then I notice that I haven't let go of his fingers. His hands are at my side. I let go. He doesn't, putting his fingers through mine.

I feel like I'm fourteen again.

We walk. I point out all the sights to him. An hour later my hand is still in his. There is a experimental theatre featuring a group of dancers from China. We go in and sit on the floor. It is very uncomfortable but as the dancers weave their tales of love and loss the pain fades away. Everything becomes a blur of bodies and red chemise.

After coffee I lead him back home. We follow the canals, watching the vignettes of life through the small portholes of the boats. Most people seem to be watching television. We stop near the Hof bridge to gaze at a garishly coloured boat drifting by, festooned with bright lights. There is a party happening on deck, discordant strains of a violin wafting through the air.

He starts singing to me. Kris Kristofferson. '*Take the ribbon from her hair, shake it loose and let it fall...*'

It is a corny, self-indulgent weepie of a song but he does it well.

The funny thing is, when I was a self-absorbed, rebellious teenager I owned a copy of Kristofferson's greatest hits, endlessly listening to Me and Bobby McGee. It was my song.

He picks me up and places me on a balustrade. I put my arms around him for balance. He kisses me. I kiss him back. After a while neither of us can breathe.

He grins and nuzzles my neck, sending shivers down my spine. Then we start all over again. And again. He slips his hands up my dress. I have no idea why I'd put on a garter and stockings, but I'm glad I did. I feel his hand on my thigh, on my mound. I feel the breath sucked out of my lungs.

I also feel my bum slipping off the rails. Then I collapse into his arms in laughter.

Outside our respective buildings there is a mental tussle, but only a minor one. I follow him upstairs to his apartment. It is completely empty except for a large, low bed on the floor of the bedroom. I kick off my shoes and walk across the bare wooden floor to the window. It is strange to see my block from this end. I cannot see my window, for which I'm glad.

He is behind me, his mouth on my neck, hands on my breasts. Then he slides my dress up to my hips, pressing against me. His hands cup the flesh of my bum, kneading them through my panties.

'I don't have any condoms,' he whispers to me.

'Neither do I,' I say, reaching for the belt of his trousers.

Chapter 16

The lights of the new high-rise apartments along the Thames look beguiling. The seaman standing next to me and I share the same thought. I can tell by the look on his face. That we would be better off sitting near a fire high up in one of those fancy apartments that you see in the Sunday supplements. Watching the world go by from up there, instead of from the depths of the river.

Laville had phoned again, the silly man. This time they had a trace. I had listened to the conversation, or rather the monologue. He was full of bluster and self-justification, protesting again about his "setup". He also lied again about being on his way to the Slovak Republic. The call was traced to a payphone at the Amsterdam docks. By the time the police had got there he had disappeared. Fortunately for us, the numerous snitches that work at the docks had fingered a boat that specialised in the cross-channel transportation of human cargo, illegal or otherwise. Apparently large numbers of people with perfectly legal documents make use of the service to avoid detection of their movements. It is a low-risk, high profit service. The boat on its way to England had left a few minutes before the police arrived.

It is a long shot. He could still be in Amsterdam, or on any number of ships leaving the harbour. Before I knew what was happening, I was in a military helicopter to London.

It's nice to know that Boehme seems to finally take me seriously.

*

I think about the best unconsummated sex I've ever had. About his hard, hairy body. His semen in my hands. His tongue exploring me.

I shiver.

'Are you cold?' asks Helm solicitously.

I nod in affirmation. He drapes his coat over my shoulders. I'm not really cold.

My mind is back is Amsterdam again.

After, he'd lit up a joint, asking me if I'd minded. That's when I knew he couldn't possibly be in the CIA.

The boat is slippery, with thin plastic railings instead of metal. The entire body seems to be made of plastic. There are triangular indentations on the deck, which helps to get a foothold. They told me to dress as if I was going hiking, but to wear black.

It is an alien vessel, a cross between a dinghy and a submarine. The 40-foot craft is coated with the same kind of black paint that makes the Stealth bomber invisible to radar. The manufacturers, showing a spectacular lack of imagination, have called it the "Stealth Assault Craft". They had first called it a "manned underwater vehicle".

A combination of reduced infrared, acoustic, electromagnetic, visual and radar signatures makes it almost impossible to detect. The signatures make it difficult for sophisticated nautical defensive systems to track the craft. From a distance it looks like one of Batman's flying gadgets. I wonder how much of its impact relies on primeval instincts; astonishment, fear and terror rather than technological wizardry. We humans have a boundless capacity for delusion.

The deck space is very small - enough for three people. We are six. Next to us are the two storage units that contain the "chariots" - diver propulsion units that allow the commandos to move independently to their targets. The Special Boat Service crew members are the elite of England's marine forces. However, a lack of suitable wars means that the outfit has to hunt down drug dealers, terrorists and smugglers of human cargo. The captain looks about eighteen, with his short cropped hair and drawn haggard face that comes from too much exercise or too much heroin. Judging from his muscles I suspect it is the former.

He also doesn't look very happy with us aboard, but it is an order from the highest authorities so he doesn't have a choice. He's on his radio, casting a lugubrious eye over us.

'Down!' he snaps suddenly. The automatic doors whirr open and the satellite dish retracts instantly. Inside the tiny cabin there is space for four people, each compartmentalised section the size of a fighter plane's cockpit, with just as many instruments glowing in the dark. There is a small armoury section where an assortment of high-tech weapons are kept. Helm and I are squeezed together. It is very uncomfortable to be wedged against all those guns, like being brushed up by a dozen men, all with erections.

We submerge. To sink into an inky blackness in a plastic boat the size of a Volkswagen is a terrifying feeling. The water sloshes ominously overhead and we duck instinctively. The glass canopy is waterproof, which somehow doesn't ease our fears. We can see the waves close above us as if they were about to come gushing in. I understand how the Egyptians must have felt after Moses willed the Red Sea down on them.

Below deck artificial eyes and ears create the world above for us. The phosphor screen is fed data from an RMU - Remote Mobile Unit, a remote-controlled flying video camera the size and shape of a football which hovers above us. It is an electro-optical device that uses infrared light to take pictures. The operator uses a joystick to manoeuvre the ball through the air around the craft. It is eerie, almost like having an external set of eyes. The craft is a light-blue boat, badly in need of a coat of paint. There are crates on the deck and we can also see two men having a smoke break on deck. The flying gadget also has a sound amplification unit built into it which provides telescopic listening. The two men are English. They are talking about the rise of house prices, moaning about their mortgages and their wives.

The seaman controlling the equipment squirms with embarrassment, as if they were talking about gang-bangs. The banal is just as bad as the obscene.

'Why', I ask the seaman, 'do you still have these green screens that look like ancient computer equipment?'

'The phosphor screen is purposefully coloured green because the human eye can differentiate more shades of green than other phosphor colours.' He breathes a sigh of relief.

The boat moves forward. It only submerges a few feet, but there is total blackness and an overwhelming sense of claustrophobia. Submerged it can travel at 50 knots per hour. I have never been in a conventional submarine so cannot say what it feels like but I do know that it would be a more pleasurable experience than this. At least there would be freedom of movement. This must be akin to flying underwater in a state-of-the-art fighter plane.

Then we stop with a sickening lurch, like an elevator with a broken cable, but in reverse. The hatch whirrs open and before Helm and I can move the SBS boys are out, shoving us out of the way. There is not a single drop of water inside the boat.

Procedure dictates that we have to stay inside. They don't want us getting shot and having to answer for it.

Outside we can hear what sounds like a polite hail in the evening. There is a two-way discussion. It is not possible to discern the words but it all sounds very civilised. One of the SBS seamen returns and motions us over. He helps me out. I climb the spidery rope ladder up to the deck of the ship. It is constructed entirely out of nylon, with no wooden steps, and I sway around dizzily. They do it so easily.

On the deck of the ship the sailors and the captain stand around gazing at us, as though we were performing an irritating but necessary chore. There is no anger or apprehension from their side. They even point out the crates that contain the alcohol, under the impression that that's what we're there for.

We're after something more important than illegal contraband.

I scan the faces. There is only one illegal immigrant on board. The rest of the passengers are a motley bunch of shifty-eyed Englishmen who, for reasons of their own, wish to enter their own country illegally.

They keep their eyes on the ground as if caught soliciting sex in a public place. Laville is nowhere to be seen.

Helm shrugs his shoulders. 'Tough luck. It was a pretty wild shot in the first place.'

The backup police boat that was lurking in the background has arrived, so we go below deck with the dogs to check out the cabins. They're tiny, squalid places. One kick of the door is all it takes to see that they're empty.

One of the officers shouts out loudly. We rush over, clattering down the passageway.

In the cabin Laville is dangling by his tie, legs flailing wildly. The officers scramble frantically to reach him.

He is alive. Blue in the face, terrified and anguished, but still alive. How is it that I end up feeling sorry for all these souls? Crooks, murderers, cheats. He collapses into the arms of the officer. A big blubbering baby.

In the stark interrogation room of Thames Division, they offer him hot tea and a blanket. He is shivering uncontrollably, in a state of shock. His head is bowed low, almost between his legs.

'It's all over, it's all over,' he mutters repeatedly. The others glance at me. He's had enough, let him sleep, their eyes say.

I shake my head. No, my eyes say. Let's question him now, while he is like this. Before his strength seeps back into him, and his arrogance returns.

The duty officer grimaces in distaste for a split second, but he is aware of the chain of command. He goes back inside. The others avoid making eye contact with me. I hope that I am right. Someone switches on the microphone. The sound of Laville's snuffles comes through.

'Right then, Laville. What we have here is a pretty serious list of problems. You're in very, very deep trouble. You have two choices. Either you help us with our enquiries or you don't. If you don't, you'll face the full consequences of British law.' He glances up at me. 'European law.'

Sergeant Potter is a throwback to those Fifties police officers who were spread far and wide in the dying days of the British empire. The ones that you see in the old movies as loyal sidekicks to Stewart Granger. Less brutal and hostile than his Victorian predecessor, but still imbued with a sense of British indomitability. He has short black hair, a severely clipped moustache and an accent from one of the English counties that I cannot place. In the old days he would have been considered very handsome. Now he looks vaguely comical. You would not want to make fun of him in his presence though. There is a brutal glint in his eye and underneath his uniform a hint of firm, hard muscle.

What Potter says is not strictly true. Laville has committed only a misdemeanour. He could walk out on us.

Laville talks. He doesn't need prompting. What he says is not entirely surprising.

Sym-Tech, via Gattschalk, was putting the screws on Biogen for twenty million dollars following the market collapse of Biogen. The large amount of Biogen shares that Sym-Tech owned were worthless. They had been close collaborators once working on many projects together, but things had turned sour after the CMV retinitis debacle. Biogen simply didn't have the money to pay, so Sym-Tech was attempting to extort cash from other major shareholders. They had even robbed one of the other directors, carting away the entire contents of his mansion in Berkshire.

One of the police officers checks immediately. The details of the police report show up on the screen. A burglary report was filed, a Mr Jonathan Pocock, entire household removed while the family were away.

He raises a puzzled head when Potter mentions the LTTE and the dead Tamils. Laville vehemently denies any knowledge of them.

There is no need for Potter to ask questions. The words come gushing out of Laville in between the sobs and the self-pity. It is a tale Boehme would find most interesting.

Potter silently signals cut to the recording team behind the opaque glass window. His eyes are on me, both accusatory and triumphant.

I write a question on a piece of paper and have it passed to him.

He reads it, then addresses Laville. 'Did you try to kill yourself or did someone try to kill you?'

'I have nothing to say.' Laville answers.

I shrug my shoulders. It has been a long night and I still have to wait for the typed report. Some of Laville's comments were unintelligible.

There is a greasy all-night café across the road. It is patronised by early morning market workers, truckers, and a couple of tired-looking young girls, gruesomely pale under the harsh lights of the restaurant.

The waitress minces towards us. 'All-day breakfast or all-day supper?'

'What's the difference?' asks Helm.

'You don't get the mini steak for breakfast,' she answers, 'and how many times do I have to tell you this?'

He grins at her.

We are both very hungry, and order more junk than is good for us. Sausages, eggs, baked beans, toast and lots of tea. All served on tin plates by the loud Cockney waitress who has no right to be so cheery at three-thirty in the morning.

'I hope you got what you wanted,' says Helm.

'I'm not sure,' I answer, taking the first sip of my tea. It is a sweet elixir, infusing my body with a warm glow.

*

The two doctors face each other across the table. It wasn't my idea. Boehme brought Laurier with him when he arrived.

'He understands what the hell this company is all about,' he answers when I ask him. It comes with a helpless shrug. Boehme is floundering, that much is plain to see. What worries me, though, is that it might not be the case itself, but something else. It is the way he reacts to situations, the lack of preciseness that he has shown in the past. He knows that I know.

Laville is wearing his sorry-but-superior look. He is now clean-shaven and upright. A neat, blue tailored suit and a flashy business tie complete his transformation. His composure has returned too. He had seen his lawyer in the morning, and this seems to have given him more confidence.

Laville's hands are raised upwards, palms turned towards the ceiling, as if he was asking forgiveness from his God.

It is hard to tell if he is genuinely contrite, or just a consummate actor. Perhaps it is both, a little portion of him that is genuinely sorry for the deception and lies he has inflicted on his good friend.

Laurier is trying hard to control his emotions, no doubt aware that he is being watched.

The tape recorder is on. Legally, it is not supposed to be, but we all pretend not to be aware of its existence, as if it were a natural phenomenon, part of the background noise.

The doctor's supplicating voice is clear. It is different from yesterday. This time I can tell he is lying. Now he is full of self-recrimination, asking forgiveness for his sins.

*

'It's about drugs,' says Boehme. 'Drugs, power, money and politics.'

He takes a swig from his cool drink can.

The view from the office is the same as that from the Stealth Assault Craft, apartments glittering in the night like baubles.

'Somebody's been talking to you,' I say.

He is still.

'They've started the ball rolling,' he finally answers.

'Who's "they"?,' I ask.

'Biogen.'

'What do they have to do with anything?'

'I didn't know at first. Then I had a chat to Laurier on the way here. This drug that they're all talking about. Biogen was developing it, with the help of Sym-Tech but all the distribution and marketing would have been carried out by third party - whoever they managed to sell it to. It is like a food chain, with the multinational corporations on top. They have the power. Although they didn't lose any money in Biogen's fall, they don't want to lose face by being associated in any way with scandal.'

*

Boehme goes to meditation classes.

There was a blue leaflet on the floor of his car once. I had stepped on it, picked it up and put it in his cubby hole - but not before taking a quick glance. It was from the Mystical Centre. Boehme had ringed 'Meditation Class - Tuesday, 7 pm. Thirty Guilders per session.' I had looked up the Mystical Centre in the telephone directory, phoned at 7:20 pm, and asked to speak to Josef Boehme. The woman said he couldn't come to the phone as he was in a class. Nosy, nasty me.

I think about it now because he is so still. He doesn't even tense up his shoulders, which is usually a dead giveaway with most people.

'Politics,' he says finally.

'I know,' I almost shout , 'and I don't care. I don't want to know. As long as I can carry on with my job. Is that understood?'

He nods almost imperceptibly. His face is sad and droopy. Like I've just broken his heart. My voice is trembling slightly. It is the trembling that comes after a fear-induced adrenaline rush.

Laurier comes out of the room. He looks like he's just staggered way from a horrible accident. I half expect to see blood on his clothes.

He stops, runs his hands through his air, as if trying to brush away the thoughts buzzing around his head. The last time he did that it was a different gesture. It was in the lecture hall, and his action then had a certain rakishness about it. It was both effete and attractive at the same time. He has an air of bereavement about him now so it's difficult to know what to say. Besides, other people's sorrow always reduces me to inarticulateness. Not to mention the fact that he avoids looking at me. Studiously.

He walks right past us and out the door. For a moment I consider following him but ennui grips me.

I have a cup of coffee instead. Boehme shrugs his shoulders helplessly at me.

Chapter 17

Biogen's headquarters are in a tall glitzy building in the Docklands area of London. It's all self-consciously new. The whole area resembles the set of a movie, from the strangely small crowds that walk determinedly through the streets to the offices that don't seem have any function other than to present a facade. At Biogen it is even worse. Everybody is carrying out their tasks normally, as if there is no thread of doom hanging over their heads. It's not that they are forcefully optimistic, merely chillily professional.

The receptionist at the front greets me with a smile and asks me to take-a-seat-he-won't-be-long. Pre-conceptions are deeply rooted in our psyches, that is why it is such a jolt to the system when they are shattered. The PR function of a company is normally headed - firstly by a woman - and if it's a major corporation - by someone under fifty but over forty. Someone who is still sexually attractive but old enough to have had responsibility. Someone who is eminently telegenic for us to believe her lies but is at the same time sexually desirable. This is how psychologists tell businesses to operate if they know what's good for them.

So I'm not really prepared for the red-faced fiftyish man in a pink and blue pinstriped suit and red braces that saunters over to me as though I'd brought him the weekly shopping. He looks at my card over the top of his glasses, then at me. I stare at his coiffured silvery mane, thinking that he spends more time on his hair than I do on mine. An appointment had been made with the head of public relations but nobody had given me a name.

He ushers me into a boardroom which has a great view of the London skyline. On the left wall there is a very large perspex board with the company logo as well a some vaguely abstract spiral bits that are meant to represent stylised DNA strands. It is the same logo I had seen on the plaque at Groningen University.

'What can I do for you, miss ...er.' He looks at my card again. 'Miss De Hoop.'

His superciliousness is annoying. I would like to tell him that for a man who works for a company that is in such serious trouble he's got no right to have the attitude that he has, but it occurs to me that he's probably a director, and, as such, already has a good chunk of his fees and gratuities stashed away somewhere safe. An account in the Cayman Islands, a beach-house in Tunisia. It's the ordinary workers who will have to take steep salary cuts, put in extra hours and then finally be made redundant. His type will just slide lubriciously into another well-paid directorship.

I open the folder before me. 'Everything. I have a letter from the SFO - the Serious Fraud Office authorising Europol access to all company records and audits, as well as to staff members. At all times.'

His face drains to a whitish pallor. Only his nose remains red, the broken capillaries from too much alcohol showing through.

'Any attempt at hindering the process and speed of the investigation will be viewed in a most serious light,' I continue.

He stares at me, his mind a battle to maintain his composure and to marshal his thoughts.

'Very well.' There is something in his eyes that is beyond hatred, a passionless desire to reach out and hit me hard across the face.

He stands up and leaves the room. It is disconcerting. It occurs to me that there may be hidden video cameras in the room, that someone is watching me being flustered.

When he returns he flings a stapled document across the shiny surface of the mahogany table. He doesn't bother hiding the contemptuous look on his face.

It is a document from the Serious Fraud Office. I flip through the pages. They have impounded all of Biogen's records. There is no unambiguity in the release. Everything. I flip the pages casually. My heart is thumping wildly.

I'm a firm believer in the dictum that for every problem there is a solution, for every door that closes another one opens, every ending entails a new beginning. There must be another start somewhere else.

I ask if I could use the bathroom.

'No,' he snarls, twisting his florid face into a skein of hatred. 'Get out.'

I pick up my folder and walk out as calmly as I can.

*

The computer geek upstairs is so happy to see me again that he practically drools all over the front of his shirt.

'It's got to be quick,' I say to him.

His nostrils flare up.

'Try me,' he challenges.

I plonk myself down next to him and give him the name of the company.

'Why the hurry?' he asks.

'The company is on the verge of closing down. I don't know how long it will be before total computer shutdown. The computers have been impounded but as far as I know, no-one's audited the data as yet.'

It's in the report that the pig had flung at me. A stroke of luck, spotting it. The audit report said that, due to a lack of technical resources, the systems audit was on hold until a suitably skilled person could be reassigned.

'Like doing this?' I ask as he types away furiously.

'Sure. We're not what the media makes us out to be, y'know.'

'Oh,' I murmur dubiously.

'Look, I have a code of honour; never intentionally delete or damage a file on a computer you hack, treat systems you hack as you would treat your own computer, notify system administrators about any security breaches you encounter, do not hack to steal money, do not distribute or collect pirated software.'

'That's more morals than I have,' I say to him.

He smiles, pleased with himself.

'Okay, let's see what we've got this time. Unix system, good. Let's use two different attack mechanisms.

'It's my own method, by the way. It's called Two-Kaauws,' he beams proudly.

'First, we use IP source address spoofing and TCP sequence number prediction to gain initial access to the workstation being used mostly as an X terminal. After root access had been obtained, the existing connection to another system is hijacked by means of a loadable kernel streams module.'

'Great,' I say, rubbing my hands in an attempt at false enthusiasm.

He downloads the entire contents of their file-server onto what hackers call a remote machine. It's basically any large, low-security computer that they can use undetected for storing large quantities of data. The computer that he uses belongs to Groningen University. It is perhaps a predictable choice, but I smile to myself at the irony of it. He provides me with login access and a password to the system so that I can log on from anywhere.

'Hullo, hullo, what's this?' he jerks his head back comically.

I lean forward.

'There's a block of data here that's been encrypted and hidden.'

'Can you get to it?' I ask.

'Depends on the file encryption method used. From the digital signature, I would say that they've used a program called Crypto File System, an encrypted file standard for Unix. It runs as a user-mode NFS server on the local machine, and passes any requests to theremote machine over an encrypted channel.'

'Can you crack it?'

'Depends on whether they used pseudo-random or chaotic numbers as a key stream. Either way, it will take a while.

'Cryptographic applications demand much more out of a pseudo-random number generator than most applications. For a source of bits to be cryptographically random, it must be computationally impossible to predict what the Nth random bit will be given complete knowledge of the algorithm or hardware generating the stream and the sequence of 0th through N-1st bits, for all N up to the lifetime of the source. A software generator has the function of expanding a truly random seed to a longer string of apparently random bits. The bottom line is: I'm going to need access to a Sparcstation 1 workstation to do this for me. It will take a few hours to run. Okay?'

'Yup,' I answer, my mind racing through a series of excuses as to why I cannot hang around this time.

His body stiffens. The blue veins on his pale neck stick out.

'Damn, damn, damn,' he shouts, banging the keyboard.

'What's wrong?' I ask in alarm.

'Alert sequence generator. It warns the systems administrator if an illegal file access is taking place. Looks like I've got a tail.'

'Can you shake him?' I ask worriedly.

He laughs at me. 'I can see that you don't know anything about computers. We don't shake a tail like the cops do. We call it ping-ping.'

He is tapping the keyboard furiously. A jumble of characters scroll down the screen. His head is thrust right up against the screen.

'Water!' he shout at me suddenly.

I stare at him dumbly.

He motions with his hand.

I hurriedly fetch him a glass of water.

It is a nerve-wracking wait. I pace behind him, watching him uttering oaths to himself. His scrawny shoulders rise and fall in a nervous tic.

Suddenly he shouts out with joy and kicks back the chair. It hits me on the chin.

He turns to me, overjoyed. I'm afraid I get caught up in the enthusiasm and throw my arms around his neck.

*

Another body has been found. It is in England, on the beach of the seaside resort of Brighton. An old couple out walking their dogs stumbled upon the corpse.

The body's hands were missing. This time there is an outcry. In the twelve hours since the discovery of the body a rally has been organised by the Tamil diaspora living in London. Helm sends me video footage again. There's a few hundred angry people chanting and waving placards around Hyde Park. With the leaders in front, I catch a glimpse of a very angry Laxman Kadirgamer. I feel uneasy.

*

The doctor is late. There's a good chance that he will not arrive. Considering what we've subjected him to, I wouldn't be surprised if he decided not to bother.

There is a knock on the door to the conference room. Ilsa ushers him in. He shuffles in, looking terrible. His face is wan, eyes circled by dark shadows. There is at least two day's growth of beard on his face.

'Traffic?' I enquire.

'No. Change of heart. And then back again.' He gives me an anguished smile. He is heartbroken, that much is plain to see.

He has a couple of books under his arm, so he looks like a reluctant schoolboy going for extra maths lessons.

'I've requested a couple of days leave from the university,' he says.

'I've brought you all the documentation that I have. It's no more than what an ordinary researcher would have access to. Also some background stuff from scientific journals.'

He has to sit next to me in order for both of us to have comfortable access to the computer screen. He stacks the books at his elbow, as if providing a barrier between myself and him.

I log in and then move through the myriad directory structures to get to the files for Biogen.

Recognition dawns on his face. 'Hang on a minute, this looks like the university computer...?'

'It is. We didn't have the disk space to download the entire contents of Biogen's computer system here.' I cannot resist a smirk. I have been infected with that peculiar brand of cockiness that hackers have.

'Miss De Hoop, you're like no-one else I've met,' he gently chides.

I explain Biogen's past and current financial position which the company had hidden the true details of to its shareholders, or at least glossed over the truth.

He is philosophical about his losses. 'I never had the money in the first place. I have always been distrustful of this whole racket. It's not like I actually went out and bought the shares.'

'This stuff is the new nirvana,' he continues. 'It's all about money. Greed is what drives these people. At the university they're trying to get us to have most of our research financed by companies. They call it private-public partnerships. They say that funding has to come from the private sector if we are to survive.'

'And you don't like it?'

'No.'

'Biogen has, or had, a number of different areas of research, as you are aware. There has been collaboration with Sym-Tech in a number of different areas of the biotechnology sector. Sym-tech offered favourable terms, once-off payments instead of a royalty amount like Biogen would be getting from organisation.'

I stop him. 'Terms for what?'

'Well, there are two ways the industry works. Let's say some big company approached Biogen and asked them to carry out research on a potential new drug. On successful completion of trials, Biogen would generally hand over all material to the company for a pre-negotiated fee. The company in turn would file for a patent on the drug and reap in the rewards. If, on the other hand, Biogen, through its own initiative, came up with its own research, and if the company was interested, Biogen would either negotiate a royalty structure, or accept a once-off payment. This relationship works in exactly the same way between Biogen and Sym-Tech, except it seems that Sym-Tech accepted shares in lieu of cash.'

'What about Sym-Tech? I couldn't find any information on them, even on the Internet.'

'Not unusual. Most of these small biotechnology companies jealously guard what they do. They don't want the publicity. They leave that to the big guys. They're obsessives. They collect patents. From what I can see, Sym-Tech's speciality lies in obtaining and refining natural remedies, patenting them and usually selling the patent to other biotechnology companies. This way they make a whack of money. The big picture however is the manufacture of drugs for gene manipulation. Both Biogen and Sym-Tech are supposed to be working together., but then again so are most of the other biotechnology companies. It's what we're doing at the university as well. This is why Biogen is so cagey about its relationship with Sym-Tech.

'What's the big picture?' I ask.

'The big picture?' He gives me another one of his quizzical looks. 'The big picture is the future of mankind.'

'Christ, you ought to be a politician.'

'I'm not exaggerating. Ever heard of the Human Genome Project? The mapping of all the genes in the human body. I'm sure you've read about it?'

'It's all over the papers,' I say.

'It is indeed. There are two projects going on at the moment to map the entire human genome. The human genome is like a computer code and genes are like particular sections of code that perform a specialised task. It is an extractive technology. In essence we are working backwards to unravel the codes. Life in the 21st

century will be moulded by what we're doing now, medically, culturally and ethically. Genetic testing will become pervasive, and with it all the associated problems.

Actually, there's a couple of projects, but they've been divided into two camps, one American, the other European. The main research on the European project is being done in England, Germany and here. The big difference is that the American one is entirely privately funded, whereas the European one, although it does receive significant private funding, also receives a big chunk of taxpayers' money via the EU.'

'Why am I not surprised,' I say

'I'm not either. Now, here comes the important stuff, namely, it's not so much the genetic mapping that counts, but what you can do with that knowledge. Once the 60 000 to 80 000 genes that we have in our cells are identified and mapped, they are linked to biological functions. It is fairly certain, for example, that there is a gene that causes Alzheimer's Disease. If any of the pharmaceutical companies could pinpoint it, discover what causes it to malfunction and then develop a drug to prevent malfunction, they would be worth billions of dollars.

The thing is, the company that maps the gene owns it. Both the US Patent Office and the European Patent Office have ruled that genepatenting is legal. Understanding and owning a particular gene means that the company can then attempt to produce the drugs that prevent those genes from malfunctioning, which is the root cause of quite a few diseases and illnesses. There is a company in the US, for example, that owns BRCA1 and BRCA2, two genes that cause breast cancer.

We're talking billions of dollars here. You must also remember that there are only between 100 and 300 genes that may used to make the most valuable drugs, big ones like diabetes, heart disease and asthma. The others are useless, commercially that is. You can see why the drug companies are desperate to get in there first. It's a gold rush. The prime patents will be worth zillions.'

'What you saying to me is that the body is a carcass and that we are simply fighting over the choicest cuts of flesh, like a pride of lions.'

'Correct. More or less.'

*

My next stop is the city centre, to talk to a broker at an investment firm. Addy van Dijken is a commodities trader and his portfolio is biotechnology. Van Dijken's work environment reinforces both the public's view as well the traders' perceptions of their job functions that they are different from the rest of us mortals. They have their own rules and regulations and deserve to be judged by their own standards.

Those of us with a bit of intelligence simply call it hubris. He perches on the very top of a circular building overlooking the ocean. The entire floor consists of cubicles manned by men and women, hands glued to phones and eyes to the screens in front of them. It is a loud and aggressive environment. Shouts and screams rent the air. It is a market environment, not much different to the local fish centre at five in the morning.

Van Dijken comes hurtling through the security doors. He is young, about twenty-seven but podgy and pasty-faced with buck teeth. His brow glistens with sweat which he wipes away with a bright yellow silk handkerchief. Very nimble on his feet, judging from the way he came through the doors. He is attired in stockbroker uniform - white shirt, red braces, navy blue trousers.

There's something of a junkie about him, his sweating, his rapid-fire speech, but I can't tell if it's caffeine or cocaine. Or perhaps a handful of Benzedrine tablets. It's the retro-drug of choice among well-heeled Amsterdammers this year. He ushers me back towards the elevators. It's the only spot where we can talk. I switch on my tape-recorder.

'Biotechnology. Not as bad as the Internet industry, but it's getting there. Both industries are built largely on hype. However, when there's money to be made, it's big money. So far it's not great. The US, for example, has invested 75 billion dollars over the past twenty-five years to create an industry with a market capitalisation of only 100 billion dollars. That's a pretty bad return for an investor, but it hasn't really deterred people, although the potential demise of Biogen has already caused problems in the marketplace. The share prices are like yo-yos. When they're up, they're really up, and when they're down it hurts. Biotechnology is still viewed as an upstart industry especially by the pharmaceutical industry, although they have started working closely together in recent years. I suppose it is the same way the mainframe computer market views the PC market.

'How's that?' I ask.

'Well, the biotech sector thrives on what they call "blockbusters" - same as in the movies. They invest large amounts of money on a single drug that they think will be a big hit, let's say a cure for Alzheimer's Disease, but if it flops, it takes everyone down with it. You know the story about Biogen and CMV retinitis.'

I nod. 'What about Sym-Tech and Biogen?'

'Their relationship is pretty much the new shape of things in the industry - or was - I'm not sure what's going to happen now. Biotech companies are usually small, high-tech organisations whereas the pharmaceutical industry is a land of dinosaurs populated by huge companies, quite a few of which have been around since Felix Hoffman first synthesised aspirin in 1897. But there's a revolution taking place.

Genomics, the study of genes in disease; combinatorial chemistry, the creation of vast compound libraries and bioinformatics, the use of computers to identify problems, have drastically altered the landscape. The big companies know that they cannot compete with the little biotech guys in these areas, but they do control access to vast amounts of money. So, they work together. The pharmaceutical companies are increasingly outsourcing their R&D to the biotech companies, and are instead concentrating on marketing and distribution. All I can say is that portfolio managers like myself are in for a rough ride.'

'But no doubt you'll make lots of money,' I add.

He answers by giving me a wolfish grin.

'What about patent problems?'

His eyes narrow. 'Screw the hippies. Patents are the *only* method of recouping the cost of an investment. Each drug needs an initial outlay of 500 million dollars. No company is going to spend that kind of money if they could not own the intellectual property rights. No rights, no development, no new drugs. We might as well be in the Dark Ages.

Patents only last twenty years anyway. After that it's public domain.

'What these fuckers don't seem to understand is that in order to get a patent a company must make its research public. Knowledge that would otherwise be kept secret is brought out in to the open. It makes for a healthier intellectual climate. You got a problem with that?'

'No,' I say. 'Thanks for your help.'

'No problemo. Any more questions, I'll be at the Blue Parrot at midnight tonight.'

'Not my kind of place,' I smile back at him.

I watch him dancing his way back to the entrance to his workspace. He looks like a hippopotamus in a tutu.

Chapter 18

The elevator is ancient. It takes such an interminably long time to reach its destination that I wonder if we're moving at all. It finally grinds to a lurching halt. We step out directly into a room. It seems to consist of four white walls, no doors, no windows. It's a disorientating confrontation. The doctor walks towards the wall directly in front of the elevator. He swipes his card through a card reader in the wall. There's a dull clink and a section of the wall in front of us swings open.

'What is this place, some sort of top-secret facility?'

'Not quite. It used to be a particle research lab for physicists, used primarily for bombarding atoms with neutrons. When funding was withdrawn, it was temporarily closed down. When we received a new grant from big business, it was turned into a series of biotechnology labs for the European Genome Project. It serves its purpose, providing both a naturally sterile environment, as well as being away from prying eyes.'

The first corridor we go down seems endless. It is like a tunnel disappearing into the distance.

'This is the area where they used to fire lasers that split atoms. It goes along for four miles,' he continues.

'Who runs this place?' I ask.

'It is nominally government funded.' He smiles ruefully.

'But...'

'The truth is, a large chunk of our financing comes from private sources...'

'And...'

'And Biogen is our biggest donor.'

'Can't bite the hand that feeds you,' I say.

'It's more than that,' he responds. 'It's a moral and ethical issue. I'm against the patenting of human genes on the somewhat quixotic grounds that it belongs to all of us. To the human race. As far as I'm concerned it's the same as patenting an arm or leg. I'm not the only one that feels this way. One HGP project currently being conducted as a global venture publishes its research immediately on the Internet for public access. This also serves to undermine the research being conducted by the private companies. The pharmaceutical industry is on the cusp of a revolution like no other we've witnessed. I know it may sound melodramatic but it's true. We have started tinkering with the fundamental building blocks of matter. The human body is the final frontier. And like all frontiers we humans encounter, we do our best to inflict as much damage as possible, with careless regard for the future.'

An old-fashioned romantic. A man after my own heart.

'The trouble with our times is that the future is not what it used to be,' I say to him.

'True,' he answers. 'You're very witty.'

'Not mine,' I answer. 'Paul Valery. French poet.'

We turn into a side room, the laboratory. There are no petri dishes in site though, just banks and banks of computers. It is totally alien to my concept of a laboratory.

The lighting in the room is unnaturally white and it is cold, like a morgue. We're surrounded by white walls. There are no windows here either. The desks consist of steel cubicles that look like gigantic stainless steel hospital bedpans. They are totally impersonal, no pictures of lovers, spouses or silly cartoons.

On the walls there are six gigantic white screens, the kind you'd find at rock concert. Around one of them, is a cluster of people in white coats. On the screen is a show that the audience finds totally engrossing. To me it resembles some kind of drug-induced fractal imagery swirling in slow motion in a pool of garish colours.

'What's happening here?' I ask.

'This is where all the really important stuff happens. About half the people here work on gene sequencing. Actually, it is the computer that does all the work.'

He waves vaguely in the direction of the screen. 'Every cell of an organism has a set of chromosomes containing the heritable genetic material that directs its development. It's our blueprint, the reason we exist, our genome. The structure of DNA was discovered by Jim Watson and Francis Crick at Cambridge University in 1953. It simultaneously explained how the genetic material is carried and how it is copied from one generation to the next. The genetic material of chromosomes is DNA. Each of the paired strands of the DNA molecule is in a linear array of subunits called nucleotides. It is our job to map the location of all the genes in every chromosome and to determine the precise sequence of the nucleotides of the entire genome. By understanding the entire genome we have a blueprint for life.

'The technical process involves duplicating the DNA using an enzyme. This is done in the presence of specially marked terminator nucleotides. The enzyme recognises these terminators and builds them onto the chains. This gives a mixture of DNA fragments of varying lengths, each length finishing with one of the four differently marked fluorescent dye molecules corresponding to the four nucleotides.

'The fragments are then driven by an electrical field through capillary tubes filled with a polymer. This sorts them by length. The order of colours that emerge - corresponding to the sequence of nucleotides in the original piece of DNA - is scanned by laser and displayed by computer.'

'Presumably you then go out and do what fashion designers do, make copies?' I say to him.

'Don't be so dismissive. In a couple of years, that will be a reasonable possibility. There might even be a gene for our biological clocks. If we tinker with that we can even achieve immortality.'

'Have you ever wondered,' I interrupt him again, 'that, if there was a "clock" gene that determined how long we lived, why, throughout the history of man, has it not malfunctioned. There ought to be examples of severe malfunction, of people, say, living for two hundred years?'

That knocks the wind out of him. He dazes at me in astonishment.

'Miss De Hoop, I am astounded by your perspicacity. Not once has that puzzle crossed my mind. If you don't mind, I'm going to use it at the next conference I go to and pretend that it's my own. That should knock the old farts out.'

He pats me on the shoulder. My ears feel hot. I've always had a problem accepting compliments.

'Basically what we do here though,' he continues, 'is interpret computer printouts. The technicians that you see wondering around are called "finishers". It is their job to check the computer printouts for patterns, anomalies and repeats. Unfortunately a computer can't decipher what the human eye can see.'

'That's very reassuring,' I say.

'The other half are doing the stuff that will bring in the money. This is the "3D Crunch" - a computer project that is being used to determine the protein structures in the genetic data. As I've said before, mapping the human genome is important enough, but it is the structure of the proteins within the genes that is important to the drug designers. Proteins are the building blocks of life. Each of the 60 000 to 80 000 genes in our body is a blueprint for a protein. By identifying how these proteins function, we can design drugs that will either enhance specific protein activity, or in cases of proteins that cause diseases, inhibit the ability of that protein to function.

'In the old days, they used to use X-rays or nuclear magnetic resonance to do this, which was a pretty slow and expensive process - the patents on the genes only last for twenty years, but now all the computers are connected to a Silicon Graphics CRAY Origin2000 server which powers a SWISS-MODEL, the protein-modelling software. We get the pictures in 3D.'

'And in full colour,' I add.

The doctor switches on one of the computers. The large screen on the wall closest to us flickers into life.

'I've been through all the pathology and research reports that were stored on the Biogen computer, including the encrypted data. That's where all the interesting stuff was, by the way.'

'Fascinating to see how much all those directors earn,' he smiles weakly.

'I studied all the research reports in the same directory. I think we've struck gold. Incredible stuff. The work that Sym-Tech has been doing for them lately seems to centre around organ transplants, more specifically transplanting animal organs into humans. It's called xenotransplantation.

'I cannot tell you what methodology Sym-Tech and Biogen were using though, even whether it was based on grafting technology like the older research methodologies, or genetically-based, but I would stake my life on the latter.

'We have found a number of pathology reports detailing the stages of the programme but no corroborative data. There seems to have been a lot of exchanges between the two parties regarding the rate of progress, Biogen being the unhappy party. That's as far as it got to.'

'What are the financial implications?' I ask.

'Enormous actually. We're taking billions of dollars worldwide in the long term. We are looking at the actual scientific details but most of the stuff seems to be with the other party. It's obvious that Sym-Tech only shared as much information with Biogen as they wanted to. On a need to know basis, so to speak.'

He presses a few buttons on a video machine. 'This is the spectrographic analysis of the actual gene transfer.

'The big problem has been the body's response to foreign organs. It doesn't like them. An animal organ is recognized within minutes and targeted by protein sentries that circulate the blood. These sentries flag the animal tissue and set in motion a cascade of events. The end result is that the blood supply to the organ is cut off and it basically starves to death. Some new research has tried to lessen the rejection by breeding transgenic pigs, which contain parts of the human immune system.

'The first time xenotransplantation was carried out was sometime in the 1600s was when a portion of dog skull was implanted into the skull of a Russian nobleman to repair damage. The graft was removed after a threat of excommunication was made by the Russian Church. The graft had been successful up until the removal.

'There have been some successes in fooling the body into thinking that the organs are human, but it doesn't last for very long. As far as I know, the closest we ever got was in 1990, when a US company altered the DNA of pigs with human genes. The human gene CD-59 was grafted into pigs. The heart of the pig was then transplanted into a human, with the hope that the body's immune system would be deceived into believing that the heart was human. It was only a partial success. That particular gene was patented, by the way. Not that it's worth a lot of money.'

All I see on the screen are a series of smudged grey lines running vertically, each line about ten centimetres.

'Okay, so it's not very exciting, but this was the end result.'

A video comes onto the screen. It is in colour, mostly bright red, and very graphic. The screen is awash with blood. It is easy to discern the heart pumping so violently, the oceans of blood rushing out in all directions.

'Baboon's heart inside a baby girl. Didn't last very long because the transplant was a ABO-blood group mismatch. The heart is a miracle of nature. No bit of mechanical equipment can sustain this much activity for so long a period. It keeps going and going. And what do we do?'

It is a rhetorical question, so I merely nod politely.

'We go out of our way to abuse it as much as possible. Then we look around for a replacement. It is the human conceit that whatever is old and worn out we throw away and get a new one.

Some day we are going to pay horribly for this.'

*

London is in the grip of chaos. Three IRA bomb threats have paralysed the city. Large swathes of the central district have been cordoned off. I start to panic. Round two of the interrogation of Laville is about to begin in twenty minutes. I have already been delayed by a late flight.

Traffic is at a standstill. Helicopters whirr ceaselessly overhead. The sound of cars hooting rent the air. The man on the radio is manic, teasing people, playing with listeners' fears. He is mean and spiteful, cracking nasty Irish jokes. There is a mood of pervasive ugliness in the air and I do not like it.

Even before we reach the New Scotland Yard headquarters at Broadway we see the thick black smoke billowing into the sky. The area has been cordoned off by a series of police cars, ambulances and fire-engines. The taxi driver curses and utters an apology to me. He tries to reverse but he is trapped. I jump out and walk a block further. Accosted by a fire-officer, I flash my badge. It doesn't work. He orders me brusquely to head back.

The firemen have taken over the area.

I spot a group of police officers huddled nearby. As I get closer I notice that they're all black, that is, they're covered in a black soot-like substance. They look like a troop of Negro minstrels. One of them breaks off and walks towards me. I double up with laughter. It is Sergeant Helm.

'Are you okay, what's happened?' I cry out.

'We had an attack. Your man is gone.

'They came in through the front door. In a plumber's van. We have them on video-tape. They didn't bother hiding their faces.'

He opens up a plastic bag and gingerly lifts out a smooth brown oval object, about the size of a grenade.

'British made. It's a combination of smoke bomb and tear gas. We export it to Third World countries, to help control the restless natives. Very effective for crowd control *and* rounding up suspects once they've fled as the black stuff doesn't wash off very easily. They also fired off a couple of AK 47s. We botched it, I'm afraid. Laville had the minimum of security. They could be anywhere by now.'

I offer him a pack of tissues.

He declines. 'It will only make it worse. Need a special detergent to get rid of the stuff.'

Out of the corner of my eye I notice a familiar shape. My heart skips a beat. I turn to make sure, hoping, praying that it is a figment of my imagination.

It is the American, deep in conversation with one of the police officers.

My knees tremble.

Helm notices. 'Are you okay?'

'I'm fine,' I answer.

He has seen me. He strides purposefully in our direction. There is nowhere to run. I feel trapped. I cannot breathe.

'Hi,' he says with a rueful smile. He looks different. Older. He is wearing a black suit, tie and laced shoes.

I answer back with a disembodied voice. It does not sound like my own. I am far away, drifting even further into the ether.

Whirling away in the back of my mind, I remember something.

The helicopter.

'I have an errand to do,' I urgently address them both. Helm is watching me with an expression of bemusement on his face. He shrugs his shoulders. I turn abruptly and walk away.

The American follows me. As we round the corner of a building, out of the view of Helm and his colleagues, I push him against the wall and hiss violently at him. A few of the passers-by stare but I am beyond caring.

'Bastard, bastard,' I shout at him. He tries to grab my arms but I push him away.

I walk briskly through the crowds, running when I can, for about fifteen minutes. Then I hail a taxi and ask the driver to take me to Heathrow.

In the cab I try to still the psychic chatter in my mind, to avoid the anxiety and terror. Exist for the moment.

Relax and take each step in its time. Still the senses. Stay within yourself at all times.

Above all, prevail.

*

The hustle and bustle of Heathrow is soothing and comforting. It ameliorates the noise in my own head. I'm almost relieved to be bumped into, shoved aside. It affirms my existence. I accost one of the security men patrolling the floors to find out where the control tower is. He gazes at me doubtfully until I show him my badge. He escorts me through a series of lifts, corridors and stairways, the security in each section getting progressively tighter. Finally we reach the main control tower.

The chief duty technician tries not to hide his laughter when I ask if an ageing Russian Kamov-32 helicopter has taken off in the last half hour. I'm pointed gently but firmly downstairs. By now, the security officer, a turbanned Sikh, and I have become quite friendly. He's started telling me about his daughter's forthcoming wedding. He is useful to have around. He gets me into the executive lounge of one of the airlines. In the business centre I send a fax to Hausenpfeff, the PR lady at Biogen. It consists of one line, 'I KNOW ABOUT SYM-TECH AND THE XENOTRANSPLANTS.'

That ought to set the cat amongst the pigeons.

The helicopter zone is away from the bigger planes. The helicopters are scattered around the enclosure like expensive toys. That's what most of them are anyway, executive toys in various shapes, sizes and colours. The security guard is getting quite proprietorial over me. He takes me through a cavernous hangar right over to the person in charge. "Malcolm Hitchens" says the tattered name-card on his desk. He's a portly owlish man sitting behind a very untidy desk, wiping his glasses on a dirty rag. He taps his computer screen with a green pencil, obviously unable to unlearn the lessons of a lifetime.

'Ka-32. We don't get many of those around. Geology team. Oil exploration. North Sea,' he rattles.

He checks the computer, typing laboriously with one finger.

'The flight plan was to Edinburgh and then to the island of North Ronaldsay, one of the Orkney Islands. It's a couple of miles off the coast of Scotland.'

He gives me the details of the flight control centre for Edinburgh. North Ronaldsay does not have a control centre, all its destinations are handled by the mainland.

The American is standing at the entrance of the hangar. I see his profile first but I know right away it is him by the way he stands.

'What the fuck are you doing here,' I shout at him.

'Followed you.'

'Well, get out of my fucking way.'

'I can help,' he says.

'You can help me,' I snarl at him, 'by disappearing. Preferably to another planet.'

'Look, I'm sorry about what happened, but I have a job to do.'

'Oh, and I suppose screwing me and then spying on me was a "job".'

'No, it wasn't. And it case you haven't noticed, I have extracted exactly zero information from you. So get off your high horse and let's work together.'

'I don't need your help.'

'Yes, you do. You need a plane. How do you propose to get one? You have no jurisdiction or authority to commandeer one here. As you've pointed out before, your organisation is mired in bureaucracy. By the time you file a request and fill in the papers, your suspects will be long gone.'

He's right. 'And I suppose you just happen to have a plane idling around here somewhere, waiting for you.'

'As I matter of fact, I do. Let's go.'

I scream silently in frustration. He's right, I have no choice.

He turns to walk away. I follow him. He waits for me. I stop. He shrugs his shoulders and turns away again. I carry on after him. It is a silly, childish reaction but it makes me feel slightly better.

The plane is a eight seater Cessna Golden Eagle. He chats to the pilot, who's fiddling with the propellor at the front, and points his thumb at me. Inside the craft he pokes his head out of the cockpit and orders me to buckle up. I hate small aeroplanes. Large planes give the illusion of indestructibility. Small planes do not. We fly below the dense clouds in a darkening sky. Below, the English channel looks smooth and unruffled.

He leaves me alone for about fifteen minutes. Upfront, he is in charge. I can hear him talking to the control centre in Edinburgh. I'd like to hurl one of the parachute frames at the back of his head.

Finally he eases himself out of his seat and comes over. 'It belongs to the company I work for,' he says. 'It's a workhorse, not very fast, but faster than a helicopter.'

Then he sits opposite me, cracks open a small bottle of whiskey, removes his tie, and proceeds to tell me what he says is God's truth.

He works for Meacham, the US drugs company. It is an organisation that is larger than Biogen, primarily because it has captured the plum US market. Biogen has more of an international presence but Meacham is catching up. 'Kinda like Coke and Pepsi,' he grins at me.

I fail to see the joke.

'How did you do that thing with Davids and McKie? I heard voices in the background.'

'Call re-routing,' he answers. 'When you dialled the Amsterdam number I gave you, the call was automatically routed to the ops centre at Meacham headquarters in Gary, Indiana. Simple trick.'

'Amazing. Your company has an entire centre devoted to dirty tricks.'

'Meacham has net profits of five hundred million dollars per annum. The company is valued at sixty billion. Why shouldn't its shareholders protect what is their property by all legal means necessary?'

Deep down inside I find it hard to disagree so I keep quiet.

'Now, if you want a dirty rotten company, try Sym-Tech. They've been involved in all kinds of rackets. Everything from selling old medical stock to African countries - from which they've raked in millions of dollars - to stealing patents. This is what they are focussing on at the moment. The drug market in Third World countries has become over-traded, now that the Russians are all over the place.'

'Why exactly is the CIA involved in all this?' I ask.

'No, wait, don't tell me,' I laugh bitterly, 'you're here to safeguard the capitalist interests of American businessmen now that the CIA doesn't have a cold war to fight.'

He looks discomfited. Good.

'I don't work for the CIA,' he snaps. 'My records that you checked up on are accurate.'

'Glad to hear that,' I say. 'Perhaps you'd care to explain why you're mixed up with Meacham. It cannot be for philanthropic reasons.'

He sighs in exasperation. 'Stop busting my balls. I'm doing a job here.

Sym-Tech has a spy in Meacham. We believe that the spy is passing details of Meacham's gene sequencing programme to Biogen.

'Unlike Biogen, which receives a whack of fat EU grants, Meacham is a business-driven enterprise,' he adds sarcastically.

'How did you find out that there was a spy from Sym-Tech in your organisation?' I ask.

He looks at me thoughtfully for a moment.

'Because we have someone working for us at Biogen.'

'Don't look so shocked,' he adds. 'It happens. You and I both know this.'

'I'm not shocked, merely puzzled by this web of deceit.'

'I used to work in counter-intelligence. Do you know which countries engaged in the most extensive economic espionage against the US?

Not China or Russia. It's France and Israel, our allies. At least France had the grace to say nothing. Israel flat-out denied it. Ironically Israel is the biggest recipient of US aid. *All* these countries are signatories to TRIPs - the Trade Related Intellectual Property Rights agreement, the treaty formulated by the World Trade Organisation. It specifically calls for the enforcement of intellectual property rights. It's kinda like putting the fox in charge of the chickens.'

'It's not the same thing,' I say.

'It's *precisely* the same thing. It is the theft of intellectual property. Everybody does it, and everybody denies it.'

'Gattschalk used to be a chemist, way back in the Seventies. What you guys don't know is that she had this racket going, counterfeit drugs smuggled back into Europe. They specialised in flooding Western Europe with cheap generic drugs manufactured in the Eastern Bloc, China and India. It was officially sanctioned, by the way. How else do you think she got that apartment in Warnemunde. They didn't hand out those places for twenty years loyal service to the state.'

'How do you know all this?' I ask.

'Ever heard of *Operation Rosenholz* [Rosewood]?' he answers.

'No.'

'Your buddy Boehme would have. Basically what happened was that immediately after the fall of the Berlin Wall in '89, the CIA, via a tradeoff with the Russians - ie, $1.5 million cash - got their grubby paws on a whole lot of Stasi archives. It was a list of thousands of Stasi operatives, and their code names. Spies, racketeers, thugs, you name it, they're all in there. The Stasi had 102 000 officials to oversee a country of only 17 million people, whereas the Gestapo had 40 000 to keep 80 million Germans in check.

'Now, your associates in Bonn - should I say Berlin - the boys at Gauck, have only recently cracked the software codes on some of the East German computer equipment, but without the names to match, it's meaningless. The CIA of course, refuses to share the info with the Germans.'

'I can't understand why,' I add dryly. 'I assume Gattschalk is on that list.'

'You assume right. She was a racketeer par excellence. Actually, the theory is that the CIA is keeping the names to themselves because some of the Stasi members are now CIA agents.'

'How did someone involved in illegal drug distribution get so big?' I ask

'Drugs?'

I tell him what we know about Gattschalk.

He roars a cynical laugh. 'Excuse my French, but that's a load of horseshit. It's all lies. Gattschalk was a senior operative in

Department IV. It was a super-secret section of the Stasi and was active right until 1989. Department IV was set up in the Sixties as a kind of elite force within the Stasi. They were known as "partisan comrades". It had a number of different units within it, each devoted to creating as much trouble in the West as possible. They specialised in different ways of destruction; portable nuclear devices, radioactivity, poisoning. They also kept a list of government offices, armament factories, hospitals, television stations, etc, that they planned to destroy. This also included a list of important West German people they planned to assassinate. The interesting thing about Department IV is that they had a great deal of help from hard-core leftists in West Germany, so you can bet your bottom dollar that she's making good use of her contacts. We don't know much about what Gattschalk actually did, but she used to be a chemist, so I would guess developing new poisons and drugs would be just up her alley.'

'What about Quetscher, the hotel doorman?' I ask.

'It's amazing the amount of lies and deception that goes on. He was probably also an operative as well, although I would say from his attitude a disgruntled former member. They didn't have a pension plan for these guys. Anyway, it would explain Gattschalk's long list of contacts. She probably also has other ex-Department IV personnel working for her.

'After 1989 Gattschalk branched out. Sym-Tech has had three name changes, but it's been the same company. She was active in South America and in South East Asia.'

'As a drug smuggler?'

'Yeah, but a drug smuggler with a difference. It was neither cocaine nor heroin and it was perfectly legal. She specialised in patenting drugs, often based on natural remedies. Her team scoured the world looking for medicines that had been used by the locals. They did a bit of gene-based research, patented the drugs, either in Europe or the US and sold off the patent to any of the pharmaceutical companies that were interested. In Thailand for example, she got her hands on a root plant called Pueraria. It is a natural oestrogen booster that the Thais had known about for decades. Admittedly she did isolate the active ingredient. Then she sold it to Meacham for 50 million dollars.'

'Seems like a lot of money,' I interrupt.

'Not to Meacham. The drug derived from the plant has been proven to enlarge breasts. Can you imagine what it is worth to the drug companies?

'When I was a teenager, one of the large pharmaceutical companies had a slogan, "Better living through chemistry". We used to fall about laughing every time we saw the billboards.'

'I had no idea Americans appreciated irony,' I reply.

He ignores my comment. 'The problem is, the Thai government, via its National Institute of Thai Traditional Medicine, got wise and protested in the strongest terms to the US government about the "plundering of their natural resources". They've called it "bio-colonialism". The end result is that the case has gone to The Hague and is being mediated by the World Trade Organisation. It also means that all development has been suspended by Meacham. It's got nothing to do with Gattschalk and it's not illegal, but you can understand why everyone's pissed. And it's not the first time this has happened. Other countries have not been so vigilant.

'The US patent office receives about 13 000 biotechnology patent applications a year. It is also currently processing 7 000 applications for entire genes. It has *already* granted 2 000 patents for genes.

'It's all about power isn't it? All a game to you people. It's not about the protection of innocent people, solving crimes. It's about who has the most information. And information has become currency. Since you people have the most, it makes you richest. Information is power, in the same way the dollar is power.'

'Isn't it a case of the pot calling the kettle black?' he shakes his head sadly at me. 'You, after all, work for an organisation that has secrecy embedded even deeper in its constitution than the CIA ever will have.'

I don't answer. To do so would mean reeling off a litany of coups, assassinations and murders that the CIA has either sanctioned or carried out itself in the name of democracy.

Instead, I change the subject. 'Do you know anything about the dead Tamils?'

'Nope. Like you I suspect it has to do with money. Gattschalk's goons and the LTTE taking their war to the streets. Told you that Gattschalk spent time in South East Asia, so it's possible that she got mixed up with the LTTE in some kinda racket, not necessarily to do with all this biotechnology stuff. You got caught in the middle.'

Chapter 19

The radio crackles into life and the pilot beckons Woods over.

'They have landed in North Ronaldsay,' he says. 'Guess we have to wait and see what happens.'

The radio screeches into life again. Woods returns to the front. I can see him getting him very agitated. He utters a stream of expletives over the radio, then an inaudible dialogue.

A couple of minutes later he returns with a map. He unfolds it over his knees. 'The bastards took off again. I had to ask for radar tracking by the flight centre at Kirkwall airport, which is on the mainland.'

'These are the co-ordinates I have.' He points to a spot in the North Atlantic. It looks like open sea to me. I say so.

'According to them, it's an oil rig,' he answers. 'One that was decommissioned in the middle Eighties. It was sold off privately. Part of the then government's privatisation drive.'

'Didn't know they sold these things.'

'They do, very often for scrap. If they are not dismantled within twelve months of purchase, they have to explain why. Purchases are only sanctioned to government-approved private organisations.'

'Why all the restrictions?' I ask.

'Well, the British government wouldn't want a foreign power gaining a plumb observation post right on their doorstep now, would they?'

*

We land in North Ronaldsay after the second try. The wind is strong and treacherous. We had almost touched the ground at the first attempt when the plane was suddenly lifted up, nose first. I had visions of us dangling from our seats in a buckled craft. It is a very small island, four miles long and two miles wide. The "airport" is a strip of concrete with three green, sturdy bunker-type structures nearby. They look as if they could withstand the strongest hurricane.

In addition to being small, the island is low, the northern-most island land mass of the Orkney Islands. An old Norse settlement, its main inhabitants are now the seaweed-eating sheep which inhabit the beach. The sky is a dark and uniform grey mass extending far into the horizon. It feels like the end of the world here, an overpowering sense of being swallowed by the ocean. Tourists visit occasionally in summer to see the migrating birds, seals and dolphins, and to rummage amongst the shipwrecks. There is a small jetty for boats, used mainly by the lobster fishermen.

The police force for the islands possess one boat. You can't miss it. It has a big blue light, with the word 'POLICE' written on the side. We are lucky to spot it. It is doing the rounds, before heading for Edinburgh. I use the shortwave radio on the boat to contact Coonrodt to find out if he has any friends in the area. He has acquaintances in most of the harbours of Western Europe. The only person he knows is in Kirkwall, but he's a fisherman who would be unwilling to spend two days away from the fishing grounds. Coonrodt's on his way back from Stockholm, where he'd been delivering a cargo plastic of Christmas trees.

He's three and a half hours away, he says, and he's free to meet us.

I hesitate. There is no time to think, so I say yes.

'I could do with a bit of English cooking,' cackles Coonrodt, before signing off.

'Sense of humour, your Dutch friend,' grins the captain of the boat.

I'm not sure if it is a joke, or if Coonrodt means it.

The pub we are staying at, The Broch House, offers basic accommodation. We book a room for the weekend. There is only one room at the pub.

'It's used mainly by blerks too drunk t' go hurrme,' says the landlady helpfully. I think she would prefer it if we stayed somewhere else. There are two other bed and breakfast places on the island but they are further inland, where the smell of rotting seaweed is not so strong. The islanders' legendary hospitality seems to have deserted them. The fishermen in the pub can tell that we're not tourists. They don't get many visitors in late October. You can see that look in their eyes, a mixture of curiosity and suspicion. Wondering whether we're EU officials checking up on quota scams. It's strange being on the other side, so to speak. To have people viewing you with suspicion, even hatred, for being a representative of a distant authority. Self-justification is the easy part. This isn't.

The room hasn't been used for while. My fears of congealing pools of vomit on the floor are unfounded. Although the room is clean, the musty air tells us that the windows have not been opened for a long time. The thin sheets are cold with damp. Even the glow from the lightbulb seems mean-spirited. The wallpaper hasn't been changed either. It is depressingly yellow with age. The sloping roof also makes it difficult for us to stand up straight in places. There is only one bed. It's not a single bed, but neither is it a double.

Woods feeds a few coins into the heating unit high up on the wall.

'I hate these things. Why are the English so mean?' he grumbles.

'They haven't gotten over the spirit of the Second World War. They scrounge and penny-pinch because they think it will start all over again soon,' I answer.

He unplugs the lamp on the small table and plugs in a square black box, about the size of a toaster. From his other case he unpacks two notebook computers. Then he starts typing.

'Catching up on your e-mail?' I ask.

'Something like that. This little baby is a Worldphone satellite phone. Weighs all of five pounds. Via its links to the constellation of INMARSAT series 3 geostationary satellites and the mini-M service, it lets you place and receive voice, fax and data calls from practically anywhere in the world. I'm contacting my buddy at the Global Resource Unit. With the co-ordinates we received from Kirkwall about the helicopter's final destination we might be able get sat-pics - that's satellites pictures. It all depends on where the sats are.

'What's the Global Resource Unit?' I ask.

'It's the CIA section unit that gathers, quantifies and disseminates information and intelligence to operatives around the world.'

'Oh, I thought it was the American equivalent of the Weather Bureau.'

'Ha, ha, ha.'

'Okay, here we go. The Lacrosse satellite system will be traversing this sector at 14:00 UTC, that's another four hours and fifty minutes. It's a radar and infrared imaging satellite, so we ought to get good pics. Gonna get my buddies to kindly forward the stuff to my computer.'

'Wake me up,' I reply, leaving him to his toys.

The bed is lumpy and hard. I still have on most of my clothes under the thin blankets, removing only my boots and overcoat. From where I'm lying I can see his back hunched over the computer, casting a shadow into the corner of the room. The light makes him look big and powerful. For the first time in a long while, I fall asleep without thinking too much.

Somebody once said that language is the skin of our thoughts. I try to remember this when I feel the fear deep inside.

*

He shakes me gently awake. The four hours that have gone by feel like four days. He has not slept, or even laid down on the bed.

'The photographs have been downloaded.' He smiles like an angel. I pull on my boots and draw up a chair next to him. The room has become colder. He takes my hands in his palms and starts to rub them. They are limp in his hands. I avoid any eye contact.

The photographs are amazingly detailed, a gradual progression from a distant height to shots that seem directly overhead. It is a big rig, as befitting one from the Seventies. They make them much smaller these days.

'The satellite can resolve objects as small as one metre wide. There's your helicopter,' he says, pointing to the craft. It is well secured by ropes on the deck, its blades folded. There are no signs of life on board. The rig has been partially stripped of its oil exploration equipment, but even at a casual glance it still looks functional. Almost too functional, as though it had been dressed up to look as if it was in working order.

'Something is missing,' I say.

'What's that?'

'Don't know. I can't quite put my finger on it.' I scan the pictures again.

'No cat on board?' he says flippantly.

'No, no, I know what it is. There are no lifeboats.'

'They're obviously not expecting to have any trouble.'

'Perhaps, but it's a maritime regulation,' I answer. 'Perhaps we can board it on that pretext.'

'Hey, take a look at this.'

He taps on his computer.

The grey screen morphs into red shapes. Slowly they change into recognisable human form.

'Heat signature close-ups. It picks up warm bodies. There are three men now on deck.'

'Three *people* on deck,' I correct him. 'I can't see men on the screen, unless these tiny blobs here are penises.'

'That's the heat from the cigarettes they're smoking. You're looking at it upside down, remember.' He purses his lips at me.

'Sorry,' I say. 'And definitely no cat.'

'Yeah, but you've got dogs.'

'Look,' he says, pointing to the slowly rotating image.

There are about a dozen recognisable shapes on screen, all prancing around each other.

'Why would they have dogs on board an oil rig?' I ask.

'They're probably guard dogs. An oil rig is a tricky place to go looking for intruders. The dogs can explore all the nooks and crannies.'

We put on our overcoats, pack away all the computer equipment and walk down to the jetty. Coonrodt is there, leaning against his cabin, puffing on his pipe. He greets the American almost shyly. Me, he almost squeezes to death. He has a present for me, badly wrapped up in garishly decorated red, silver and black paper. It is tied up with silver ribbon into a bow.

'It's a Christmas present,' he says. 'Remind me to give it to you when I leave, but you are not to open it until Christmas Day.'

We stow our gear on board the boat and stroll back to buy supplies. The fishermen glance at us from their small boats with that same mixture of suspicion and curiosity. We ignore them, but Coonrodt, blissfully unaware of the latent tension, hails them with a hearty greeting.

The island's only general store is still open. It has an incongruous neon Coke sign that flashes above its low door. Goods of all kinds are crammed onto its crowded shelves in an alarmingly haphazard manner; fresh bread next to boot polish, sanitary towels alongside boxes of cakes, tea next to drain cleaner. Coonrodt behaves as though he were in Harrods. He packs English chocolate bars, baked beans and white bread into his basket with an expression of sheer pleasure on his face.

He answers the bemused looks on our faces by confessing a deep and abiding passion for English foods.

It is 11 pm by the time we leave. The rig is about two hours away so we ought to get there by 1 am. Coonrodt lets me pilot the boat. I have done it often enough in the past, the first time when I was twelve. At first it was his treat to me. As I grew older I simply asked and most of the time he let me. Gradually I worked out that the only times he wouldn't let me pilot the boat was when he wasn't too happy with himself.

The rhythm of the boat feels different when you are at the helm turning the wheel, feeling the force of the sea in your hands. The flow of the ocean takes on a new cadence, like looking at the stars from a spaceship as opposed to through a telescope.

Coonrodt has the position mapped out on his grubby charts, which he leaves next to me. Below, he is emitting groans of ecstasy. Woods is showing him the computer and satellite gadgetry. I smile to myself. It strikes me that a notebook computer is what I ought to get Coonrodt for Christmas. I also feel a twinge of jealousy. In order for us to get hold of the kind of equipment Woods has, we have to fill in about five requisition forms and even that is no guarantee.

Fortunately for us, it is a foggy night. This means we can spend more time idling in the vicinity of the rig, instead of pretending that we're on our way somewhere. The boat is too low for radar detection. The only problem would be an underwater sonar device, possibly installed on the sea bed or on one of the pylons of the rig.

The fog is thick and swirling, but every now and then it breaks up into big chunks, as if swatted by a gigantic hand. They say that fog is only water with a variance of property. I disagree. Its smell is different to me. Fog has a musty odour, like old cobwebs caught in the rain.

The first flicker of lights comes into view whenever the fog breaks. They're just disconnected spots in the distance, as though there was a palace floating on the ocean.

I alert the two below. Coonrodt reluctantly takes over from me. We maintain a distance of about two miles.

Woods has something in his hand that looks like an Martian firearm, or a dildo. A pair of headphones runs from the instrument to his body. Tucked into his belt is a cigarette-pack sized metal box

'Shotgun microphone,' he says. 'It is a sound amplification unit that picks up directional noise from a distance. The adjustable filter allows emphasis on high frequency sounds *and* it has a wind shield. The unit has a radius of three miles, provided there are no obstacles in-between. The ocean is perfect.'

'What are they saying?' asks Coonrodt eagerly.

'They speaking Russian,' he answers.

Coonrodt groans. 'Well, I suppose that toy is not going to do us any good.'

'I speak a bit of Russian,' smiles Woods.

He shakes his head at us. 'You two ought to see the looks on your faces. Yup, I'm an American who speaks more than one language. Three, as a matter of fact. I speak a bit of Chinese as well. It's shameful.'

He is right. It is cultural prejudice on our part. Both Coonrodt and I apologise.

'The only American who spoke a foreign language was a soldier who stayed after the war, and it took him fifteen years,' mutters Coonrodt under his breath.

'So, what are they're saying?' I shout impatiently.

'Uhm, I can't really tell. They're talking about...biology. Cell division.

A lot of Russian scientific terms. Wait, one of them's just asked the other for a cigarette.'

'It's no use,' I groan. 'It looks like they only come out for smoke breaks.'

'What are they doing on the rig?' asks Coonrodt.

Woods shrugs and looks at me, as if I have the answers. Then only does the futility of our actions engulf me. It is an enormous emptiness that chills me inside. I want to phone Boehme and hear his peremptory voice order me back to Amsterdam, hear him say that I have no right to be in the cold North Sea in the middle of the night. They probably have a formidable arsenal of weapons on board the rig and all we have are Woods's Remington semi-automatic pistol and Coonrodt's old bolt-action rifle.

'If we sit out here they are bound to spot us. We ought to turn back or...' Woods interrupts my panic attack.

The rig lights twinkle in the distance. They look comforting, almost beguiling. We could hail them like lost souls and be fed and warmed.

We turn back.

Coonrodt insists on spending the night on the boat. I decide to stay with him. Woods trudges back to the pub. I watch him pulling his jacket tightly around him. It is bitterly cold. He turns to wave. Coonrodt waves back.

In the gallery Coonrodt opens one of his new purchases, a tin of Bourneville cocoa. He pours a large quantity of condensed milk into two tin cups and heats the resulting sludge, adding only the smallest amount of water. It tastes surprisingly good. We chat for a few minutes, the aimless chatter of two exhausted people. He tells me about his northern trip.

Coonrodt has probably been at sea for eighteen hours without rest.

He has a narrow bunk bed in the cabin. Normally he sleeps on the bottom bed and uses the top bed for an assortment of junk material. I clear away the oily rags and old magazines. The bedclothes are not the cleanest but it is ineffably snug in the cabin. I fall into a blissful sleep, disturbed only by Coonrodt's fitful grunts.

Coonrodt shakes me awake. It is 8:30 am. Woods is outside making an unholy racket. I put on my coat and clamber on deck. Woods is jogging on the spot. He has on black tracksuit pants and a grey T-shirt that says US NAVY.

'I've already been around the island,' he hails.

'It's only four miles,' I shout back sullenly.

'Breakfast for three is almost ready,' he grins, waving his arms up and down his sides.

I decide not to be so churlish towards him.

Coonrodt's presence helps thaw the atmosphere at the pub. The landlady is considerably friendlier towards us. Coonrodt is overly enthusiastic about her cooking, much to her pleasure. Unfortunately she starts to ask questions. To my astonishment Coonrodt says that we're an advance team from an American oil exploration company, revisiting the old oil rig. She knows about it. A few islanders from the mainland lost jobs when it was decommissioned by the British government.

When she leaves, Coonrodt winks at me. I'm still staring at him in open-mouthed astonishment. Woods is equally impressed.

After breakfast I have a bath in the room upstairs. A thin stream of lukewarm water trickles out of the shower for about five minutes. I violently curse the woman downstairs.

The bed is crumpled, blankets in a heap. He has tossed and turned all night. On impulse I press my face to the pillow his head had rested on. Then I am overcome by shame and embarrassment.

I go for a long walk to ease my irritability, leaving the two of them sitting at the wooden table outside swooning over Woods's electronic gadgetry. It serves the added advantage of being good camouflage. EU inspectors definitely don't carry all that equipment around.

It is a brilliantly clear morning. The sea sparkles as though it has been washed. Even the seagulls seem to be screeching happily overhead.

We have a day to kill.

I walk along the beach. A few scrawny sheep eye me. There is a drystone dyke that keeps them along the shore at all times and I follow the wall, clambering over occasionally to get a better view. Some sections of the wall are reputed to date from before 1000 BC. I can see bits of ruined buildings, as well as farmers cottages. A grey-slated lighthouse rears its head against the turquoise sky. The sense of isolation is deep and profound. At the same time it is indescribably beautiful.

When I return, my body and spirit are rested, a warm squirt of fuzziness injected into the soul. I have a smile on my face.

The boys are still at it. Woods has downloaded a second set of pictures, or sat-pics, as he calls them. They are disappointingly familiar.

'Anything new at all,' I ask hopefully.

'Nope, not unless you count the fact that two of them seem to have played "catch" on deck.'

'Any idea how many people are on board?'

'Could be three, could be thirty. There's only ever been three people on deck at the same time. It's possible that they take turns.'

'Aren't you going to call Boehme?' he adds as an afterthought.

'No, I'm going to tell him I had communications problems,' I smile wryly.

'D you always have communications problems?'

'Marlon,' I say, 'if this conversation is heading in the direction I think it is, forget it.'

'Just checking to make sure you're okay,' he answers.

It is a foggy night again, as Coonrodt had predicted in the morning.

He knows the mood of the sea. It is his world. He has traversed this stretch of ocean so many times that all he needs to do is sniff the air and sense its plans.

Again, we are two miles away from the rig. Woods hooks up his sound equipment.

'Anything juicy,' asks Coonrodt.

'Overtime pay,' says Woods puzzled. 'I sure hope this rig *is* out of action and we're not eavesdropping on some Russian-English scientific co-operative endeavour.'

'It's either that or there's a bunch of disgruntled former communists on board getting ready to launch nuclear missiles on London,' I say flippantly.

The flood of light is so bright that I am temporarily blinded. My hands reach out blindly hoping to grip onto something. I try to avoid moving.

One step in the wrong direction and I could be in the sea. Then I feel Coonrodt's gnarled hand take mine. He shouts into the night. Somewhere in the back I can hear Woods's voice as well. A spray of water hits me across the face. The boat must be sinking. At the back of my mind a discordant refrain is thinking, 'this is what panic feels like'.

Then the noise, the hypnotic thud of helicopter blades. It is an overwhelming and overpowering sound, like being trapped inside a drum being banged on by an orgy of revellers. In the hazy distance looms a dark and sinister shape. A gigantic two-legged creature with a bulbous head and the eyes of a fly. It moves towards us. It occurs to me that my maker has come to meet me. And I am terrified.

Another sensation, a sharp, acrid smell that burns the nostrils.

That is the last I remember.

When I awake I am in a cold metal cell. It is about four by two metres, painted in a dull grey colour. A naked lightbulb dangles above my head, burning dimly. In the corner there is a steel toilet bowl. The bed consists of a thin mattress and a single brown blanket. The door has a perspex window with iron bars on it. My head throbs violently. I want to retch. I struggle to sit up but my legs have turned to rubber. There is a salty taste of blood on my lips.

A shadow crosses the window. The outline of a head is visible.

'Don't bother getting up,' says a female voice. It is thick and guttural.

The door swing opens and Charlotta Gattschalk steps in carefully over the frame. It is an exaggeratedly dainty step and it fills me with rage and hatred. She is wearing a grey boiler suit and a pair of black boots. A pair of black gloves is tucked into her belt. Her wiry, greying hair is cut above her neck and swept severely back off her head. She is jowly, heavier than in her photograph. Her breasts are large. There are also dark bags under her eyes, which make her look tired and old. She has a podgy, dour face that could belong to anyone. A downtrodden housewife, a mass murderer.

'Where are Coonrodt and Woods?'

She raises her hand peremptorily at me. 'The American is next door. The old man was of no use to us. His boat is outside. We will dispose of it later, at a far-away place. We do not want the police sniffing around investigating flotsam.'

The rage that explodes inside me consumes all my thoughts and actions. I hurl myself at her legs. She is surprisingly nimble. All I feel is a blow to the back of my head. Then she slams her knee into my face. My head hits the back of the wall and I slump to the ground, stunned. Blood spurts out of my nose.

'The only reason you two are alive is that I want to know what you and the American know. Everything.' She beckons to the young man standing behind her.

'He is your lover, ja?' she curls her mouth slyly at me. The look of hatred on my face leaves her unfazed.

The guard enters, grabs me by the ankles and places a pair of shackles on my legs. Handcuffs snap on my wrists. Then he hauls me up. I fall against the wall, still unable to stand on my feet.

'Come,' she beckons.

We walk slowly down the passageway, she in front, the guard behind.

I shuffle along in the middle. We pass beneath three hatchways. The forth leads into a work area, probably where all the sensitive anti-corrosive equipment was stored when the rig was still in use. It has now been turned into a high-tech laboratory. It is a small-scale version of Laurier's lab at Groningen University. The computers and the screens are the same. There are about a dozen young people in white coats sitting around, working and chatting. They have the air of bright postgraduate students in prime form. From the soft murmur of their voices, these must be the Russians. It is a relaxed atmosphere, nobody looks like a killer, or as if they are being held against their will. I uneasily remember Woods's words, about the rig being used for scientific research. All sorts of permutations go through my mind. Perhaps Gattschalk is part of of some sort of international scientific endeavour and nobody knows about her previous life. Some of the workers gaze curiously at me but I might as well be a casual passer-by.

Gattschalk smiles and addresses them in Russian, to which they respond with a burst of laughter. It sounds like a joke. My head is spinning.

'EU grant,' she chortles at me, waving her hand over her domain.

We reach another door. This time she swipes a card through the unit on the wall. The door clicks open. It is another makeshift laboratory, smaller, cosier, and with more security.

Laville is at the elongated desk, bending over his microscope. There are books, two computers, petri dishes and an assortment of scientific instruments scattered all around him.

He looks up, surprised and slightly annoyed to see us, as though we'd interrupted the rhythm of his work. Even here, in the middle of the ocean, he is wearing a white shirt and a black and gold striped tie, the absolute antithesis of a mad genius.

He gives a cursory grunt to Gattschalk. Me, he ignores, as if I was invisible.

He is as much a prisoner as we are. I can see it in his eyes. His attempt to assert his independence by showing annoyance is a sham, like a dog growling at his master. Inside, he's quaking with fear like me, like I am.

'So,' I sneer at him. 'First they try to murder you, and now you're in chains like me.'

He squirms uncomfortably and glances at Gattschalk but he doesn't say anything.

There are rows of built-in steel shelves above his head. They contain jars with green lids, the old-fashioned kind that children keep tadpoles in. At least we used to when I was growing up.

They are filled with hands.

At first glance they're not immediately recognisable as hands. They're that grey indefinable mass that characterises old laboratory specimens.

They could be ox lungs, rats, bits of sheep. All schools have rows of them in biology class, and the teachers use them year after year, hauling down the dusty bottles to demonstrate the circulation of blood, the intricacies of reproduction.

The palms are shapeless, shrivelled and wrinkled, as round as tennis balls. It's the fingers that give it away. They are like claws, starkly played out as if reaching out in desperation for help. The white tips where the fingernails are, are like markers.

I try to put my hand over my mouth, but I cannot. The chains are too heavy to lift up. The stream of vomit comes out the side of my mouth. I attempt to wipe the corners of my mouth on my shoulders. Gattschalk pretends not to notice, but she is gloating, revelling in my horror.

'Why hands,' I hear myself saying dumbly, 'why not heads, feet?'

'Portability. They fit easily into those jars. Perhaps the doctor will care to explain the scientific details.'

A flicker of distaste passes over Laville's face but he pulls himself together.

'The hands have been eviscerated,' he begins. 'All we need is the bone marrow. The bone marrow is rich in certain type of cells that produce an excess of a protein called Rentium B. The gene JH-35, that produces the protein, is found only in Tamils. Now Rentium B has an interesting property. Normally it specialises in attacking non-primate animal tissue. The defence mechanisms of the human body are well organised and regulated, like an army.

Think of Rentium B as the commando unit. What we do is graft the gene into the embryos of pigs. We then rear the pigs until a healthy age is reached. Then we graft pig tissue onto human tissue and see what the reaction is. The specially reared pigs obviously start producing Rentium B. This tricks the body's immune system into believing that the pig tissue is human tissue. Hey presto, transgenic pigs.'

'And you first injected the victims with Mescoan to prevent the blood from clotting?' I find myself saying.

'Clever girl,' he grins smarmily at me.

I remember what I've learnt. Extend right hand forward, hand upraised and palm flattened. Fingers straight up but not stiffened. Go with the flow. Strike the lower part of the palm between upper lip and nose. Use it like a blade. Ignore the pain because the enemy's will be infinitely worse.

I have the satisfaction of seeing the look of shock on his face and the blooding trickling down onto his crisp white shirt.

Gattschalk pushes me roughly from the back. We go though another door. She steps into a small cabin. It has been stripped of everything except a table and a chair. The guard forces me down on the chair and handcuffs me from the back. Gattschalk seats herself on the table, close to me. I can see her big thighs spread out through her boiler suit.

She lifts my chin up so that my eyes meet hers.

'Don't insult my intelligence. I have been in this business since before you were born. You will tell me everything. Most important of all you will tell me why the CIA is interested in me.'

She doesn't know that Woods is now private. 'Will you promise to set me free if I do?'

I see the flame of anger in her eyes. I almost regret saying it. Being hit in the face hurts. Her face is a mastery of self-control. She sighs, almost sadly and gets up.

'I will wait,' she says ominously. 'You will learn the hard way.'

I cannot remember walking back to my cell. Or the hours or days that went by. There is a black hole at the centre of me.

*

Different sounds filter through the door. My mind had become used to the metal clang twice a day, and nothing else except an inordinately faint pulsating whoosh, the sound of the distant sea. Now I hear the thump of boots on the metal floor, the barking of orders, doors clanging shut. The sounds impose on my senses, forcing me to listen. The door to my cell opens. The man who had earlier put the handcuffs on me steps in. Behind him there is another guard. He doesn't exactly take out the handgun from the holster at his waist but his hand hovers nearby. I get the message.

The first guard places the chains on me all over again. He also tapes my mouth. He lifts me up and pushes me roughly in front, down a passage, up a set of metal rungs and though the hatch.

My eyes blink in the dark. I suck in the salty air. There is a wind blowing and the sea is choppy. Grey balls of cloud move rapidly across the sky like a flotilla of spaceships. Now and then a full moon glistens through.

All the commotion becomes clear. The Russian helicopter is a burnt, black wreck on the deck, its blades forlornly sagging to the ground. The fire has been put out but it still smoulders, little hisses emanating from the wreck, accompanied by the occasional spark. Two of the guards circle the craft warily with fire extinguishers in their hands.

I become conscious of an overpowering smell permeating the air. It the smell of animal dung. I look around. There is a rudimentary pen in a corner of the platform, from which the squeals of pigs emanate. Recognition dawns. This is what we saw on the satellite thermal maps.

Gattschalk is standing near the helicopter, hands on her hips, surveying the wreckage.

'This is the work of your American colleague,' she smiles grimly at me, 'but we will flush him out.'

The two guards wrench open the rusty hatch on the floor of the deck. There is a pulley next to it with a length of steel cable, normally used for wheeling equipment to and from the sea surface. The guard clips the end of the cable to my handcuffs.

Gattschalk has a flat black object in her hand. It is about the size and shape of a portable CD player with nobs on the front.

'This is a motion-detecting bomb. Any attempt by your friend to rescue you, and boom. You have a choice of being blown up or drowning.'

'Surprise me,' I spit vehemently in her face.

She responds by hitting me hard. A punch in the solar plexus. She knows the spot that hurts the most. It must be years of training. First the air is sucked out of me, leaving me gasping for breath. Then the sharp, unbearable pain, like a stab in the gut. I double up, clutching my stomach and sinking to my knees. I want to retch, but I have not eaten for two days.

The guard picks me up from behind, his arms under my shoulders. He eases me through the hatch very carefully, as if afraid to damage me.

Then he lets go. The plunge is terrifying. I feel myself free-falling through the air. Everything else is a blur.

I am dangling in the air. Still.

The ocean is below me, waves crashing violently against the pillars. The roar is deafening, amplified by the roof of the rig.

I look into the floodlights to see Gattschalk closing the hatch. The bomb is attached to the cable. It is halfway between the end of the cable and the hatch. The cable is swaying slightly. I have no idea what strength of motion is required to set it off.

Coonrodt's boat is chained to one of the pillars. Every now and then it smacks violently against concrete. Only the rubber edges that Coonrodt had fashioned from old tires prevents it from being damaged. The weather is relatively calm at the moment. The rubber edges are no protection in even a moderate storm.

A seagull flutters close by, buffeted into a drunken stagger by the wind.

I close my eyes and pray.

I hear a voice. Imploring me, pleading with me. My relationship with God has had its ups and downs. I have only sporadically paid attention to my spiritual needs. It has not been a wilful neglect. I simply have been unable to summon up the deep will to surrender myself.

I hear the voice again. This time I open my eyes. Woods is on the boat, waving his arms at me as if trying to attract my attention. Then I see him struggling to put on a yellow life jacket.

I am completely and utterly puzzled.

He picks up the gun and aims it at me. It occurs to me that he might be doing me a favour, putting me out of my misery, so to speak. When I was a child I saw a western movie where the hero shoots his wife as she is being carried away by Indian raiders, to spare her the horror of being a slave to the savages.

I want to laugh out loud, but my mouth is taped.

There is a blinding flash of light. A loud bang almost shatters my eardrums.

I am falling.

My arms and legs try to flay out instinctively but the shackles prevent any movement. It feels like a long time, like a hundred storeys are passing by in slow motion.

As I hit the water the cold wraps around me like a steel blanket. My lungs are crushed. I can feel the water in my nostrils already cutting of my supply of air.

I resign myself to a watery death for the second time in forty-eight hours. They say that your life flashes past in moments of extreme terror, that it is biologically based. Something to do with the production of adrenaline. I can vouch for that fact. I see whole episodes flashing by.

His arms are around me, dragging me up. He rips the tape away from my mouth, and I take desperate gulps of the salty, moist air. There is a rope attached from him to the boat. I grab onto it, but there's not much else I can do with handcuffs on. He struggles to help me, but there's nothing he can do either. He swims off, leaving me spluttering in the water again, clutching the rope with all my life. He hauls himself aboard. Then he takes hold of the rope and pulls. I cling desperately to it. He grabs me by the arms and hauls me into the boat.

I wince. My arms feel like they've been pulled out of their sockets.

'Quick, I need your help to start this goddamn boat,' he shouts at me. I cannot feel my hands or feet, let alone assist him. They are frozen.

I gaze helplessly at him and then at my handcuffs.

He grabs me roughly and shoves me towards the cockpit. Clumsily I switch on the ignition and power the throttle. The boat lurches dangerously towards the nearest pillar but a wave causes it to sheer sharply away.

He grabs the wheel, twisting it violently away from the pillar. We still manage bang into it but it is a glancing blow. The boat bounces away like a frightened deer.

We are out from beneath the rig.

They start shooting at us, bullets ricocheting off the side of the cabin. I duck instinctively but there is nowhere to hide. We are out in the open.

Woods grabs the flare gun and fires in the direction of the rig.

'That will keep them quiet,' he shouts.

The flare careers over the rig and onto the other side.

'Try another one,' I shout.

'No, the damage is done.'

'They were wearing night-vision goggles.' He responds to the quizzical look on my face. 'It works by amplifying external light, mostly from the moon and stars. The light from the flare is equivalent to staring directly at the sun. It will temporarily blind them. And give them a serious headache.'

Woods helps me take off my clothes. I am standing in front of him in my underwear, indescribably cold, grief-stricken, miserable beyond belief, and all I can think of is my modesty. We are both wet and cold. Woods grabs a couple of blankets from the bunk and gives them to me. He has on a pair of Coonrodt's trousers. And his navy blue jersey.

This is the first time as an adult that I have been on Coonrodt's boat without him. I burst into tears, sobbing uncontrollably. The pain eats into my heart. I cannot for one moment envisage life without him.

'The body has probably been weighted and dropped into the ocean,' says Woods, reading my mind. He puts a hand on my shoulder and hands me a mug of powdery hot chocolate. His eyes are moist.

'Don't blame yourself.' He attempts a weak smile in my direction. I am unable to will the tears to stop.

*

On the horizon a thin line of orange is appearing. The truism that only when we come so close to being denied the reasons for existence that we truly appreciate it, becomes, in an instant, all too real. I want to wrap my arms around the sun, feel its warmth, its strength.

'How did you know,' I address Woods, 'that the bomb wouldn't have killed me first?'

'Had a look with the binoculars. The actual explosive charge was very small. Those gadgets work using a signal processing technology called True Motion Recognition. They have built-in computers that only respond to the presence of a human body, either by heat detection or the strength of electrical signals emitted by the human body. That's why the bird didn't set it off. Besides, I had to take a chance. I didn't know how to start this boat.'

We both laugh. I want to cry so badly that it hurts.

Epilogue

Woods contacted MI5 in London and in a joint operation with the Special Boat Service they raided the oil rig. Boehme was, as usual, granted observer status, as the rig was in British territorial waters. Benschop-Fehr and I watched the action on video. A few members of the SBS unit were equipped with digital cameras built into their helmets. It was like watching a television action series, or rather a montage of all the exciting bits. A view of a starry sky as someone looked up. A jumble of words hurtling through the air. The violent motion of the motorised dinghies crashing through the waves. Another dizzy climb to the top of the rig. Somebody lobs a smoke grenade. This is where the plots gets lost. All hell breaks loose. Amidst the billowing smoke there is general mayhem. Screams and shots rent the air. It is impossible to see who the enemy is, compounded by the fact that both parties are dressed in black. The screen is a blur of arms, legs and other body parts. Then abruptly it all stops, with the speed of a tropical squall. I catch a glimpse of Boehme on the deck, machine pistol casually at his side. He looks directly at the camera. In reality it is the cameraman who swivels his head in Boehme's direction, but such is the power of illusion. It is a revelation. Boehme's eyes have a sparkle of elation. He is thrilled. And yet so calm. I experience an inexplicable surge of happiness for him.

They did not find Charlotta Gattschalk. She simply vanished. Investigations are continuing into her whereabouts. The Russians, technologists, chemists and scientists that she had recruited, were also illegal immigrants . They had been very well paid - in dollars - by her company. The price they paid for their illegal status was absolute silence. Laville was on board. He surrendered quietly. I watched him on the video. His reaction to the attack was exactly the same as when I walked in as a prisoner, that mixture of superciliousness, annoyance and arrogance. He looked up, took off his glasses in exasperation and stepped forward to be arrested.

His life was over when he was first arrested anyway. Success for a person like Laville is measured in affirmation; in how other people view his life, his rise from humble beginnings, his triumphant achievements. He would not be able to have had plastic surgery and live as a non-entity on some tropical island in the West Indies.

His is the story of Phaethon, the son of Clymene and Helios, whose schoolfriends wouldn't believe he was the son of a god. When Phaethon did manage to persuade his father to let him ride the golden chariot through the heavens, he gloated and went wild, destroying fields and rivers until eventually he was shot down by Zeus. Today we see him in the meteor that blazes across the sky.

*

I paid a few more visits to Laurier. He introduced me to a cardiac specialist, Professor Roland Eakin, a member of the European Committee for the Propagation of Scientific Research, who explained a few interesting facts about xenotransplantation to me. The main problem is that pigs harbor retroviruses and every retrovirus has the possibility of causing cancer. Retroviruses are a major concern, because they can exist in the host for a long period of time before becoming apparent. Retroviruses are a particularly insidious form of viral strand because they allow for the reverse transfer of genetic material, that is, viral DNA strands are incorporated into the host's cells for the production of new retroviruses. This means that an animal's genes can slowly migrate into the human gene pool. The end result could be the creation of Chimeras.

Some might say that mankind would deserve a fate such as this.

Another factor is that even though a pig's heart may be similar to that of a human's heart, there is no real long-term evidence that the pig's heart will function effectively in a human being. There are some important physiological and anatomical differences, for example, the pig's heart is normally on the same level as its head, but the human brain is 15 to 18 inches above the heart. The pig's heart could well struggle to provide enough blood for the human brain to function properly.

Laurier says that it opens up a whole new can of worms, and in the wake of the numerous animal related virus scandals that have rocked the West, it is unlikely that the US and the European governments will sanction xenotransplants other than for research purposes.

The monstrous absurdity does not pass me by. A great number of people have been killed in pursuit of an infinitesimally small fragment of their bodies. One gene, JH- 35 to be precise.

I will not pretend that I understand much of this. In the words of the singer Iris DeMent, 'Think I'll just let the mystery be.'

*

I have tried to rouse in me a spirit of revulsion and horror about what the pharmaceutical companies are engaged in but I cannot muster much more than outraged indignation. As much as I agree with Laurier about mammon being the possessor of our destinies, behind it all there is the yearning for an understanding of our universe. Why and how we came to be what we are. We have always lived at the edge of the abyss. Thomas Aquinas and his contemporaries were profoundly disgusted at the age in which they lived. In their eyes the thirteenth century was a period of decadence, greed and immorality. We do not think of their misery now. We only see the great medieval churches of Europe that make our hearts soar. For that we have to thank the thousands of unknown cathedral builders. The relationship of the individual to history will always be a one-sided affair. It is the inherently syncretic nature of our own selves that we fail to understand this. I hope Laurier does.

Biogen *had* tried to get me fired. They sent a letter to the Co-ordinator in Paris. I was not supposed to see it but Boehme wangled it so that I did.

Actually, he didn't really wangle anything. He simply showed me the letter that he received from the Co-ordinator - and told me what he'd do to me if I ever went public with it, ie rip my guts out with a Bavarian hunting knife. It was an extraordinary letter. In it, a group of nameless

"Executive officers" outlined the "irreparable damage" done to Europe's chances of winning the genetic race. They ascribed our interference as delivering a "mortal blow" to the prestige of European scientists and researchers.

They waved around the fax I sent to Hausenpfeff as proof of my "gross incompetence". The case is still pending in the European Public Prosecutor's office. Boehme says I have nothing to worry about. Although I trust him I have nagging doubts. He is also not very happy with me for not notifying him about my jaunt to the Orkney Islands, but he said that he was prepared to overlook it due to the rapid unfolding of circumstances. Something like that. One can never be sure what Boehme actually means.

I have also learnt something else. There are no grand conspiracies in the world, only groups of people who cumulate for periods of mutual benefit. Nothing more, nothing less.

It is a biological imperative.

Scientists call it "the selfish gene". Ha, ha, ha.

*

I have also tried to play matchmaker. It struck me that Laurier's idealism meshes very well with Benschop-Fehr's rough-edged view of the world so I introduced the two of them.

They clicked right away. I could see by the awkward way they circled each other, like Tarzan and Jane. Neither of them seemed to have gone out in years. I know that they have been on at least one date, but Benschop-Fehr will not divulge any details.

They never found Coonrodt's body. I'd like to think that it is at the bottom of the ocean. He always told me that he wanted to be cremated and have his ashes scattered on the sea.

'Fish food,' he used to cackle hideously.

Coonrodt, despite all his eccentricities, did make a will. The boat he left to me. He donated most of his surprisingly substantial savings to the Seaman's Association. He left money to me for the upkeep of the boat. The boat has been moved to the Amsterdam docks. One of Coonrodt's old friends rents a section of an inlet which he uses for barge repairs and he has kindly allowed me to keep the boat there at a nominal cost. I would not have been able to travel to his old place in Rotterdam anyway. There are too many memories there.

Woods is spending Christmas in Miami with his father. I will join him there for two weeks after Christmas. The old man has a smallish yacht in the Florida Keys, he had told me. Spends his time fishing for sailfish and tarpon in the waters off the Florida Straights.

He stayed behind for a while, pretending he had work to wrap up. At first I barricaded myself in my flat for four days. I'd look out the window and see him there, like a lost puppy. Sometimes he'd go off for walks, or a jog. The way I figured it, I would either have to phone the police to have him arrested as a stalker, or go out and meet him.

I went out.

He made me laugh even when I didn't feel like it. Silly jokes, James Brown impressions, notes stuck in my postbox.

I started holding his hand again.

But I worry. I have no idea how this will work out. I am addicted to beginnings and endings. It's the middle parts I can't handle.

*

But first I phoned my mother, told her that Coonrodt was dead. There was silence on the other end for about ten minutes. It felt like an eternity.

Then she started to cry. To wail and sob like I've never heard before.

I was shocked. I had never witnessed such an outpouring of emotion from her. My solid-as-a-rock mother, who had more faith in the golden cross around her neck than anything else. Then just as suddenly as she had started, she stopped. It was back to normal. I will never understand my parents and neither will they understand me. I read the other day that the generation gap is closing, that children today have much more in common with their parents than previous generations did; mothers buy the T-shirts that their daughters wear, fathers and sons go to Rolling Stones concerts.

There are clearly defined limits to my horizon. But sometimes I fantasize.

I told her that I would be spending Christmas with her, my first in five years. She had greeted this piece of news with a choking sob. I had maintained my silence. Sometimes the mind's response to overwhelming emotion is to reflect on the banal and the inconsequential.

She had promised to make up the spare room. I will sit there on Christmas Eve and unwrap Coonrodt's present. I have already gazed into the heavens and promised him that I will not cry.

Printed in the United Kingdom
by Lightning Source UK Ltd.
1550